Faith

Book 3 of The Feather Trilogy

Laurie Lyons

RING OF FIRE PUBLISHING

ISBN-13: 978-0615979748
ISBN-10: 0615979742

Faith

©2014 Laurie Lyons. All rights reserved. No part of this book may be reproduced or transferred without the express written consent of the author.

Published by
Ring of Fire Publishing
Seattle, Washington, U.S.A.

This is a work of fiction. Any similarity with real persons or events is purely coincidental. Persons, events, and locations are either the product of the author's imagination, or used fictitiously.

Edited by Marissa Litak.
Cover image by Sheila VooDoo. Cover design by Stephen Penner.

Acknowledgements

The title of this book is 'Faith' and, although it took forever to come to that title, it's perfect.

Faith is a difficult concept for us humans to understand. Sometimes we have faith in proven things, like oxygen and gravity, scientific proofs that have been verified time and time again. Usually though, we have to have faith in things that are less substantial, less proven. It is these things that we struggle to have faith in. I struggled with this book. I am not ashamed to say that I considered more than once throwing it out the window. I stopped myself, though because if I don't believe in my words, no one else is going to. So the title is just as much about me having faith in myself and my work as it is about Lucy having faith in Nathaniel.

I have so many people to thank for making this act of faith a reality. I must always thank Stephen Penner and the team at Ring of Fire Publishing for always having faith in my stories. A personal nod of gratitude goes out to my editor Marissa Litak for her keen eyes and insistence on perfection. You are a grammar superstar. Thank you to my fellow writers who took late night texts of doubt and despair, particularly Margarita Gakis and Grant Lafleche who often put their own work on hold to read for me.

Thank you to my supportive family, particularly my brother Robb and sister Christie, who have always had faith not only in my work but in me as a person. Thank you to my amazing children, Ethan and Julia, who tell me every day that I am the best writer in the world even though they aren't old enough to read anything I write. That's faith for you.

Lastly, as always, I need to thank my soul mate and partner in crime, Trevor Lyons for sitting up late helping with edits, bringing me countless cups of coffee, reminding me that I have a talent to share and telling me when I need to take a break. No one has faith in me like he does.

For my readers, thank you for having faith in The Feather Trilogy and the magic of Lucy and Nathaniel. Thank you for your kind reviews and emails and tweets pushing me to finish this book and make it just right. Thank you for your love of my work and the stories I tell you.

It is because of all these people that I found the title of this book and faith in myself. I am eternally grateful for that.

I hope you love this book, because although I didn't always love it, I always believed in it because you believed in me.

True Love,
Laurie

Prologue

March 20
The Spring Equinox

The sky was streaked black and blue like someone had beat it into submission, and the air was thick with humidity. The world around had gone silent, paused by celestial hands for this crucial slice of time. After it was all settled, the unsuspecting humans might go about their business as if nothing had changed, or they would be dead.

It would be all or nothing.

There they stood, shoulder to shoulder, or more so, wing to wing. The army went on as far as the eye could see. Miles of black leathery wings, twitching and clawing at the sand. A deep rumble emitted from the soldiers as they gnashed their teeth and dug their clawed feet into the sand. They had been eager for this war since the dawn of time. In the water, rather, on the water stood a line of white feathered wings. They did not move, or twitch or snarl but stood strong and still. Their eyes blazing with fierceness that radiated out like a wall. Both sides were equally terrifying.

She only had a second to decide what to do. Somehow it had

all come down to her. Her legs flexed and every muscle engaged. She was strong now -- she had developed the physique of an athlete in the last few months. Not by choice. Her bare feet dug into the sand and it pushed up between her toes. Enough thinking, enough worrying, enough panicking, this was it – no more fear.

She took a deep breath and sprinted….straight into the middle of the battle.

Chapter One
Despair

"Love is better than anger.
Hope is better than fear.
Optimism is better than despair."
~ Jack Layton

December 21 This Year

This is Hell, Lucy thought. *This is absolute Hell.* If she hadn't already been there, she would have sworn to it, but she had first-hand knowledge of the horrors of Hell and knew better. She had cried herself completely dry and yet her eyes were the only dry thing about her; everything else was waterlogged. Lucy's adrenaline was still racing so the cold hadn't quite sunk in yet, but her hands were beginning to shake. She knew she should move from this fetal position but she was too frightened to even shift an inch. If Lucy moved then it all became true -- if she just stayed here, on the wet dock crying in the freezing drizzle, then maybe time would just stop. Maybe Roman and Nathaniel weren't on their way to their deaths, maybe Anastasia wasn't already dead, and maybe just maybe, it wasn't all her fault.

Lucy had no idea how much time had passed but she knew the sun had gone down since she realized that Anastasia was the target for all the recent attacks. She had used her photographic memory to replay all the events in slow motion and came to the horrific conclusion that the true motivation of the creature they called the Wrath was to kill Anastasia. They also discovered that it wasn't the Wrath at all but some Demon named Malachi who was after Roman. Anastasia was at her parents' home in Chicago getting ready for their Christmas party and was completely vulnerable to any attack. Lucy thought of what a Demon would do to her beautiful best friend and the sobs renewed themselves. The creature known as Fate had left her some time ago, having had its fill of human behavior for the century. Lucy had just lain down where she had collapsed, incapable of handling anything else.

And still the future sat there for her, waiting, like a beacon of despair. What was she going to do now? Sit and wait here in the rain for Roman and Nathaniel to come back for her? Get to the nearest airport and try to catch a flight to Chicago, knowing that by the time she got there, everything would have been decided already? Her friends could be dead, the city could be destroyed or any number of other horrors. A Demon was capable of such a great deal of destruction, and this one especially had shown little concern over the loss of human life.

And then there was the deepest reason for her tears: she had just sent Nathaniel to his death. Her Nathaniel, her Angel, her heart, her soul, her everything…was gone. He had been in such a hurry to get to Anastasia that there was no time before he flew away. Nathaniel might be dead and Lucy didn't even get to say goodbye. Pain ripped through her body anew as she curled up tighter upon herself and once again she became lost in her anguish. Eventually, the rain stopped and still Lucy laid there on the dock in the dark of night.

Finally, her inner voice spoke to her, urging her to save herself. She had stopped shaking and understood from her extensive knowledge that this was a very bad thing. Lucy could be in serious trouble if she didn't get out of this situation. She had to find Nathaniel, and she couldn't do that if she was dead. So with a deep breath, Lucy forced herself to roll onto her stomach and begin to push herself up. She grunted with effort and pain as fire ripped through her frozen hands. Slowly, she moved to kneeling and then pushed herself to a hunched-over stand. She shoved her auburn hair back from where it had slicked to her cheeks and neck. This small movement made her stumble sideways, but she caught herself as feeling re-entered her feet.

Lucy stood, getting her bearings, and felt her energy and resolve begin to return. Her mind seemed incapable of thinking anything productive so she decided to make small goals for now that could help her get to a point where a plan could be made. Get somewhere warm, get dry. That was the goal of the moment, and once that was accomplished she could move on to something more, but not much more. Lucy didn't feel that she could make an important decision. Get somewhere warm and get dry that was the focus …how? She began to scan her surroundings when her eye caught on an object discarded on the dock. With a shaky groan she slowly bent over to pick it up.

It was a wallet, Nathaniel's wallet. It wasn't wet and Lucy realized that she had been laying on it this whole time. She breathed a cautious sigh of relief; Nathaniel must have dropped it at some point. Thankfully, Lucy knew all of Nathaniel's passwords – she helped set them up. Nathaniel's accounts were usually very well stocked so now, money was not her biggest problem. Lucy had her own wallet, although it held her passport and ID, it sadly had very little money in it. Her biggest problem was still that she was very cold and very wet and as the blood began to move around her extremities, it became apparent that hypothermia was a definite possibility.

Lucy slowly lifted the wallet and sniffed at the leather. There it was, that wonderful scent of honey, sunshine, and salt water: Nathaniel's smell. She closed her eyes and breathed him in, allowing her mind to bring up his image. His strong jaw, high cheek bones, ebony hair, and grey crystalline eyes. She repressed the pain trying to surge through her torso with a deep sigh. She would see Nathaniel again, feel him, and smell him. She had faith in that. She had to.

Looking around again, Lucy realized that the town was completely abandoned and not a soul stirred. She had just been laying on her side in a very public place for hours and no one had come to her aid. Lucy hadn't looked if there were any open hotels in the area when she suggested this town as the location for their organized coup on Fate, but judging from the fact that the gas station was closed, a cozy bed and breakfast was unlikely. Having all this money was no good if there was nowhere to spend it. Calling Doctor Hannon would be a complete last resort; he would ask far too many questions…questions that Lucy was unable to answer. Her mother too, was not an option for she was still on her honeymoon cruise. Thankfully.

Lucy had suggested this town because her lab partner Gavin had told her about it. His family owned a house up here. If Lucy couldn't find a hotel to stay at, maybe she could find Gavin's summer house or at least call him from somewhere and ask for his help. He would certainly know where she could go. With this small goal in mind, Lucy shoved the wallet into her pocket and stumbled back to solid ground. The rickety wood of the dock had done nothing to ease her steps, and her stability increased as she hit the parking lot. She stopped for a moment and retrieved a memory. She was sitting with Gavin in the lab and they were supposed to be recording the results of the experiment at hand. Gavin, having done this particular lab before, had simply recorded their answers. Lucy, having no interest whatsoever in science, allowed him to do all the work and merely looked at his laptop to record the results in her photographic memory. Gavin was telling her about the first time he tried to get up on water skis. He had an easy, charming way of telling a story that made it both completely fascinating and totally hilarious.

"So we have this ugly ass wind sock at the end of our dock," he said through laughs, "and I, in my infinite wisdom of eight years old, thought that if I held on to it, Dad wouldn't be able to drive the boat away and I would not have to learn how to ski."

"You didn't want to learn how to water ski?" Lucy asked.

"I would like to make it clear that I was a terribly logical child," he grinned, "a genius really, and I knew that flying over water at a rapid rate on two tiny sticks is foolish."

"And yet this same genius child-wonder thought that a wind sock tied to a stick at the end of a dock would stop a speed boat in its tracks?" Lucy's voice dripped with sarcasm.

"I was eight, Lucy," he challenged seriously. "Don't be an asshole."

Lucy nodded soberly. "I am so sorry."

"You should be." He sounded hurt and Lucy stared to giggle.

"Please continue," she said, holding back a grin.

"Thank you, I will," he said harshly, then grinned. "So there

I am, holding onto the rope with one hand and reaching for the wind sock with the other and Dad hits it. I spin sideways, now pay attention here, Lucy, because my physical prowess and agility was deeply evident even at an early age, grab the wind sock and yet do not let go of the rope. I end up, going twenty miles an hour, backward across the ocean streaming a rainbow cat-shaped wind sock over my head."

Lucy maintained her strong face and managed, "You cried like a little girl, didn't you?"

"No!" Gavin protested, then hung his head sheepishly. "Yes….and I peed a little. My mom put the sock back as a charming memento." That was it and they both lost it and laughed until the rest of the lab had shushed them into submission.

Lucy came back to the present. Yes, Gavin was a great choice for an ally right now. He might not even ask that many questions and at this point, Lucy most likely wasn't even able to speak enough to tell him much of anything. She scanned the beach and rows of docks. About four houses in, there it was, floating in the now peaceful air, a rainbow cat-shaped wind sock. There had to be only one. Lucy gravitated toward it.

The cold wind picked up again and her shakes began again in earnest. Lucy picked up her pace. She made a harsh decision that she would simply break into Gavin's cabin and get warm. She would leave a note or something explaining and take the consequences later. The chances of her being caught seemed fairly slim seeing how law enforcement in this town looked completely obsolete. Her energy faded steadily and Lucy slowed as she struggled to put one foot in front of the other. She stumbled and came down on her knees in the wet sand. Grunting, she forced herself to stand and struggled to keep walking.

Finally, she lifted her eyes and blinked in disbelief. A warm glow was emanating from Gavin's family cabin. In this completely empty town, there was one sign of life and it was at the one home where she needed it to be. Of course, how she would explain her appearance or her presence, Lucy had no idea. She only needed to fulfill her first goals. Get dry, get warm, and she added one extra task from the smells coming from the cabin, to eat. Lucy hobbled up the porch steps toward the sliding glass doors that emitted a bright, warm glow. She was slightly blinded by the lights as she approached and she ended up just running into the doors with a weak thump. Her legs gave out on her and she slid down the glass to her knees. It suddenly got darker and Lucy realized with detachment that she had closed her eyes.

Chapter Two
Stories

*"If history were taught in the form of stories
it would never be forgotten."
~ Rudyard Kipling*

Lucy came to when she felt her body being lifted and her name being called. Opening her eyes a crack, she saw one of the best things she had ever seen. Gavin's face was creased with concern, but it was there and Lucy rejoiced.

"Oh thank God," she mumbled. Figuring she was almost incapable of completing her first two tasks alone at this point, she added, "Get warm, get dry."

"Gee thanks," Gavin replied. "Being bossy, of course."

"Hmph," Lucy grunted. They were in a bright bathroom with all white tiles. Gavin set Lucy down on the white carpet and she glanced down at her filthy clothes and matted hair now marring the perfect surface. "Oh no," she grumbled and attempted to roll away. Gavin's solid hand was on her shoulder.

"Stop," he said kindly. "It's a stupid rug. Only my mother

would put a white rug in a place where people poo."

"Ha," Lucy half laughed and half sighed. She was already warming up when she heard the bath water running. After a bit she heard Gavin's voice again.

"Red," he said quietly, shaking her shoulder, "the bath is ready, are you okay to get in on your own?"

"Yup," Lucy muttered drunkenly, as she sat up and began pulling off her coat. "Got it."

"Now are you hurt anywhere?" he inquired with worry seeping into his tone.

"No no no," she mumbled while wiggling out of her coat. At some point, Gavin had pulled off her boots and socks so that was one less thing she had to worry about and she started pulling at her shirt. "Just cold, just wet, just sad."

"Okay," he sighed, stepping past her to the door. "Get in the bath, warm up, wash up and I am going to be back in a minute with some warm clothes for you."

"Mmmmm," Lucy mumbled and as she pulled off her shirt, she heard the door respectfully close behind her. She undressed completely and crawled to the gleaming white tub. She lifted herself up and slid blessedly into the tub's embrace. At first, her skin protested and every nerve came alive with fervor, stinging her from neck to toe. After a moment though, it eased and she felt her blood pump fresh life into her extremities and organs. After a few moments, she was able to move again and after lifting her eyes realized that she had never been that dirty in her life.

She managed to wash her body and with each layer of sand and dirt that left her, her resolve and energy returned. It was as if she was shedding off a shell and with it, doubt and fear. She had to find Nathaniel and Anastasia and yes, Roman, she had to find him too. She would find them. She didn't know how yet, but Nathaniel was always telling her to trust that the answer would come and so that was what she was going to do. Thinking of Nathaniel made the tears come again and she let them drip down, mixing with the bathwater, releasing them. Then she sniffed, splashed water on her face and forced herself to stop. She reminded her inner self that it might be sometime before she would see Nathaniel again and though she could not hold her pain bottled up, she could not just sob the whole time. She dunked her head and found the shampoo and washed her thick red hair back to life.

There was a soft knock at the door and Lucy slunk down into the tub.

"Come in?" she called and Gavin's soft brown curls poked out from the door, his eyes closed.

"Hey Red," he said, "you doing better?"

"Much," she answered, "thank you."

"Here's some clothes." He dropped the folded items on the floor. "Come out when you want to. I have some food for you."

"Thank you," Lucy answered, her gratitude pressed through her voice and it cracked. "I don't know what I would have done if you weren't here."

"No worries," he said as he started to close the door. "You can repay me when you tell me what the Hell is going on and what in God's name you were doing outside in one of the worst storms I have ever seen." He closed the door.

Lucy sank further down in the water. What was she going to tell Gavin? She began to concoct a story in her mind about a trip with Nathaniel to the seaside and what, he abandoned her? Or that she came to see Gavin? For what reason? A study session? She came up with many different stories but none of them made any sense. Maybe it would have been better if the cabin had been empty and she would have had to break in. Less questions.

Sighing but now completely starving, Lucy pushed herself out of the water and dried off with a towel. She had ruined her nails by digging them into the soft wood on the dock. She found a set of nail clippers and cut them down to the quick, then she dressed in the warm plaid shirt and jeans that Gavin had left. She found a hair brush and eventually dragged it though her unruly red curls. Lucy observed herself in the mirror. Her eyes were swollen and there were some cuts and scrapes on her face and hands but overall, on the outside anyway, she looked okay. Inside, she was a ragged mess. Eating was the next goal and she focused on that with all she had. Just eat; then thinking would be much easier.

She padded out into the hall and took in the seaside house for the first time. It was lovely. Bright windows and colorful fabrics lit up an open airy living room and the kitchen. Gavin was sitting on the soft couch with his elbows resting on his knees. His head hung down between his shoulders.

"Hey buddy," Lucy said quietly.

He lifted his head and his face rearranged to an expression of sheer relief. "Hey Red, you okay pal?"

Lucy nodded. "Hungry."

Gavin jumped up and guided her to the couch; he was talking the whole way.

"Okay, good, because I have a ton of stew for you. Come over here, have a seat and I will get you some food. Do you feel okay?"

Lucy nodded and sat down with a small grunt. Her muscles were starting to stiffen up. How long had she been out there?

"What time is it?" Lucy asked, her voice hoarse from screaming and crying, and she winced at the harsh tone of it.

"Late, very late," Gavin replied while moving easily around the bright kitchen.

"Are you alone here?" Lucy asked, looking around.

"Yeah," he answered while heading back to the couch with a plate and a glass of water. He put it all in front of her on the coffee table. Lucy's mouth began to water at the smell of meat and potatoes. Throwing politeness to the wind, she sat down on the floor in front of the coffee table and started to dig in.

Gavin smiled. "You're a savage, Lucy. My family is coming in a couple days. I wanted some peace and quiet before the brood gets here for Christmas."

Lucy nodded while throwing the food in her mouth. Within moments her plate was empty and she sat back to exhale with satisfaction.

"Thank you so much," she mumbled with her eyes closed. "You are a life saver."

"Feel better?" Gavin said with a small laugh.

"Yup," Lucy replied. She stretched and scooted back up to the couch. She could feel her strength returning and she stretched again, finally feeling more like herself.

"Excellent," Gavin smiled and then turned serious. "Now, would you like to tell me what the hell you were doing wandering around the ocean in the middle of winter all alone? How did you get here? Why?"

Lucy sighed; she hadn't thought of a lie yet. Then suddenly, her mouth opened and she started to talk. She told the truth, the whole truth, and nothing but the truth. Once it started spilling out, there was no stopping it, there was no filtering it. It was all coming out. She told Gavin how she met Nathaniel when she literally ran into him in the quad. How she fell in love with him from the beginning and how she soon discovered that he was invisible. She told him about discovering that he was a fallen Angel. She told him about the Demon Roman and how he used to mock and frighten

Lucy. She talked about the day Roman took her hostage to force Nathaniel to sell his soul to the Devil and how originally Lucy had sent Nathaniel back to Heaven. She paused and swallowed, recalling the pain of that moment. She told him about Gabriel coming down to make Nathaniel mortal again and Roman being dragged back to Hell.

Then she talked about the last few months and all the "accidents" that Lucy had been involved in. How Roman had returned, calmer, different, almost tolerable. How the accidents continued with increasing danger until the theatre at the school was blown up by an invisible assailant, something Nathaniel and Roman called "The Wrath." She explained that the Wrath is the great defender of Fate. That Fate sends the creature with the body of a dragon and the head of a lion when someone has dodged Fate. She painfully explained their dark and frightening time in Hell and the insane Demon known as Random who tried to tell them that there was no Wrath. She cried a little when she told him that they should have listened to the crazed creature but they didn't. They decided to invoke the anger of Fate itself. They came to this town because it was so quiet and Nathaniel and Roman had created a hurricane so Fate would appear to stop them. When Fate appeared, Roman killed Lucy so that Fate would see that she was dead and call off the Wrath.

She began sobbing when she told him about Nathaniel bringing her back from the dead only to tell her that they were wrong, Fate had no interest in Lucy being dead, that there was no Wrath and something else must be after Lucy. She only barely spoke when she told Gavin about how she had used her memory to discover the horrible truth that something was after Anastasia. She choked out that she had screamed at Roman and Nathaniel to go protect the vulnerable Anastasia and they had flown away hours ago and had not returned. She had her head in her hands when she told him that they were all most likely dead and she was all alone. Gavin sat silent and unmoving through the whole thing, not even nodding. Lucy cried herself out again, sniffed and looked up.

"I'm sure you don't believe that story," she said, swallowing, "but it's all true."

Gavin nodded and stood up. He walked over to the front door and started to put on his coat.

"Where are you going?" Lucy asked.

"To the dock," Gavin said shortly. "I need to see this for myself,"

"There isn't anything there!" Lucy exclaimed. "Fate left hours ago. There isn't anything to see."

"I just need to go look." Gavin explained, opening the door. "Stay here." He slammed the door behind him.

Lucy sank back into the couch. It was a stupid idea to tell Gavin but she hadn't been able to stop herself. It had felt so good to let it all out. Lucy hadn't even told Anastasia or her mother about any of this and it was such a release for her to share it with someone. Sadly, she had shared it with someone who clearly did not believe her and really, could she blame him? Lucy wondered if maybe she should leave now, before he had time to call the police or the hospital and have her locked up. Again though, this town was completely deserted, the chances that Gavin could get civic assistance anytime tonight would be unlikely. Lucy would judge his mood and sneak out in the morning.

The door opened and Gavin walked back in, slowly. He took off his coat, hung it on a peg, slipped off his boots and walked back over to Lucy. He sat down on the couch beside her and faced her.

"Well?" Lucy pushed, "nothing, right? Gavin, you have to just trust me on this one and if you don't believe me that's fine, just let me go because I have to do something about it all."

Gavin didn't respond but pulled one single huge white feather from the sleeve of his sweater. "Lucy, I grew up here, and never in all my life have I ever seen a bird that is large enough to produce a feather this enormous." His voice was calm but his hand was shaking lightly.

Lucy reached up and let her finger travel lightly up the side of it. She smiled ruefully. "That belongs to Nathaniel," she said quietly. "That's one of his wing feathers."

"The guy I played Xbox with two days ago!" Gavin exclaimed and shook the feather, "this, this is his? His Halloween costume? Real?" Lucy just nodded. "And Roman, Anastasia's boyfriend, is a Demon and he took you to Hell to talk to another Demon about the actions of Fate? And now Roman and Nathaniel have flown off to Chicago to save Anastasia from another Demon who is trying to hurt Roman?" Lucy nodded again. Gavin's voice had become strained and tight. "And, and, there are Demons wandering around the world trying to get us to do bad things to each other and the Angels are in Heaven trying to do the opposite?" He was yelling now. "And you are in the middle of all this?" Lucy nodded. Gavin dropped his head and blew out a huge gust of air. He was quiet for a long time. "Oh Red," he whispered. "What were you thinking?" He looked up with such sympathy in his eyes that relief swept through her. "Come here." He reached out and put a protective arm over her shoulders in a tight sideways hug.

Lucy rested her head against his shoulder and sighed herself.

"I am so sorry to burden you with all this," she said quietly. "It was selfish of me."

"Hey now," Gavin said, pulling away and looking at her, "you did the right thing by telling me. You can't do all this alone. I will go with you and help figure everything out."

Lucy started shaking her head. "Don't be silly, Gavin, you aren't coming with me."

"I don't think that you are in a position to argue with me even a little bit on this. If I were Nathaniel, I wouldn't want you alone right now." He paused. "Hey, I'm no Angel or Demon or anything, but I would like to think I'm a pretty good man to have in a crisis."

Lucy smiled at him. It was true, Gavin certainly did seem to be a solid guy to have in a time of trouble and Nathaniel definitely would prefer her to have some protection.

"But your family," Lucy protested, "your Christmas."

"Lame!" Gavin exclaimed. "Like I wouldn't rather come on an adventure with you than sit and play crib with my cousin Holly Halitosis."

Lucy started to giggle. "Holly Halitosis?"

"Yup." He shook his head. "The girl has problems let me tell you."

Lucy laughed. "But I don't know how much of an adventure it will be."

Gavin shrugged. "Better than here, man. We leave first thing in the morning. Where are we going?"

"That's a good question." Lucy sat back on the couch and thought for a minute. "We could go to Chicago but I would think we missed whatever happened there."

"So you assume this Demon guy has taken Anastasia somewhere and Roman and Nathaniel are trying to find her."

"Yup," Lucy replied. "And that's the *best* case scenario." Neither one mentioned the worst case scenario; it was too much to talk about right now, or ever really. "But I have no idea where to go from here."

Gavin sat and thought for a second. "Okay, well, let's get some sleep and think about it. You need to rest. After that, your piddly little brain there might come up with an answer."

"Right into the insults, hey?" Lucy said with a grin.

Gavin spread his arms wide. "I gotta be me!"

Lucy laughed and stood up and as she did so, exhaustion sank into her bones. She let out a massive yawn. Telling Gavin everything had a cathartic effect and Lucy was ready to rest.

"I banish you to siesta, Red," Gavin said, pointing toward the hall. "Go to the master bedroom and get some shut eye."

Lucy was too exhausted to argue or even speak; she just nodded and stumbled down the hall. The master was a huge room with one wall completely covered in windows. Lucy beheld the black Atlantic Ocean and sky beyond as she crawled over the massive bed. Her head hit the pillow and she had enough time to whisper, "Please, tell me what to do," before falling into a profound sleep.

Lucy knew where she was, and she didn't like it. She immediately felt the air; hot, dry and toxic pressing down upon her and she knew that she was back in Hell. On some level, Lucy was certainly aware that this was some sort of dream but since she had never dreamt before, it was possible that this was her current, horrific, reality.

She stood in a dark foyer of an equally dark house. She was alone and the only thing around was a tall rickety staircase that carried up beyond her sight. From her previous visit, Lucy knew that she only had two choices, to go up or to go out. She knew that the atmosphere outside was dreadful but up the stairs was no better. Lucy decided to go up. She climbed and climbed for what seemed like hours. The only sound was her shoes clanging against the black metal stairs. Finally, she came to the top and stood facing the familiar red door, willing herself to open it. She took a deep breath, stopped herself from coughing, and walked in the door.

The room was the same, completely empty but for a black claw footed bathtub that sat in the middle of the room. The only light came from a single bulb that hung down from the ceiling. Lucy knew who, well, what was in that bath tub. Slowly, with the utmost of caution, Lucy tried to approach the tub. The more she walked though, the further she felt for it began to draw away from her. Lucy increased her pace, walking faster, but the tub just went faster. Finally, Lucy broke into a jog and then a run but yet the tub still stayed in the middle of the room, not getting any closer. Finally Lucy burst into a sprint, running as fast as her legs would carry her. She gained on it at first but then it started to pull away again. Not ready to admit defeat, Lucy jumped and finally felt the smooth, cold cast iron beneath her palms.

The ground dropped out from beneath her and she was hanging off the side of the tub to nothing but blackness below. She grunted as she clutched at the tub and kicked her feet, desperately trying to get some sort of bearing. Lucy screamed as the tub began to tip toward her. She knew that this tub was not filled with water. It pitched closer and closer until Lucy could see the swirls and depth of the mercury inside as it crept toward her face in a thick metallic wave. She would have to drop to get away from it. She had no idea what was below but would have to take the risk at whatever horrors awaited in the darkness. Still, Lucy waited until the very last second, just before the mercury touched her fingers, to grit her teeth and let go. She closed her eyes in expectation of the fall that did not come.

Something was holding her hands.

With a shudder and a swallow Lucy forced her eyes open. An inch from her face was the stretched, distorted, mangled face of Random. He grinned at her, his teeth black flecks in a mouth that reeked of garbage.

"TURNER!" Random screeched in Lucy's face and then let her hands go. Lucy shrieked as she fell, kicking and swimming through the dark.

She sat up, a scream caught in her throat as she realized where she was.

Sweat poured off her and a chill ran down her spine. Lucy had never had a dream before but knew that she still hadn't had one.

That was no nightmare, that was a message.

Chapter Three
Quest

*"The eternal quest of the individual human being
is to shatter his loneliness."*
~ Norman Cousins

"So let me get this straight," Gavin said as he stirred his coffee. "You know two Demons?"

"I do," Lucy said carefully. "I actually know three if you count the one in the bathtub."

"Of mercury."

"Yes," Lucy replied plainly, "I would know more by sight from the ones I saw in Hell. There is also Bael."

"The one that was trying to kill you and you well…" Gavin shrugged.

"Yes, that one too."

"Hmmm," he paused, thinking carefully. "And you would like to go and visit one of these Demons because the one in the bathtub came to you in a dream and told you to."

"Yes," Lucy said cautiously, "although I don't dream so it

couldn't have been a dream."

"Have you considered that this is a trap?" Gavin countered thoughtfully.

"Of course," Lucy agreed, "but I don't think that we have another choice." She paused. "And Demon's aren't all bad."

"Did you just say the sentence, 'Demons aren't all bad?'" Gavin challenged with a bit of a grin. "Have you lost your mind, Red?"

"Not really," Lucy replied. "Nathaniel says that they have a soul, it's just misguided. Random, well, he, I guess, liked me."

"I just threw up in my mouth," Gavin said with his deadpan face, "but if you wanna go to Kansas, as offensive as Kansas on Christmas is for me, to see some old lady that you say is a Demon, fine, we can go. But I am warning you, Red, if I have to drink blood or dance with a dead chicken, I am out."

Lucy laughed out loud. "Don't even pretend that you have standards."

"This is true," he replied, nodding. "Kansas it is."

With a bit of time on his laptop and a couple phone calls, Lucy and Gavin were booked on a holiday flight to Wichita where they could then rent a car to travel to Stonecreek. Within an hour they were in Gavin's car on their way to Cross Keys Airport in New Jersey. Lucy had nothing else to wear, so she was still wearing the borrowed outfit Gavin had given her. She didn't really care at this point. She had a purpose and that was all she needed right now. As crazy and as bizarre as it felt, she was totally relieved. She was relieved to actually be doing something, as misguided as this task most likely was, she was happy to be active. Lucy always felt better when she was doing something. She may not have Nathaniel or Anastasia or even Roman, but she would have at least something to do that occupied her mind enough to fill the gap, for now anyway.

Lucy looked at Gavin. "I'm really happy that you're here." She smiled at him and Gavin smiled back, his boyish face an open book. "I would not want to do this alone."

"Hey, listen, the moment anyone says, 'Angels, Demons and prima donna dancers?' I think 'party.'"

Lucy giggled and then sat back in silence for a while. She brought up an image in her mind's eye of Nathaniel. Tall, dark, handsome with those crystal grey eyes that always cut straight through her. A shudder ran through Lucy as she thought of something happening to him. She sighed and swallowed back the tears threatening to come.

"Whatcha thinking about?" Gavin prompted from the driver's seat.

"Nathaniel," Lucy said quietly. "I'm so worried that this is all for nothing."

"Hey, hey now," Gavin interjected, "we have to think positive. Let's assume that they are fine and we just have to meet up with them and then we will all go for a steak sandwich, okay?"

Lucy smiled.

Soon they arrived at the airport and were thrown into the absolute chaos of holiday travel. They made their way through security only to be faced with more crowds. Gavin reached down and grabbed Lucy's hand to pull her through the throng of people. Lucy held on tight, glad to not be alone. When they finally got on the plane and in the air, they both breathed a sigh of relief.

"So tell me about this Turner character we are off to see," Gavin prompted.

"Well," Lucy replied, "Nathaniel said that she is a very old Demon, that she might have even known Egyptian Kings. He also warned me never to irritate her in any way because she is so powerful."

"So we are off to pester her," Gavin said with a smirk. "What a great idea."

"Yeah," Lucy agreed, "this does not seem like the best plan I have ever had. But I really feel like Random was trying to tell me something."

"Your nightmare does seem to be far more clear and specific than most nightmares I have had. But then again, it might be your memory that is making it more vivid, who knows. I agree that it seems the only logical place to start." Lucy nodded. "I'm going to take a nap because, well, to be honest, we are on a plane and I am bored with you," Gavin said with a wink and sat back and closed his eyes.

Lucy stared out the window and sighed – this was not a good plan, at all. It was such a bad plan that it could get them both killed before it even started. Lucy wished she could locate Nathaniel the way he could find her. Lucy shook her head. Maybe Mrs. Turner would be able to tell them something. Anything at this point would be helpful. Lucy closed her eyes and let herself drift off.

She awoke with Gavin lightly shaking her shoulder.

"Hey Red," he whispered, "we're here." She opened her eyes. The plane was almost empty and Gavin was up and collecting their items. Lucy stood up and stretched. They made their way to the car rental counter. Lucy remembered the girl behind the counter. She was the same person who took care of she and Nathaniel when they came at Thanksgiving. The girl remembered Lucy too and kept looking around, clearly hoping that the gorgeous Nathaniel was with her again. Nathaniel often had this effect on women.

"No Calvin Klein model today," Gavin interjected, practically reading the girls mind. "She's with me. Pretty crappy, hey?"

This flustered the girl to no end and they ended up with a much better vehicle for a great price. Lucy burst out laughing as they climbed into the car.

"Seriously!" Gavin said as he turned the key. "What is wrong with that chick? Make a guy feel inadequate much?"

Lucy laughed. "Nathaniel has a way about him that leaves a mark on people."

"Well, at least I know that he's not even human. That actually makes me feel better, but really, I am going to get a complex hanging out with you, Red."

Lucy laughed again and directed Gavin to the highway that would take them to Lucy's hometown of Stonecreek. They drove in silence for a while.

"Wow Lucy," Gavin interjected sardonically as he peered out at the snowy, barren farmer's fields, "I wonder why you moved, this place is pretty amazing."

"Shut up!" Lucy pretended to be hurt. "I bet your home town isn't any better."

"Yeah," Gavin said, "New York is pretty lame compared to this action."

"You're from New York?" Lucy asked. "I didn't know that."

"Born and raised on the Upper East Side. It was awesome."

"What do your parents do?"

"My dad is a stock trader and my mom is an actress."

"An actress?" Lucy asked. "Where?"

"Broadway."

"No way!" Lucy said.

"Yes way," Gavin said, "she has played Grizabella in Cats for the last decade or so. We get to see any show we want whenever we want. She's actually really famous but because of all the makeup on her, no one knows what she actually looks like."

"That's so cool!" Lucy exclaimed. "But did you like growing up in the city?"

"Oh yeah. It was awesome. I had a really fun childhood. We had a roof top garden on our building and me and the other kids from the floor would go up and throw stuff off."

Lucy laughed. "Sounds like good times."

"It was."

"So why Mulbridge?"

Gavin shrugged. "I could have gone to NYU but I kind of wanted to get away on my own, you know?"

"I know exactly what you mean," Lucy said, nodding. "It's like you start to feel completely smothered no matter how great your parents are."

Gavin nodded. "Exactly. And you know, I like Mulbridge. My lab partner is a total loser but you can't win them all."

"Ha!" Lucy laughed, "I bet it ain't so easy for her either. Here's Stonecreek."

Gavin slowed as they approached the main street. "Now this is worth a letter home," he said while leaning forward and looking all around them. Main Street was completely ready for the arrival of Santa – each lamp post was strung with wreaths and lights and holly. The entire downtown was glittery and peaceful. Snow fell softly and the lights twinkled in the night air. "This is gorgeous, Red," he said, "You Stonecreek people know your small town charm."

"That we do," Lucy said wistfully as they made their way down the quaint street.

"So what now?" Gavin asked, "Should we go see the old lady? It's past nine o'clock."

"Hmmm," Lucy considered. "I don't think I could sleep

before we see her anyway."

"Does she know we are here?"

"Most likely," Lucy replied, trying to sound confident like Nathaniel did when they talked about stuff like this. She didn't pull it off.

"Creep-tastic," Gavin mumbled as they made their way down Main Street. Suddenly, he pulled the car over and got out. Lucy watched in confusion as he approached a police car idling in front of the closed hardware store. The police officer opened his window and Gavin leaned in and seemed to have some sort of affable chat with him. Lucy just shook her head. Did he have to make friends everywhere they went? Did he not understand that they were on a schedule of sorts? A few moments later, Gavin shook the police officer's hand, smiled, and made his way back to the car and climbed in.

"What's up with that?" Lucy said, trying to hide the irritation in her voice.

"Just getting directions," Gavin explained as he pulled back out on to the street. He waved at the cruiser as they passed.

"We don't need directions!" Lucy yelled.

"Simmer down, Red," Gavin answered calmly. "You are traveling with a man who likes to get directions. Be happy with that."

Lucy rolled her eyes. As they made their way to Lucy's old street and Mrs. Turner's house, she peeked down the street to confirm that her mother and Miles were indeed still away. At least if Turner were going to blow the whole town up, Lucy's mother would not be among the victims.

"This couldn't look less like the house of a Demon," Gavin mused as he took in the small cottage-style bungalow with the blue trim.

"I know, right?" Lucy said as they got out of the car. They stood side by side on the front walk.

"Do you have any idea what we are going to do after we ring the bell?"

"None," Lucy said with a sigh. "I'm going to wing it."

"Solid," Gavin said as he reached down and took her hand. "Let's go get ourselves killed." He winked at her and with that they walked up the path and rang the bell.

There was silence. Lucy and Gavin waited. Neither one moved and Lucy's breath came in shallow gasps. They looked at each other. Gavin reached up and knocked lightly on the door. Lucy winced at the sharpness of it against the silence.

"It's the most polite knock I could do!" he whispered out of the side of his mouth. The handle started to turn and the door gradually creaked open. Lucy held her breath, Gavin's hand felt like a vice around hers. Standing there was one of the oldest and most dangerous Demons in the world and she could not look any more like Grandma Moses if she tried. She wore a pink cardigan with a frilly white blouse underneath, paired with polyester pink pants and sensible, thick-soled shoes. Mrs. Turner, resident Demon, had recently had her silver hair washed and curled.

Her eyes lit up in a pleasant smile. "Well, little Lucy Bower," she cooed. "How have you been?"

"I'm fine, Mrs. Turner," Lucy replied shortly. She had no patience for any games. "Can we come in please? I wanted to talk to you."

Mrs. Turner's eyes narrowed slightly but she maintained the polite demeanor. "Is everything all right, dear?"

"Nathaniel has gone missing," Lucy said, deciding to omit Roman's involvement. If Hell didn't know what was going on, there was no reason to cause more trouble. Mrs. Turner just stared at

Lucy blankly.

"Hi there," Gavin interjected affably, showing no signs of fright at all, "I'm Gavin McFarlane."

Mrs. Turner smiled kindly at him.

"Well, kids," she almost sang, "it is late and I have my shows to watch."

"Mrs. Turner," Lucy interjected; she was not going to be turned away. "Gavin knows everything. I need to talk to you."

The smile disappeared and a sneer replaced it. As, Mrs. Turner trained her eyes on Lucy, they turned from a light blue to a deep black. "Really?" she growled. All politeness was completely gone and in its place was something very unpleasant indeed. She shook her head and walked back into her house. "Close the door, you fools," she cracked over her shoulder as she made her way through her pink living room to the dining room. She sat down at the lace covered dining table. Lucy and Gavin sat down across from her. Mrs. Turner snapped her fingers and every blind in the house shut with a bang. Now the only light in the house came from a dim lamp on the china hutch.

An ashtray and a glass filled with amber liquid materialized in front of Mrs. Turner on the table and a lit cigarette appeared between her two fingers. She sat back, took a long drag and blew the smoke out. It covered her face and clouded the air and rather than dissipating, remained like a veil, shadowing Turner to nothing more than a grey outline. Lucy stifled a cough.

"What do you want, stupid?" Her gravelly voice cut through the smoky haze.

Lucy bristled. "Why am I stupid?"

"For many reasons," the Demon replied, her face still mostly hidden by darkness and smoke. "First, for having a crush on an Angel; foolish, mindless, singular creatures that they are, second, for losing said Angel, and third for now dragging some new poor sap into your long line of unfortunate decisions."

Lucy nodded; she was right of course. She had lost her Angel and had now dragged poor unsuspecting Gavin into the mix. She sighed.

"Can you help me find him?" she asked softly.

"Who?" the Demon replied.

"Nathaniel, of course."

"Oh," Mrs. Turner said, trying to sound surprised, "the puppy isn't coming when he is called?"

"Please don't be cruel," Lucy pleaded, "I need your help."

The Demon leaned forward, her wrinkled, sharp features pressed out of the smoke for a second and she was suddenly within inches of Lucy's face.

"Why should I help you?" she screamed. Lucy jumped back but within a second Mrs. Turner had retreated behind her veil of smoke again.

Lucy took a deep breath. This could either help or get them killed but the truth was always the best course of action, even with a Demon. "Random sent me."

There was a long pause.

"What did you say, stupid?" Mrs. Turner almost whispered.

"I said Random sent me," Lucy explained. "He came to me in a dream and told me to come to you."

"Really?" Mrs. Turner almost cooed. "Well then, you can certainly tell me what Random was wearing."

"Nothing," Lucy tried to not sound victorious. "Random lives in a bathtub of mercury." There was a sharp intake of breath and Lucy allowed herself to smile a little.

"What do you want to know?" the tone was suddenly very terse.

"Do you know who was after Roman and Anastasia?"

Lucy could tell that Mrs. Turner was choosing her words carefully--when she spoke again it was with great care. Mrs. Turner was afraid of who she was talking about.

"Malachi," she said quietly. Lucy nodded; that was the same name that Roman had said on the dock. "The crime that Roman pays for is no ordinary crime. He had the great misfortune of murdering someone that should not have been murdered. Roman just caught the man off guard and therefore was able to kill him. When a Demon is murdered while in human form, he is sent to the depths for an indeterminate amount of time. Malachi has just been released and is not pleased."

"So Roman murdered a Demon in his human form? Not a man?"

"Yes," Mrs. Turner almost whispered. "I would hazard a guess that the same is true for your little Angel. If he is killed while in mortal form, he's going back."

"How kind of you to remind me," Lucy said tightly.

"Roman's case is perhaps the most unlucky stroke of misfortune I have ever heard of," Mrs. Turner added, her voice dripping with irony. "The thought that he could even catch a Demon that powerful off guard is astounding. Still, despite his power, Malachi was sent to the depths to sit and plot how he would get his revenge on Roman. I would assume that Malachi has them all."

"So where are they?" Lucy asked in a very small voice.

"How would I know?" Mrs. Turner demanded.

"But I thought--"

"That's your problem, stupid, you think too much."

"Please stop calling me stupid," Lucy said in a small voice.

"I can't," Mrs. Turner replied, almost sounding apologetic,

"it's the best way to insult you and I have to insult you. I can't help it. It is in my nature." Lucy shook her head but did not respond. "You think too much, stop thinking so much."

"Are they alive?" Lucy asked. She was being very careful to not provoke Mrs. Turner.

"Well, Roman is already dead so that doesn't make sense, the Angel could be killed but it would take a lot of effort and the human with them is none of my concern." Lucy stifled a sigh. There was a pause and Mrs. Turner added quietly, "Malachi had gone to great trouble to get the human girl, it would not be logical for him to kill her…right away." Lucy swallowed her terror. Was Anastasia being tortured right now?

"Is there a way for me to find them?"

"You mean him," Mrs. Turner cut in. "Be honest. We Demons might have our faults but we are at the very least, honest."

"Yes, him," Lucy almost whispered. Mrs. Turner took a drag of her cigarette and blew more smoke in the air. There was a prolonged pause.

"You claim to be his soul mate, you tell me." She said *soul mate* like it was offensive.

"I….I…" Lucy stumbled on her words, "I don't have the ability to find him like he can find me."

"Because you don't know who he is, stupid!" Mrs. Turner yelled again, her raspy voice jarring into Lucy's teeth. Lucy didn't understand and indeed felt stupid. Mrs. Turner realized that she had to explain further and her irritation increased with every word. "You have no idea who he is, where he came from, where he was born, where he died, how he died! You don't even know his name!"

"But how do I find that out?" Lucy pleaded.

"Well, from the Book of the Dead, of course, stupid! That will tell you how he died!" Mrs. Turner was yelling now.

"Where is the Book of the De--"

"Purgatory, stupid! Did he teach you nothing? Has he told you nothing?" Mrs. Turner leaned forward and screamed through the smoke again. "You have to die and go to Purgatory and find him in the Book of the Dead! Then you have to come back and then you will be able to find him! You can't have a soul mate if you don't know who he is!"

Lucy recoiled back.

Mrs. Turner sat back again. "But it won't do you any good really," she said quietly. "Malachi will prevail, he always does. You most likely won't get there in time and even if you do, no one is powerful enough to beat him." There was a long pause. "You might not even make it out of this house alive," she added softly, like she was speaking to a sleepy child.

A chill ran down Lucy's spine and her stomach clenched in fear. She knew that Mrs. Turner could kill them with a thought. Lucy started to speak but could think of nothing to say that might help the situation. She was in fact stupid and this entire quest was completely foolish and most likely useless. There was nothing Lucy could do now, and maybe it would be easier for Mrs. Turner to kill her. She sighed in defeat.

"Hey, Mrs. Turner," came a subtle voice beside her. Lucy had somehow forgotten that Gavin was even there. He leaned forward and rested one hand on the table cloth. "Remember me? The poor sap who has been drawn into this line of unfortunate events?" He smiled as he leaned even more forward. The smoke around Mrs. Turner cleared slightly and her facial features become clearer. She was looking at Gavin with curiosity. "Hi, there you are," he said kindly. "By the way, I love this town. It is really something else and your home is beautiful, were those Floribunda rose bushes I saw on your lawn?" He didn't wait for a response. "I didn't know that you could protect them from the frost with potato sacks, what an ingenious idea!"

"It's an old trick," Mrs. Turner replied quietly. She was absolutely fascinated with this character. Lucy just stared, completely confused. Gavin was either a mastermind or he was going to get them killed.

Gavin shook his head in amazement. "I bet they are gorgeous come July. A lot of work, I tell ya." He paused and smiled again. "And those roses are pretty popular around this town. Notorious, if you will." The smoke around Mrs. Turner was completely missing now. She still smoked but the smoke dissipated normally. She took another drag and squinted her eyes at Gavin, suspicious of where he was going. "Yup, I was just talking to Officer Miller down on Main Street and he knew exactly which house was yours. Isn't that nice?"

Silence.

"So, we are just going to head out now," he said politely while standing. "We really can't thank you enough for all your help. We will get going on that project right away." He stepped smoothly back from the table and took Lucy's hand to guide her with him. "This is really, just a lovely home, great town, and I hope to come back and see those roses real soon." He flashed that disarming smile again and pulled Lucy toward the door. He reached behind them for the handle. They were going to get away, alive.

Suddenly, there was a flash and Mrs. Turner wasn't at the table anymore, she was standing right in front of them with a dark grin on her face. Lucy stifled a yelp of terror. Mrs. Turner's black eyes glared as she gripped the door knob with one claw-like hand and surprisingly, pulled it open for them to walk out.

"Now, this one is not stupid, Lucy. You should drop the Angel and stick with him. Out."

Lucy and Gavin darted out the door and down the walk toward the car. Gavin opened her door for her and all but shoved Lucy inside. He moved quickly around to the driver's side and jumped in. Just as Gavin's door slammed closed, they heard Mrs. Turner call out in the sweetest voice possible, "You kids have a Merry Christmas now!"

"Drive!" Lucy growled and Gavin hit the gas.

After they left, Mrs. Turner closed the door and walked slowly over to the table. She finished her drink. Then she moved to her china cabinet and opened the delicate glass door. Inside was an antique phone. It wasn't plugged in; the handset wasn't even attached to the base with a cord anymore. She slowly, deliberately, lifted the handset to her ear and waited a moment.

"They just left," she said carefully, "I did what I could. She has a clever boy with her." She nodded, "I see. Well, I still believe it is a great deal of trouble for an exceptionally common girl." She winced as a male voice in deep rage blasted out of the handset. "I understand." She hung up the handset and carefully closed the glass door with a sigh. She sat back down at her table and another cigarette materialized in her hand. Mrs. Turner looked out at the Christmas lights.

"Floribunda roses," she muttered with a small chuckle and she took a drag.

Chapter Four
Run

"If you want to live, you must walk.
If you want to live long, you must run."
~ Jinabhai Navik

They drove in silence for a long time before Gavin finally spoke.

"Holy crap that was the most terrifying thing I have ever seen!" he yelled at the windshield.

Lucy nodded fervently. She now, more than ever, needed Nathaniel. She hadn't understood half of what Mrs. Turner had even said. Lucy didn't know Nathaniel? What was she talking about? She knew everything about Nathaniel! Everything. But then, Mrs. Turner was right that Lucy didn't even know if Nathaniel was his real name, she didn't know where he was born or even how he died. It had never actually been a problem before today.

"Wait!" Lucy yelled when she saw how far out of town they were. Gavin half looked at her but kept going. "We have to go back to my house! I need clothes and stuff!"

"Sorry kiddo," Gavin said, shaking his head. "I am not going back there!"

"You have to go back!" Lucy yelled, "I need my stuff! I can't wear the same clothes for the next God only knows how long!"

Gavin glanced sideways at her and rolled his eyes. "We are not staying there overnight." He started to pull a U-turn.

"Deal," Lucy replied.

"We are not even staying there for 20 minutes," Gavin explained again. Lucy smiled, totally relieved that she would get some comforts.

They approached Lucy's street and Gavin slowed the car as Lucy directed him to her childhood home. The porch light was on but Lucy knew that was only on a timer. They parked in the driveway and got out of the car.

"Do you think she can hear us?" Gavin whispered as Lucy directed him to the backyard.

Lucy shrugged. "Nathaniel can hear rain coming," she whispered back.

Gavin stopped walking and looked at her. "Seriously?" He shook his head and kept moving.

They walked around to the back of the house where it was pitch black but Lucy moved easily. She had a perfect image of the backyard in her head. She led Gavin to the back porch and bent down to lift the silver flower pot to reveal a key. Lucy fit the key into the back door and within moments they were in Lucy's mother's kitchen. She flipped on all the lights and gave Gavin a smile.

"That's better, hey?" she said brightly.

"Nope, nope, nope," Gavin said with conviction. "This house is lovely too; unfortunately it happens to be within a few houses of a Demon, therefore its curb appeal and resale value just plummeted in my books."

Lucy smiled at him. "It's okay," she said reassuringly. "If she wanted us dead, she would have killed us."

"Wow that's so much better!" Gavin exploded sarcastically. "Move fast, Red, you have ten minutes before I leave with or without you."

Lucy tried to think about what Nathaniel would tell her in this instance. It would most likely be something about him loving her so much, which would not be appropriate. She decided just to move quickly.

She ran upstairs with Gavin right behind her. She grabbed a bag from the hall closet and filled it with clothes from her drawers in her old bedroom. Thankfully, Lucy's wardrobe was so extensive that she had more than enough to choose from. She pilfered some makeup and products from her mother's bathroom and her mother's warm wool coat from the front closet. Finally, she scrawled a vague yet happy note to her mom about the cabin being snowed in and a change in plans for her and Nathaniel. She offered no further details; hopefully, it would all be sorted out by the time Sandra returned home.

She did all this with Gavin protectively beside her, silently but urgently pushing her to go faster. Finally, Lucy retrieved some emergency items from the basement: candles, flares, matches and bottled water. From the kitchen, she took some dry goods like crackers and cereal. After all was done, she pulled on her coat, her boots and looked at Gavin.

"I think we are ready." He nodded silently and grabbed all of her stuff himself. They let themselves back out the door, Lucy locked it, and they skulked quietly back to the car. It wasn't until they had Stonecreek sufficiently behind them on the highway that they both felt the tension release. Gavin let out an audible breath of air.

"Where are we going?" Lucy asked, hoping that Gavin had a plan. She certainly didn't have one yet.

"Back to Wichita, we will get some food and sleep at a hotel or something," Gavin replied with assurance.

"That whole thing with the police officer was amazing, Gavin," Lucy replied.

He shrugged. "I know everyone remembers Nathaniel because he looks like a movie star," he looked over at Lucy while he drove, "people remember me because I am funny. If I can make someone laugh, they will know who I am forever. I figured that it would help that someone at least knows where we are."

"It was genius really," Lucy answered. Gavin shrugged again.

"Are you doing okay with all this?" she prodded.

Gavin shook his head. "I gotta tell ya Red, I thought you were a little off your rocker. I thought that maybe you were speaking metaphorically, like Nathaniel is your savior and therefore he is *like* an Angel to you and Roman is a jackass and therefore *reminded* you of a Demon. I thought you were being a little delusional about the storm at the dock. I thought, well, I don't know what I thought. I honestly had no idea how deep into this we were."

"You thought I was making it all up and you still came all this way with me?" Lucy asked incredulously. "Why? Why didn't you just tell me to take a hike?"

"Because you are my friend," Gavin said, "and you are all alone and whether or not I believed you had nothing to do with you believing it yourself."

"That's amazing," Lucy replied.

"Obviously, if the roles were reversed, you would have told

me to go pound sand, good to know." He grinned.

"Well, I have to say that you are handling it all very well," Lucy said with relief, "I don't think I could do this with someone who is a basket case."

"Don't count me out yet buddy," he said slyly and Lucy smiled. "But it's all true? There are Demons wandering around the Earth giving us the choice to do the wrong thing and Angels are up in Heaven giving us the choice to do the right thing?" Lucy nodded. "Yowza." Lucy smiled again.

"I know it's all a lot to take in, trust me I know."

"How did you take it all?"

"I had Nathaniel."

Gavin nodded. They had arrived in Wichita and Gavin pulled into a hotel that had a pub attached. As they entered the lobby, Gavin said, "I am only getting one room. Nathaniel would kill me if I let you out of my sight, but we will for sure get two beds." Lucy nodded in agreement. "I can't have you getting all fresh with me in the middle of the night." He elbowed her jovially. "I know I must be pretty irresistible after the tall dark Angel." Lucy laughed out loud.

They checked in using Gavin's credit card and went up to the room. Lucy insisted on taking a shower and putting on her own clothes and afterward they headed down to the pub to eat. The pub was marginally busy but it was dark and warm and very cozy, and the pair settled in to a booth in the corner. The waitress appeared and Gavin ordered two beers and a pound of wings to start with.

"If you don't like wings and beer," Gavin said, "we can't be friends."

"If you don't like very large steaks," Lucy replied with a wink, "we can't be friends."

Gavin laughed out loud as the beers arrived. They both

drank and sat back and relaxed slightly.

"All right, Red," Gavin said when the waitress had left, "talk to me."

"Okay," Lucy started to think, "I don't think she was lying, do you?"

"Not exactly, but that whole, 'I can't help being cruel' attitude really throws a wrench into the works. Everything she said could have been a lie just to mess with us."

"True," Lucy agreed, "but we really have no other choice but to believe her."

They fell into a thoughtful silence.

"You know what I find to be weird?" Gavin supposed out loud. "That Anastasia's parents haven't reported her missing. I watched the news in the airport and nothing was said about a missing debutant."

"Good point," Lucy agreed. She took Gavin's phone and used her memory to dial the Rookes' number in Chicago. The phone rang and within a moment Mrs. Rooke picked up.

"Hello?"

"Hi Mrs. Rooke," Lucy replied, relieved to hear her sound so, well, alive. "I am so sorry to call so late but can I speak to Anastasia? Her phone isn't um…picking up."

"Oh no it wouldn't dear," Mrs. Rooke replied, "she had it shut off for the trip."

"The trip?" Lucy asked, trying to sound light. Gavin leaned in.

"Oh my goodness, she left so quickly she didn't even have a chance to tell you!" Mrs. Rooke cooed, "She has headed to Europe for the Christmas holidays!"

"Without you?" Lucy's skin had gone cold. Her eyes looked pleadingly at Gavin's and he reached out and solidly held her hand.

Mrs. Rooke laughed. "No dear, with Alexander! Her new fiancé? I'm sure she told you about her engagement."

"Of course," Lucy choked out, "her fiancé." Gavin's mouth fell open. Lucy continued in almost a whisper, "Would you happen to have a contact number for Alexander? I don't even know his last name."

"Oh, his last name is Maleachee," Mrs. Rooke said, "They called yesterday to check in. Of course the phones went down for a bit the night of our party because of the fire in the apartment next door." Lucy knew that would have been Nathaniel and Roman. "She's just having a wonderful time but warned that they are moving out of cell range so might not call for a bit. I will make sure to tell her to call you the next time they check in."

Lucy swallowed. "That would be great." She was barely breathing. "Mrs. Rooke, could you spell Maleachee for me? I would like to send them a gift."

"Oh, of course." Lucy pulled a pen from her bag and flipped a coaster over to write on it, "M-A-L-A-C-H-I." Lucy's hand was shaking so badly that the pen dropped out of it.

"Thanks so much, Mrs. Rooke," Lucy forced out.

"Merry Christmas dear!"

"Merry Christmas." Lucy's heart broke for the woman who most likely would never see her only child again. She hung up the phone and dropped her head into her hands.

"Who is Alexander?" Gavin asked quietly.

Lucy sighed and leaned back against the booth. "He's a guy who's been hanging around Anastasia's parents for the last while. They have been trying to set him up with Anastasia but she kept telling them that she was dating Roman. It must have been Malachi all the time, trying to get her to love him to torture Roman and simultaneously trying to kill her and make it look like an accident.

When that didn't work, he turned himself into something that looked like what the Wrath is supposed to look like and tried to just kill them both."

"When that didn't work, he went back to Anastasia again."

Lucy nodded.

"And that's the Demon that Roman murdered to get into Hell?" Gavin asked.

Lucy nodded. "He raped and murdered Roman's sister. Roman came upon them and went wild. It was the 1800's, I think in London. Roman was executed for his crimes. Malachi was sent to the depths of Hell. And like Turner said, once he was released, he started his plan. I wonder if Roman has figured it all out."

"Bet he has now."

"Yup," Lucy said ruefully.

"Why would Anastasia agree to marry that guy?"

Lucy shook her head. "She must have made some deal with him. She wouldn't have agreed to marry anyone. She must have gone with him to save her parents or," Lucy choked back a sob, "me."

Gavin leaned forward. "Red, the most important thing is that she is alive." Lucy nodded. "And Roman and Nathaniel are most likely alive too or else Mrs. Rooke would have talked about the two dead guys on her street." Lucy nodded again. He was right.

She sniffed and took a deep breath. She leaned forward and drank the rest of her beer.

"Okay," she breathed, "they're alive. Now we have to find them."

"Yeah," Gavin said, grabbing a wing, "I think that whole 'Book of the Dead' stuff was fairly useless."

"Oh no!" Lucy exclaimed, "That I do believe. I just have to figure out a way to die and go to Purgatory."

Gavin stopped chewing. "Are you out of your mind?"

"Oh, it can be done!" Lucy exclaimed. "I told you that Roman and Nathaniel killed me and brought me back to life to try to convince fate to leave us alone."

"Yeah, babe, they aren't here!" Gavin exclaimed, "I could most likely figure out a way to kill you but I certainly have no way to bring you back!"

"I think I might know someone who can do it," Lucy posed.

"You can't possibly know more than one person who can kill you and bring you back to life." Gavin sounded sick.

"Sadly, I do," Lucy replied. She realized that she was completely starving and dug into her wings. "I think I know some people at MIT who might be able to help us."

Gavin shook his head. "It's a bad idea."

"It's our only idea," Lucy argued.

"No it isn't," Gavin replied, "what about Dr. Hannon?"

"Are you nuts?" Lucy protested. "He would never have anything to do with any of this. He would call my mom and it would become a big thing."

Gavin sighed, "I still don't like it."

"I don't know if I have to die though," Lucy pondered, "I wonder if I could just be deeply hypnotized and my soul will find a way to get where it needs to go."

Gavin nodded, "I like that idea better, a lot better."

"So we will leave in the morning," Lucy said. She pushed her plate away.

"Boston sounds lovely," Gavin agreed. "We should drive, that crowded airport was enough to drive me mental."

"I figured as much." Lucy looked around at the normal people enjoying their holidays, sitting with friends or catching up with family. Gavin seemed to read her mind.

"They are totally oblivious, hey?" he said, glancing around the room too.

Lucy nodded.

"You just want to get up and shake them," she mumbled, "tell them to make the right choices, because it could end very badly."

"You figure Hell is a bad place, I don't know if I ever thought about what that meant," Gavin pondered.

"Oh it's bad, really bad," Lucy said, "but you won't go there. You helping me is one of those things that get you into Heaven."

"Good to know," Gavin smiled, "I guess you are stuck with me then. I have to get the points where I can."

Lucy smiled and yawned. Gavin yawned as well and motioned for the waitress for the bill. He paid while ignoring Lucy's protests and they headed up to the room. Lucy changed into her pajamas in the bathroom and took a good look at herself. She looked tired but not beat. Her ivory skin looked healthy enough, although she looked terribly pale and she had dark circles under her green eyes. Sighing, she left the bathroom. Gavin was sitting on his bed, he had turned on the TV to a hockey game, and he smiled when she came in.

"Just checking the scores," he said, sitting up and reaching for the remote.

"No, leave it," Lucy replied, "it's fine. I like hockey."

Gavin walked past her to the bathroom and Lucy sat on her own bed. She pulled out her ponytail and started brushing out her auburn locks. She watched the game blankly for a few seconds. The Flames were winning in the third against LA. Suddenly she froze as an unexpected pain ripped through her midsection. She doubled over and stifled a scream but she allowed the tears to rain down off her face and onto the bed covers. She heard the shower turn on and let the sob continue.

"I miss you," she sobbed. "I miss you so much I can't even breathe. Oh Nathaniel, where are you?" Her body rocked back and forth as it allowed the pain to wash over her. Finally, it began to subside and Lucy sat back up and wiped her face with a Kleenex, she took a deep shuddering breath and began brushing her hair again just as Gavin stepped out of the steamy bathroom. He wore a pair of plaid pajama pants and a tank top.

"You still brushing your hair?" he exclaimed jovially, "Lady, get yourself a hobby."

Lucy forced a smile. "What, like I need your crappy hair cut?"

Gavin looked hurt as he observed his own tawny short curls in the mirror, "I will have you know that the lady at 'Cuts a Lot' is a magician and only charges me fifteen bucks."

She put the brush on the side table and slid down under the covers.

Gavin smiled down at her, "Go to sleep, Red, I got ya."

She smiled again and rolled over. "Thanks again for coming with me. I don't know what I would do without you." Her recent release had left her totally empty and she started to drift off.

She heard Gavin get into bed and turn off the lights and the TV. Lucy drifted further into sleep and her breathing slowed. Gavin must have thought that she was already out.

"I'm trying to get her to you in one piece, my friend," he whispered into the dark. "I just hope I can do it without getting both of us killed."

Lucy smiled. Gavin was so worried about her and it was nice to have someone worry about her. She wished Nathaniel could somehow hear Gavin; it would make him sleep a bit easier. She let the darkness of sleep overtake her.

Chapter Five
Road Trip

*"You got to be careful if you don't know where
you're going, because you might not get there."*
~ *Yogi Berra*

Lucy woke up feeling like she had been asleep for a year. Sitting up, she looked at the clock and saw that it was past noon. She yawned and stretched, feeling like her body was stronger than it had been in a long time. She figured that the sleep was more than needed. She swung her legs over the side of the bed to see that Gavin's bed was empty. Lucy stood and opened the curtains, wincing at the blinding sun. There was frost on the window but the sky was a clear blue. Lucy couldn't resist letting in a little fresh air. She unlocked and pushed open the frozen window and stood breathing in the chilled freshness. Then something caught her eye.

She turned her head and there, on the edge of the window, was a butterfly. A Palos Verdes Blue butterfly to be exact. It was amazing that a butterfly would exist in the dead of winter in Wichita, Kansas, and it was even more amazing when Lucy considered what type of buttery fly it was. The Palos Verdes Blue butterfly was so rare it was thought to be extinct for a decade. It didn't even live anywhere near Kansas, it was only known to live in one place, the Palos Verdes Peninsula near Los Angeles. Lucy grinned and laid her hand out. The butterfly landed softly onto her palm – it was so gentle that she barely felt its touch. Tears ran down Lucy's face as she stared at the beautiful indigo wings, so delicate, they were almost transparent. This could mean only one thing. Gavin came in the room, carrying bags of food.

"Nathaniel's alive!" Lucy screamed at him, holding out the butterfly. "Look what he sent me!"

Gavin dropped the bags and hurried over.

"No way!" he grinned at her, "Red! That is awesome!" The butterfly, obviously feeling like it had done its job, left Lucy's hand and flew off due west to warmer weather.

Lucy dropped her face into her hands and sobbed. Gavin wrapped her in a tight hug.

"Hey buddy," he said quietly, "this is a good thing. He still has some powers and he's okay and he wants you to know that. Maybe he just can't get to you right now. I don't know, but I really think we should be happy."

"I am happy," Lucy sobbed, "it's just such a relief to know for sure." She lifted her head and let out a deep breath. Gavin handed her a tissue and she cleaned herself up. "What have you been up to?"

"Well," said Gavin, closing the window. "I woke up about an hour ago and you were still dead to the world, so I got us some breakfast and provisions for the car."

Turns out that Gavin believed that eating only junk food was a requirement for road trips because the bags were full of nothing but crap. Lucy grinned at it all.

"We are going to be a hundred pounds heavier when we get there," she mused as she came out of the bathroom dressed for the day.

Gavin shrugged, "It's my best way to defend you, make you unattractive." Lucy laughed and threw a towel at him that he dodged easily. "Hey, and I was going to get a map but I figured you would have some sort of internal GPS or something."

Lucy stopped and brought up a road map of the Eastern United States, "We will head toward Kansas City first on the I-35 then to the I-435 East through Missouri, then we will take the I-70 through St. Louis and Illinois and through Indiana and Ohio. Then we should change to the I-71 North toward Cleveland then the I-90 East to Pennsylvania, then the I-86 and the I-88 through New York but back to the I-90 East to Boston, Massachusetts." She smiled and nodded.

Gavin just started at her.

"I wasn't paying attention, could you repeat that?" Lucy laughed and they packed up to head out. "How long will it take?"

"Actual distance is 1651 miles, so we should be able to make it in two or three days."

"Just in time for Christmas!" Gavin said brightly. They headed down to the lobby and he added, "Oh, and the GPS in my car back home is programmed to speak in a French accent when she gives me directions. You should do the same thing, please, if you wish for me to listen to you."

"I will try my best," Lucy replied seriously. Gavin grinned.

They checked out and drove for a while in silence.

"Lucy, can I ask you a question?" Gavin asked.

Lucy turned to face him. "It must be serious for you to call me Lucy and not Red."

Gavin smiled. "I don't want to pester or be too inquisitive."

"Let's get something straight here," Lucy began, "you are risking everything to come on this quest with me. You may ask me any question ever, about anything, for any reason at all. You may tell me when I am being annoying or dumb. I beg of you to tell me when I am wrong too because I need that every once in a while. Okay?"

Gavin chuckled, "Fair enough." He paused, choosing his words. "Do you really not know who Nathaniel is? Was that Demon lady right?"

"No, I don't," Lucy answered. "I don't know where he was born or where he died or even at what age he died. I know that age means very little in Heaven. He could have been a ninety year old man for all I know. I don't even know if Nathaniel is his real name."

"Doesn't that bug you?" Gavin asked. "It would drive me nuts and I certainly don't have your, shall we say, desperation for knowledge."

"It did at first," Lucy admitted, "It was brutal but I got used to it. I mean really, what other option did I have? Well, I had one option, Roman, and that didn't feel right so I took the option of Nathaniel."

"Roman?" Gavin asked incredulously, "Roman and you?"

Lucy laughed, "He asked me out. Mainly to figure out what involvement I had in all this because he knew I had something to do with Nathaniel."

"Sneaky bugger,"

"Yup," Lucy smiled, "and when I turned him down, he asked Anastasia out."

"I still can't believe that Anastasia is dating a Demon," Gavin exclaimed.

"He's not that bad really," Lucy explained, "he used to be really horrible when Nathaniel was tied to Heaven. He hated our guts but since then, he's I guess what you would call a friend."

"What I would call a friend in no way resembles that creature we saw in Stonecreek."

"And Roman doesn't resemble her at all," Lucy clarified. "Most of the time anyway. I have certainly been hard on him these last few months and I shouldn't have been. He was with us the whole way, brought us to Hell and back safely and defended me with as much fervor as Nathaniel did." She paused. "When he went to kill me, I swear he hesitated. He did not want to do it."

"Okay, so say this whole thing works out and you find out who Nathaniel is and you don't like him?" Gavin queried, "Then what?"

Lucy thought. "I don't know, I guess we will just have to cross that bridge when we come to it. I love Nathaniel for who he is today, not for who he was. I doubt it would make much of a difference."

"Lucy," Gavin said seriously, "what if he was a jerk or a lunatic or the guy who invented hyper-color shirts? That wouldn't bring him down a couple notches in your mind? You should be prepared. I can't imagine any human could be as perfect as he is as an Angel."

"I see your point," Lucy agreed, "but I really don't think it will make any difference."

"Good to know," Gavin said quietly, "I could be a serial killer and you would forgive me."

Lucy laughed. They were quiet for a minute. Lucy didn't want to talk about Nathaniel anymore. She could feel the pain starting pulse under the surface. She strangled it and changed the subject. "Tell me about you in high school," Lucy asked.

"Oh high school?" Gavin shook his head, "Nightmarish place really. Horrible. I sat somewhere between the science and math geeks and the class clowns. None of the groups that girls were interested in. I didn't go to my prom."

"No way!" Lucy exclaimed.

"Nope," Gavin answered, "stayed home and watched movies. I didn't really have anyone to ask and I didn't think anyone would say yes if I did."

"Ahh, that's so sad." Lucy offered. "I can't imagine why anyone would say no to you."

"Well, if I get a second prom, I guess you are coming with me."

"You bet!" Lucy exclaimed.

"Wait!" Gavin yelled and turned up the radio. "My favorite song is on the radio and you will sing or get out."

"You are so bossy!" Lucy yelled as Elvis' song "Suspicious Minds" blasted through the speakers.

"We can't go on together!" they yelled at the top of their lungs, "With suspicious minds. And we can't build our dreams on suspicious minds!" They sang to the end of the song and Lucy was tearing up with laughing. Gavin turned the volume back down and turned to look at Lucy.

"Will you remember that, Lucy? Just like it happened?"

Lucy slowed her laughs and looked at his suddenly serious face. "I'll remember that. I promise."

Gavin nodded and turned the radio back up to a listening level.

The rest of the day passed at the same pace. Lucy and Gavin talked easily about school and friends and family. It was nice talking like that with someone. Lucy never talked too much about her past because it was strange when Nathaniel couldn't share anything from his side. Of course, Lucy knew that he would listen to her all day but it felt so silly when he couldn't share anything back.

The sun had gone down when they reached St. Louis, Missouri and decided to stay the night. They rented another hotel and went again to the attached restaurant for dinner. They sat down and ordered. Suddenly Gavin yelled out at the bartender, "Excuse me friend," he called, "could you turn that up please?" The bartender shrugged and used the remote to turn up the TV. It was a news report on Mulbridge University. A solemn reporter stood in front of what used to be the student union building. All that remained was a charred and ruined shadow of the former structure. Lucy gasped as the camera panned around the quad.

In addition to the student union building, the theatre, the dorms, the sciences buildings and, most horribly, the library were burned basically to the ground. When Lucy had escaped the University, she knew that the theatre was on fire but she had no idea that the damage was this extensive. The oldest, most beautiful buildings had been destroyed. A tear came to Lucy's eye. Gavin reached out and laid his hand on hers, she smiled at the comfort of it.

"Mulbridge University has finally made a decision on the state of the school today," the reporter announced, "They have decided to cancel all classes for the following semester." Then the school's president was on the screen, a small man with beady eyes by the name of Crowne.

"Due to the extensive damage made to our campus, most notably to the student union building where the student records were kept, it is with a sad heart and a deep sense of regret that I close Mulbridge University for the Winter Semester. Our plan is to reopen in the spring for regular classes once we rebuild." Crowne's voice was cracking slightly; this could not be his best moment. Lucy sighed as the reporter appeared back on the screen.

"The University suffered extensive damage as a result of a vicious fire that tore through the century old buildings on December 15. There were no injuries reported, but damages are estimated to be over ten million dollars. The cause of the fire is not known, but foul play is not suspected. Students will receive full credit for all classes taken in the fall semester and may either take classes on-line or receive a credit for their next semester." The program moved on to another story. Gavin nodded to the bartender who promptly turned the set down again.

"Well," Gavin said heavily, "that sucks. I assume that was The Wrath you were talking about?"

"It was Malachi or Alexander, rather, posing as the Wrath and trying to kill Roman and Anastasia." She wiped a tear away. "I loved that library," Lucy said with deep sadness.

"I know you did, Red," Gavin said, "and all our stuff in the dorms."

Lucy shook her head. "That sucks too," she looked at him sideways, "not to be a diva here, but I had some really fantastic shoes in that room."

"So did I," Gavin said with a wink, "at least no one was hurt."

"Yeah," Lucy agreed as their food arrived, "that's a blessing at least."

"And we get a whole semester off school to hunt down evil Demons and save good Demons and Angels and dancers," Gavin replied brightly.

"You know," Lucy said with a grin, "you really make this sound like a stupid TV show when you talk like that."

"I aim for my life to be like a stupid TV show," Gavin said with a grin, "it makes it all more interesting. Although," he added after taking a bite of his burger, "I don't know that I have to make it sound more far-fetched."

Lucy smiled ruefully. "Sadly, my life lately has resembled a fairly eventful television show."

Gavin tilted his head, "You don't sound so thrilled with that."

"Would you be?" she challenged. "I'm just tired of it all. Not that Nathaniel isn't worth it," she clarified and Gavin nodded understanding, "it's just so much. Nathaniel and I had barely settled into a normal routine when I started having all the accidents and then The Wrath showed up and it was all downhill from there."

"Most chicks would have fallen apart by now," Gavin said proudly. Lucy thought of her breakdown last night.

She sucked in a deep breath and blinked a couple times. "I'm fine," she said brightly, "it's going to be okay." She picked up her burger and took a huge bite.

"Of course it's going to be fine," Gavin said with more conviction than Lucy felt.

They finished off their meal and headed up to their room where they took their same routine of Lucy taking the bathroom and then Gavin taking a shower. While he was in the shower, as if on cue, Lucy's fear and sadness overwhelmed her again. She curled up in the bed and sobbed until her throat was ravaged and her stomach hurt. Finally, the pain eased off enough for her to compose herself. Gavin stepped out of the bathroom and looked at Lucy.

"You okay, Red?" he asked carefully, most likely noting her suddenly puffy eyes.

"I'm okay," she assured him. He wasn't convinced but he let it go.

"Get some sleep," he said kindly, "I got ya, Red."

She nodded and snuggled down in the sheets and soon fell fast asleep.

Lucy woke up. She was in a river, standing up to her knees as the cool water washed past her. She was wearing a simple white linen dress. She looked around her and saw that a beautiful forest lined both banks of the shallow river. It was peaceful and calm and her body instantly relaxed. Lucy sat down in the water and let it wash over her back and arms. She breathed deeply and felt peace creep deep into her soul. Smiling, she glanced sideways to notice a fox sitting on a rock on the bank of the river. He was watching her with deep grey, thoughtful eyes.

"Well, hello," *Lucy said with a hint of surprise.*

"Hello Lucy," *the fox replied in a bright voice.*

"You can talk?" *Lucy was astonished.*

"In dreams, yes, I can talk," *the fox replied.*

"Oh," *Lucy corrected,* "I don't dream."

"This is a special dream," *the fox said.*

Lucy thought of her terrifying vision of Random while sleeping at Gavin's cabin, and nodded understanding. That dream was so terrifying and this one so lovely that it had to mean only one thing. "Did Nathaniel send you?" *she asked hopefully,* "Does he have a message for me?"

"No," *the Fox said sadly,* "but he is alive. You would know if he wasn't."

Lucy relaxed further. "And Roman and Anastasia?" *she prompted.*

"Alive as well," *the Fox said clearly.* "But I am here to warn you, Lucy."

She shook her head in confusion. "About what?"

The Fox dropped his snout down and stared deeply at Lucy, "You need to know that things will not work out the way you want them to."

"How so?" *Lucy demanded. Was Nathaniel going to die? Was she going to die? Was something going to happen to Anastasia or Roman?*

"I don't know that, for I do not see the future. I can only report what I have been told," the Fox answered. "Things will not work out the way you want them to. It is important though," he clarified, "to understand that things will work out for the best, Lucy. You will not understand at the time. Your memory allows us to tell you now, so you can look back on this moment and hear my words again. What will happen is what is best." He nodded at her. "Do you understand that, Lucy?"

"I understand what you are saying, but I don't see how that could be. I am trying to find Nathaniel so we can be together forever...." She trailed off as the Fox shook his snout at her.

"Again, Lucy dear," he said with such kindness it hurt, "Please understand that I do not know what will happen, for I would tell you if I did. I only know that you need to remember that things will work out for the best even if they are not what you wanted." Lucy just stared at him uncomprehendingly and he smiled. "We love you so much, Lucy. Please know that."

"I know that," Lucy said quickly, "I know that and I will remember what you told me." She could feel herself waking but really didn't want to leave this quiet peaceful place. She dropped her hands into the water and grasped at the slippery cold rocks to no avail. Within seconds, the bank and the Fox faded away. Lucy opened her eyes to Gavin shaking her softly awake.

Chapter Six
Breakdown

"Madness need not be all breakdown.
It may also be break-through."
~ R.D. Laing

Lucy waited until they were on the road to tell Gavin about her latest dream.

"This is very interesting, Red," Gavin said after she finished, "What do you think it means?"

Lucy shook her head. "I have no idea. I don't know what the Fox was talking about when he said 'things won't work out.' What 'things' is he talking about?" she wondered out loud, "Is he talking about you and me on this mission to save them? Will they be found by police before we get there? Will my conversation with Roger at MIT not go well and he refuse to help us?" She shrugged. "I don't know."

"Well," Gavin said, "I guess you should just store that into your brain for when you need it. That is obviously the point they were trying to make. Although, I don't know who *they* are."

"It was Gabriel," Lucy explained, "I couldn't see it during the dream but the Fox had his eyes. *They* are the Angels."

"Of course the Fox had Gabriel's eyes," Gavin grinned, "Only you, Red. Okay, but what about this entire new dreaming thing? It's like you are clairvoyant or something."

"I don't know," Lucy said with a head shake. "This dream last night was actually pretty nice, very relaxing. The one the other night? Not so much."

"Hmm," Gavin said thoughtfully, "it just really doesn't sound like any dream I have ever had. It seemed far more cohesive, clear and purposeful." He shook his head, "But that might just be your memory and how exact it is. But I don't think I have ever had a dream where I felt like I was being communicated with for higher purpose. This is cool though. The whole, 'message from the other side.' I hope you aren't too bummed when we have burgers for lunch instead of tacos."

"Is that what you think?" Lucy challenged with a laugh, "that the Angel Gabriel took the form of a Fox to warn me to not be too disappointed with my mid-day meal?"

"Honey," Gavin raised his eyebrows at her, "you seem to commune with the heavenly on a regular basis. How the Hell (pardon the pun) would I know what you talk about?"

Lucy laughed out loud. "You Gavin," she said with a smile, "make me laugh."

"Excellent," Gavin said with a nod, "now, if I could get you to stop snoring, then I am a happy roomie."

"Ha!" Lucy laughed. They sat in silence for a while, until Lucy saw a sign at the side of the road. "Turn in here!" she almost screamed.

Gavin obeyed immediately and veered the car to the right, taking the exit toward Terre Haute, Indiana. "What?" he exclaimed after they had swerved manically onto the main road. "What's going on?"

"Don't get too excited," Lucy said seriously, "but there is something very cool here."

Gavin, sensing Lucy's sarcasm, yelled out loud, "I thought it was an emergency! For pete's sake, Red! If there is a shoe sale, just tell me to pull over!"

"Better than that!" Lucy shrieked. "They have Stiffy!"

There was a pause.

"I will refrain from giggling like a kid in grade three and ask you," Gavin tightened his lips, "What is Stiffy?"

"Stiffy the Green Eyed Dog!" Lucy yelled, "I read this book once on the quirky attractions of America and Stiffy the Green Eyed Dog is one of them and he is here in Terre Haute and we are taking a field trip."

"A dog with green eyes?" Gavin said, "Don't toy with me Lucy."

"It's stuffed. "

"I'm in."

So within the hour they were in the basement of Historical Museum of the Wabash Valley staring into the eyes of a taxidermic green eyed dog.

"Do you think the eyes are real?" Gavin whispered as he tucked his hands in his pockets, "I had marbles once that were precisely that color."

"This is the most legit thing I have ever seen," Lucy said, trying to sound serious as she started to giggle.

"This is the biggest load of crap I have ever seen," Gavin whispered back.

They stood in silence. Lucy suddenly felt the weight of everything pressing down on her. It was unbearable.

"Gavin?" Lucy whispered. "Can I tell you a secret?"

He glanced at her sideways, his eyes serious. "Any time, Red."

"Every night when you take a shower I sob until I want to die." Her voice was barely audible. "I want to die Gavin, all the time. You are literally the only thing holding me together. You and my memories. I feel so guilty when we laugh, when we have fun. I feel," she choked on her thoughts. "I have to cry every day or else I might shatter."

The sob came surging though her as her face twisted in agony. The force of it knocked her to her knees. Gavin caught her softly and sat with her draped over his lap, his strong arms encircling her as her pain released itself in earnest. Lucy howled and wailed until all of the anguish and the guilt and the hurt drained out, leaving her feeling hollow down to her core.

"I know, Red," Gavin whispered into her ear when she was quiet, "I know that you cry. That's why I take such long showers. I figured you'd need the privacy but no more, Red." He pushed her hair back and slipped his hand under her cheek to turn her face to look at him. His eyes were determined. "No more hiding, no more secrets, no more. If we are going to make it through this in one piece, you have to trust me." Lucy nodded and a smile touched his kind face. "We do this together, okay? Plus, I have a secret for you." He paused and sighed. "I have never registered for a poetry class."

"What?" Lucy demanded as she sat up and faced him, "Of course you have. You had poetry with me last semester, after our science class. I proofread all your papers."

"I didn't say I didn't *take* a poetry class," Gavin clarified. "I said that I haven't registered for one."

"You weren't registered for that class?" Lucy stared incredulously at him.

"No," he said sheepishly, "that first day, I was, if you remember, trying to ask you out and I thought a little extra time together wouldn't hurt. So I lied about the class. But pretty soon I found out you were with Nathaniel and anyway," he winked, "I decided you aren't as pretty as I first thought but I kind of liked the class so I stayed with it."

Lucy shook her head. "I don't believe it."

"Scouts honor," Gavin put his hand over his heart. "You can tell that I am telling the truth by how embarrassing this story is." He ran a hand over the back of his neck and blushed. "So now we are equal."

"Thanks," Lucy sighed. She looked around. "How long have we been here? They are going to kick us out."

"Maybe," Gavin said while standing and pulling Lucy with him, "the lady came in like three times while you were crying and I shooed her away. She thinks we are both insane and might be calling the cops as we speak. So we should probably leave this dog to his own devices." Lucy nodded. "But I don't think we should keep driving. I think we, well, you need a break. Let's just stop and take a mini Christmas break. It will be good for your psyche." Lucy opened her mouth to protest but he cut her off, "I kind of made that sound like it was an option; it wasn't. We are taking a break, no arguments." He cast Lucy a steely glare and she snapped her mouth shut.

"Good," he smiled and started pulling her out the door.

"You were a cub scout?" Lucy asked as they made their way through the lobby, smiling unassumingly at the lady behind the counter who simply glared at them.

"For about seven seconds before they kicked me out for bad behavior," Gavin admitted and Lucy grinned.

Within the hour, they had checked into another hotel and

were wandering the pre-Christmas festivities in town. It was nice but crowded and Lucy had to hold Gavin's hand to keep from losing him. They stood in the town square around a roaring hot fire sipping hot chocolate and watching an ice sculptor create a beautiful statue of an owl. Lucy sighed and looked up at Gavin's smiling face, and he wrapped a comforting arm over her shoulders. It felt nice to have someone close to her. She really was lucky to have Gavin on this trip with her. She didn't know what she would have done without him. He was doing it all to be a good friend to her and to Nathaniel. Lucy was suddenly struck with the loveliness of that. She looked up at him and yelled over the chainsaw, "Thank you!"

"For what?" Gavin was confused.

"For everything," Lucy said with a grin and tucked her arm around him and gave him a squeeze. He smiled down at her as snow flew from the chainsaw into the sky all around them.

Chapter Seven
Christmas

"'Maybe,' the Grinch thought,
'Christmas doesn't come from the store.'"
~ Dr. Seuss

"What day is it?" he whispered. "I think it might be Christmas day."

"What am I, some sort of calendar?" was the sarcastic reply. "I can't see the sun, Angel."

"It's up though," he replied with melancholy.

"Yeah?" The darkness around them was oppressive. Far off, there was a faint dripping.

"Yeah," he sighed, "I can smell it."

"What a talent," he said drolly. There was silence except for a light clanging of a manacle as one of them shifted. There had been mostly silence. What was there to say? "Are you all right?"

"I am in pain," was the honest reply, "you?"

"Same," there was no energy for jovial mocking or poking fun. "Did you see her dress last night? She looked beautiful." There was hope in his voice, real hope.

"She did look beautiful," the Angel replied and it was obvious he was trying to sound supportive but the sadness in his voice dripped through.

"Can you sense her at all?" the Demon asked, trying not to betray his doubt.

"I can't feel her. I don't know where she is." Silence again. He changed his voice to a whisper, "I sent her something though. So she would know that we are still alive. I don't know if she received it though. I can't see past whatever he has around us. I can't…" he trailed off, frustration giving way to sadness yet again.

"She'll come," the Demon said with reassurance.

"That's what I am afraid of," the Angel sighed.

"MERRY CHRISTMAS!" Lucy woke to Gavin screaming in her face and shaking the bed.

"Ugh," Lucy murmured.

"Not very festive!" Gavin yelled, "and today I DEMAND festive!"

"I don't want to be festive," Lucy grunted and tried to roll over but Gavin pulled her pillow out from under her head and started smacking her with it.

"MERRY CHRISTMAS!" he yelled again while beating her.

Finally, Lucy had had enough and leapt up, snatched the pillow from him and smacked him in the face with it.

"Merry Christmas, you annoying jerk!" she hollered with a grin.

"Ahh!" Gavin yelled as he fell over sideways off the bed. He bounced back up and reached under the bed to produce a small wrapped box. "Merry Christmas, you nasty wench." He beamed and tossed the present on the bed.

"Oh you did not!" Lucy shrieked. "I am so sorry, Gavin, but I didn't get you anything! When did you find the time to get this?"

He shrugged, "Yesterday, while you were looking at those boots downtown."

Lucy shook her head. "I am so sorry."

"Don't be," Gavin interjected, "I just got you something because I am a bit of a sap for this whole holiday thing."

"Which makes it even worse that I didn't get you anything!" Lucy was apologetic.

"Open it, you selfish witch." He motioned to the box.

Lucy grinned despite herself and ripped at the paper. It was a small box and Lucy pried it open to reveal a silver bracelet. Hanging off the bracelet was a perfect set of angel wings dangling down the side.

"It's gorgeous," Lucy gasped as she pulled it out and gently fingered the links.

"I saw it in the window and I thought that it would be just perfect for you. It felt like one of those kismet things, right? Like the bracelet was talking to me and wanted me to buy it."

"I just love it," Lucy gushed. She slipped it on and reached her arms out to wrap them around his neck. "Thank you," she whispered into his shoulder. "It's just wonderful."

Gavin hugged her tight. "I know he can't be here but at least you can have something that he might have given you."

"Thank you," she whispered through tears. Gavin stood up and looked out the window.

"Let's get out of here and find something fun to do okay?" he grinned at her as the morning sun glinted in his eyes. Lucy grinned back and jumped for the shower.

"Merry Christmas!" she hollered on her way.

The pair decided to just wander the town and find their own

fun, which seemed fairly easy to do. They found an open movie theatre and watched some loud, obnoxious action comedy that they just made fun of the whole time. Then they went for a huge dinner at a Chinese food place. As they made their way back to the hotel, Lucy saw that a nativity play was starting soon in front of the town cathedral.

"Oh, stop, please," she pointed to the church, "can we stop and watch?"

"Sure, Red," Gavin said as he pulled over to a side street. They hurried to join the crowd of happy Christmas revelers on the lawn. It was set up with a life sized stable and even a live goat and a live sheep sat quietly in the piles of straw. As the sun was just going down, the entire scene was lit with bright spot lights set up in front. Lucy and Gavin joined the audience. The show started with a little boy, dressed as a shepherd, who came out and began to narrate.

"There was in Galilee an enumeration of all the people. So Joseph and Mary had to return to Bethlehem." Then Mary and Joseph appeared in the traditional costumes. Mary was carrying a donkey cut out. Lucy guessed the sheep and the goat were the only animals the local farm had.

"What's an enumeration?" Gavin whispered and Lucy elbowed him.

"Shush," she hissed but giggled.

The play continued on until the narrator said,

"An angel of the Lord appeared to them, and the glory of the Lord shone around them, and they were terrified. But the angel said to them, 'Do not be afraid. I bring you good news of great joy that will be for all the people. Today in the town of David a Savior has been born to you; he is Christ the Lord. This will be a sign to you: You will find a baby wrapped in cloths and lying in a manger.'" Lucy smiled. She liked all the Angel talk. It made her think that Nathaniel was safe somewhere. Despite the warm thoughts of Nathaniel, something cold invaded her thoughts and a chill ran through her. Something wasn't right. Something wasn't right at all.

Looking around her, Lucy immediately discovered what it was. There was a woman on the other side of the crowd. She was tall, blond, exquisitely beautiful, and wearing a full length stunning bright red fur coat. Lucy had seen her earlier in the month. The woman was a Demon. She rewound her memory to that horrific time in Hell. This woman had been sitting in a bar that the Demons frequented to get away from the horrors of the streets of Hell. She had been sitting at a table with another Demon and had cooed about Lucy and Nathaniel being "fresh meat" when she had seen them.

The Demon was watching the play with interest.

Lucy gripped Gavin's arm in a panic and dug her nails into his arm even through his bulging winter coat.

"Ouch!" Gavin exclaimed as he started to yank his arm back but after looking at Lucy's terrified expression leaned in. "What? What is it?" he whispered.

"Demon," Lucy whispered back, never taking her eyes off the woman.

"Where?" Gavin asked back. "Are you sure?"

"Yes," she whispered again, "she's one of the ones I saw in that bar in Hell. I remember."

"Of course you do," Gavin said in an undertone. "Here's what we are going to do, we are going to crouch down, very slowly, and move away using the crowd to hide us. Yes?" Lucy nodded. "Which lady is it?" he asked as he surreptitiously glanced through the crowd. Lucy was about to give a short description of the Demon when suddenly the Demon turned and looked directly at them.

The Demon grinned.

"Oh," Gavin whispered, "that would be her."

"I think she can hear us," Lucy murmured while not moving her lips.

In response, the Demon nodded slowly while still grinning at them. It was a knowing grin just a hairsbreadth away from positively warm and Lucy almost threw up with fear. Gavin swallowed audibly beside her. Without deciding to, the pair just turned calmly and made their way back through the crowd and to the street where they broke into a sprint back to the car. Gavin started the car and hit the gas before Lucy even had her door all the way closed. They drove back to the hotel and up to their room in silence. Every muscle in Lucy's body was tense with fear. It wasn't until Gavin had closed and bolted the door and pulled the curtains tight across the windows that he spoke again.

"What do we do?" he asked while peeking out the crack in the curtain. He shrugged and shut it. "What am I looking out there for?" he demanded, almost of himself. "We are on the 15th floor."

"They can fly," Lucy said with a sigh.

"Argh!" Gavin exploded, "you're right. We have to leave. Now."

"Listen," Lucy said calmly. Gavin ignored her and started throwing things back into his bag. "There are Demons everywhere, Gavin. We can't avoid them."

He tossed the bag down on the bed and pointed at the window. "She *saw* us, Red!" he yelled. "She knows that we know and that can't be good. Maybe she can smell Nathaniel on you or something like Nathaniel can smell rain. How the bloody Hell am I supposed to know? I just know that I came damn close to wetting my pants back there and I have no interest in her hunting us down."

"She can find us anywhere, Gavin, and if she wanted us

dead, she would just kill us!" Lucy challenged.

"Let's not give her the chance," Gavin shot back as he started to pack Lucy's stuff now. "You said that they have areas that they patrol, right? Well, let's get as far from her region as we can."

He headed into the bathroom to start throwing all their toiletries in the bag as well. Lucy raised her voice to be heard.

"Would you simmer down for a second?" she pleaded.

He popped his head out of the bathroom and fixed her with a hard stare. "Lucy, I have no magical powers. I have no way of defending you. I think you are being pretty slack about this because you are used to being around Nathaniel. I have none of the talents that he has and if we have an altercation with that Demon, WE WILL BOTH DIE! Now finish packing your stuff, we are leaving."

"But," Lucy started to plead.

"Now!" Gavin yelled.

"Don't yell at me!"

"Don't make me yell at you!" he exploded while coming back out of the bathroom. "Are you kidding me, Lucy?" he said in a softer tone. "Do you have a death wish or something? We are in danger here. *Real* danger, not like, oh I didn't wear a bike helmet danger, but tangible danger and I have no way to protect you. Please be aware of how horrible that is for me. All I can do is run. So that is what we are going to do."

Lucy sighed. Gavin was right. Being around Nathaniel gave Lucy a real sense of security. Nothing could happen to her while he was around. Gavin did not have Angelic powers and if that Demon decided to come after them, just for fun even, they would die, no question.

"All right," she sighed while getting up and grabbing her bag, "you win."

Gavin nodded and headed back into the bathroom. They

moved quickly and silently as they packed up and took the back stairs down to the parking garage and drove out into the night. They didn't speak again until they saw the "Thanks for Visiting Terra Haute" sign in the rear-view mirror.

"Merry Christmas, Lucy," Gavin said. He held out his hand and Lucy slipped hers into it. "And just one thing you ought to know about me?"

Lucy looked at him sideways. "Hmm?"

"I always win."

"I'm starting to get that impression." Lucy grinned at him. She sighed and brought up her internal map. "It's another 17 hours to Boston."

"Excellent," Gavin replied. "Go to sleep, I will wake you when I start to get tired. We are driving straight through."

"Really?" Lucy asked.

"Yup," Gavin shook his head. "I should not have slowed us down. That Demon has scared the crap out of me. You, *we*, need to find Nathaniel and the sooner the better."

Lucy balled up her jacket and tucked it under her head and settled in to close her eyes. "I couldn't agree more," she mumbled.

Chapter Eight
Lying

"We tell lies, yet it is easy to show that lying is immoral."
~ *Epictetus*

Back in Terra Haute, Octavia the Demon removed herself from the nauseating scene around her. The things she did in the name of her craft amazed her sometimes. She made her way down the street, attracting many stares along the way. Two of which were from some police officers standing casually waiting for the play to let out and help direct traffic. Octavia swallowed her distaste for their motivations and approached them smiling.

"Excuse me, officers," she batted her eyelashes coyly. They both stood up straight and puffed up their sagging chests. "Would you happen to have a piece of paper and a pen that I could jot a quick note on?" Her voice was like melting wax.

"Well, of course!" one exclaimed, being quicker on the draw than his partner and producing his note pad and pen from his front pocket with a flourish.

"Thank you oh so much." She took the items, wrote

something on the first piece of paper, ripped it off and handed the items back to the officer. "Much appreciated." She smiled while restraining herself from clawing at their faces. The officer nodded as Octavia moved away.

"Merry Christmas miss," he grinned at her back.

Octavia glanced back over her shoulder and smiled lightly. "Is it, though?" she called before sauntering away. She walked a block down to a park that sat black and cold in the night. Perched on the arm of a wooden bench was a very large crow. Octavia didn't slow as she produced the note for the crow to snap into its beak. "Turner," she whispered as she moved smoothly past. The bird blinked before launching into the air, headed due west, the note gripped tightly in its beak. Octavia kept walking, intent on finding a warm drink and a warmer body with which to spend this hateful night. She passed a man crumpled in addiction and slumped in the snow. No reason the day had to be an entire waste.

Octavia slowed as she passed him and because of whom she was and because the poor man had fallen prey to a Demon once or twice before, his eyes opened toward her. Octavia smiled kindly while turning his attention to the convenience store across the street. It was, for now, quite busy with people grabbing last minute things for their house guests but in an hour or so, it would be very empty indeed. The young new girl would be left alone and vulnerable to robbery. Octavia saw the flicker of light in the man's wobbling eyes and knew that the officers down the way wouldn't have a merry Christmas after all.

"Pity," she grinned slyly to herself as she strode away, leaving the poor soul behind wondering if he had seen anything at all.

Lucy was grateful that she didn't have any more vivid

images while sleeping. She woke up with the sun shining brightly in the window. Gavin was still driving but had been active; the floor was littered with coffee cups and to go food containers.

"You okay?" Lucy said while stretching.

"Yup!" Gavin replied brightly. "We actually just got started again. I did stop and take a nap a bit ago."

"Why didn't you wake me?" Lucy challenged.

"I tried," Gavin said with a sideways grin. "You would *not* wake up so I just stopped at a parking lot and had a break."

"Pull over," Lucy said while picking up the coffee cup closest to her and drank it. She was happy to find that it was still lukewarm. "I can drive for a bit."

"Nah," Gavin shook his head, "I'm good, we only have three hours to go."

"You are bad ass," Lucy said with appreciation and Gavin smiled.

"Hey listen," he elbowed her jovially, "I'm sorry I yelled last night. I shouldn't have raised my voice to you."

Lucy shook her head. "No," she conceded, "I was being incredibly stubborn, which is kind of my way of things. You're right, we aren't safe and we have to keep moving."

"Well, to be fair, I overreacted a little," he laughed, "but so many Demons in such a short time has totally unnerved me."

"Me too," Lucy admitted, "it makes me think that there is a pattern here."

"Do you think they are watching us?"

"I don't know," Lucy said thoughtfully, "it just seems odd you know? And one thing that Nathaniel has taught me is that there are no accidents in this world. There are no coincidences or chances. Everything is for a reason, everything has a purpose and nothing is for nothing."

"Really?" Gavin challenged, "there are no random events, no odd ones out?"

Lucy shook her head, "Nope, everything happens for a reason."

"Huh," Gavin said lightly.

The drive continued thankfully uneventfully until they approached the outer edges of Boston.

"So now where?" Gavin leaned forward and looked at the street signs.

"Follow the signs for MIT," Lucy prompted.

"Do you really think this Roger guy is going to be at work?"

"You don't know this guy," Lucy offered, "if he's not there, there is someone who knows where he is."

Lucy was right. After they got on the campus, they found the psychology building and lo and behold, there was a lonely freshman who with a bright smile from Lucy happily handed over Roger's home address. They drove through the streets and approached a neat and orderly brownstone that looked exactly like its neighbor.

They peered through the sunset at the house.

"Plan?" Gavin asked.

"Nope," Lucy tied her wild red hair up in an effort to appear saner. She flipped down the visor to peer at herself in the mirror and realized that there was no point. What was going to come out of her mouth was going to be ludicrous and therefore it didn't matter what she looked like.

"Let's do this then," Gavin said optimistically and he bounded out of the car. He opened Lucy's door and they walked side by side up the slate grey pathway. They approached the door and Lucy sucked in a deep breath before reaching out and ringing the bell. Immediately, there was a soft scuffling noise from inside.

The handle clicked and the door crept open to reveal the pinched face of Dr. Roger Hatfield.

"Hi there," Lucy started but he cut her off.

"No caroling, no donations...I am deeply against western rules of charity and religious notions of celebration during the month of December," Roger stated. It was clear that he had said this particular statement many times before. He started to close the door but Lucy reached out her hand.

"No," Lucy replied as she leaned in slightly to catch his eye, "I don't know if you remember me, but a couple of months ago, you came to visit me at Mulbridge U."

She locked eyes with Roger and noticed his lids narrow significantly as he sucked in a sharp breath. "Of course I remember you, Lucy Bower." His tone implied that Lucy was being insulting.

"Sure," Lucy said. There was silence and she started to shake her leg, unsure of where to start. Once again, Gavin saved the day.

"Hello there, Dr. Hatfield," he respectfully stuck out his hand, "I'm Gavin MacFarlane and I am a big fan." Roger's eyebrows went up. "I read your paper on The Stanford Prison Experiment. It was awesome."

"Really?" Roger replied and he opened the door slightly more. He was wearing a plaid shirt under a brown cardigan with brown cords. Not the usual for a twenty-something man hanging out alone on Boxing Day. Lucy's dislike for him increased but Gavin was certainly making headway. He was chatting about the paper like he had read it yesterday, and with every word, Roger opened the door wider and wider.

Suddenly, Gavin shifted the conversation effortlessly. "Lucy and I need your help, Roger, and I assure you it is something you, after meeting her, have been wanting to do."

"Pardon?" Roger challenged.

"I would like you to kill her," Gavin said with an impish grin.

Roger laughed out loud and shook his head.

"Very funny, you two," he started to close the door again, "But I am not falling for any tricks. Go tell Dr. Hannon he isn't going to ruin my recent application for grants."

"No!" Lucy yelled, "Please Roger, please listen to me!" He paused but didn't look at her. Lucy took this as a sign that he was at least listening. "I want you to hypnotize me, deeply hypnotize me. You can do any readings you want on my brain while I am under and you can do whatever you want with the results." The thought of Roger getting any notoriety from Lucy's talent make her a little nauseous but she had little options now.

"Why?" Roger demanded, still not looking at her.

"I," Lucy paused, scrambling for an answer.

"She wants to find memories from further back, like the womb." Gavin offered. Lucy stifled a disgusted look. Who would want to remember the womb? Roger however, seemed deeply intrigued. He finally looked at them again.

"That would be fascinating." He said to them but his mind was obviously elsewhere. "To know when fetal consciousness actually begins? That would be revolutionary. A real game changer." They had lost him to his own thoughts completely now. Lucy assumed he was daydreaming of standing on stage getting flowers thrown at him. She refrained from rolling her eyes.

"Well, Roger," Gavin continued. "Dr. Hannon said it was 'too dangerous' and 'radical' so he won't do it. Lucy said she should go to the best of the best and we drove right here."

"Is that true?" Roger trained his eyes on Lucy.

"Yes," Lucy said slowly.

Roger stood regarding them silently for a minute, neither one of them moved or even breathed.

"Fine, come in," he ordered and opened the door completely. Lucy and Gavin moved into the dark hallway. If Lucy didn't know better, she would have assumed that an old lady lived in this house. It was all dark wood, with expensive looking but useless knick knacks placed carefully and perfectly around the foyer and the living room. A hallway and staircase stretched before them that led to other rooms of the house. Lucy could not have cared less what the rest of the house looked like. "The items you see around you are from my extensive travels around the world. They are more expensive than you are, do not touch anything." Roger said over his shoulder as he led them into the living room and gestured for Lucy to sit on the couch. He did not indicate a place for Gavin, so he just stood. "You are lucky I have equipment at home. I shall set everything up. You should just sit and relax, Lucy, it will make hypnotizing you easier."

He left the room and Lucy let out a gust of air. Gavin leaned over the back of the couch and whispered lightly in her ear.

"Good job, Red, getting us in with Dr. Drab here. This place is off the chain." Lucy smiled and shook her head.

"How did you know about his paper?" Lucy whispered back.

"Have you ever heard of a little thing called Google?" Gavin grinned at her.

Lucy chucked softly. Now that they were actually here, the weight of what she was about to do hit her. Did she even want this to work?

"I hope this works," she sighed.

"It will work," Gavin said with his usual optimism.

"I am so happy you are here. I don't want anything creepy

to happen while I am under," Lucy whispered.

"You are completely safe," Gavin rested his hands on her shoulders. "I ain't no Angel, but, sweetheart, I could totally take *this* guy."

"You think so?" Lucy joked over her shoulder.

"I can take anyone who isn't a Demon, Red. My name is Gavin and my mom is on Broadway. Trust me, I can kick ass, especially Dr. Doufenshmertz here. He's right, you should relax though. Start thinking of where you want to go and why, that might help."

Lucy nodded and took a few deep breaths. Roger returned with a cart full of electronics. He busied himself setting an entire lab up on his coffee table in a matter of minutes. Lucy admitted that it was pretty impressive. He attached wires to Lucy's head, neck and one over her heart and instructed her to lie down as he fired up the whole intricate system.

"Okay Lucy," Roger began, "just relax." He sounded far more pleasant now that he was getting something he wanted. "I have hypnotized many people. I am going to put you very very deep but you are totally safe. Don't worry about a thing."

Lucy closed her eyes and reached one hand up in the air. Gavin's fingers slid between hers. "Don't you go anywhere, Gavin."

"I'm here forever if you need," he said softly, "I've got ya, Red."

"Okay Lucy," Roger began, "just listen to my voice and nothing else. I need you to relax completely and totally. I need you to let the couch support you entirely. I need you to breathe evenly and deeply. Imagine you are in a long tunnel and it is warm and comforting. Walk down that tunnel, Lucy, and imagine that where you want to be is at the other end. It is quiet and peaceful. Go to the tunnel, Lucy, and focus on your destination."

And so she did.

Lucy opened her eyes. The tunnel was warm because it seemed to be made of a soft fabric. If she just actually went back to the womb, she would be pissed. She walked down the tunnel towards a faint brightness at the other end. She recalled the bright light of Heaven that she had seen before and knew that this was not the same thing. She was certainly in a different place than Heaven and certainly a different place than Hell. She approached the source of the brightness and came upon a set of simple frosted glass doors. Lucy took note of her emotions. She was not frightened in any way but she certainly wasn't elated. She just, was.

Lucy opened one of the doors and stepped through.

Chapter Nine
Purgatory

*"When all the world dissolves,
And every creature shall be purified,
All places shall be hell that is not heaven."
~ Christopher Marlowe*

She had never seen a room so large. In fact, it was so large that Lucy couldn't see walls or a ceiling so maybe she should not have called it a room. She could only be in one place, though. Lucy was in Purgatory, no doubt about it. There really wasn't much to Purgatory. It wasn't white but a calming and somewhat boring beige. The rest was just chairs really; rows and rows of thousands, no, millions of simple wooden chairs all facing the same direction. In those chairs were people, sitting. That was pretty much it.

"It's a waiting room," Lucy whispered to herself.

"Yup," came a voice beside her. The man in the closest chair was looking at her. He wore a plain grey suit. Lucy noticed that like in Hell, it appeared as though everyone was wearing what they were buried in. However, unlike Hell, nothing was causing the ruin of the clothing here so everyone sat in their Sunday best looking fresh and new. People of all colors and cultures stretched out before her. A woman close by wore a gorgeous African headdress, and the man beside her was in full Naval regalia. Looking from forward to back, Lucy could see a distinctive change in clothing style. She was currently in the early fifties section because a lady to her right wore a typical pill box hat. Craning her neck and looking further forward, Lucy saw older clothing, bowler hats and petty coats. There was a soft murmuring around her and Lucy realized that although no one was outright chatting, a few people seemed to be making pleasant conversation in hushed tones. "Just a waiting room." The man continued. "You have to go to the back for an empty seat. It gets a little boring but it's not too bad. If you get overly bored, you can always look at the book but really, that gets boring too."

The Book! Lucy thought. That's what she needed. He had to mean the Book of the Dead.

"Thanks," Lucy replied and the man nodded his assent. She looked around but could not see any book. "Um, could you tell me where the Book is?" she asked.

"You should really go get your spot," the man prompted but then shrugged, "it's up at the front," he motioned with his chin forward.

"Thanks again," Lucy said and started off at a quick pace between the chairs toward the front. Lucy could see no end of chairs in sight so the front could be miles away. She quickened her pace, letting the rows of chairs turn into a blur beside her. Finally after about ten minutes, the chairs stopped and without warning, Lucy had arrived at the front.

The front row of chairs held people of the sixteenth century or maybe a little earlier. They looked just as calm as the man she had talked to. She stopped at the front of the line and looked around. There was still no wall but on the beige background of light sat another completely boring door. A man stood beside it in a beige suit that indicated no particular century.

Suddenly, there was a soft ping, like the sound of the bell at the butchers shop and the woman in the first chair, wearing Elizabethan ruffles, stood and walked regally to the door. The man smiled kindly at her.

"How was your wait?" he asked softly.

"Neither lovely nor horrific I do say," the woman said with a polite smile.

"Welcome," the man replied and opened the door for her. The woman stepped through and disappeared.

Beside Lucy, there was a great shuffling in the chairs as everyone moved one spot over to take their new place. There were so many millions of people that it sounded like a massive crashing wave. After a few moments the sound subsided and the same low quiet murmuring filled the air. Lucy looked away from the door and immediately saw The Book. It was on a pedestal about fifty feet from the door. Lucy approached it slowly.

The Book of the Dead sat open and was easily five feet across. The cover seemed to be made of a deep burgundy leather and the paper was thick and coarse. It was quite plain considering it would be the most vital book to all of man-kind. As Lucy got closer she paused and saw that there was nothing on the pages. She was looking at least for a list of names or pictures or really, something, but there was absolutely nothing. The Book of the Dead was blank.

Lucy walked right up to it, wondering what to do next. With a tentative hand, she reached out and took hold of one page. The paper was heavy and Lucy lifted it a few inches to peek at the next page and saw with dismay that it too was blank. She felt like she was running out of time and Roger could wake her at any second.

With a frustrated exhalation, she looked around her at the row of people who were presumably, in the front of the line. She locked eyes with a young man wearing the clothes of a stable boy. Rather than speaking, she just shrugged hoping that this universal symbol was clear from centuries ago.

The young man smiled kindly and simply whispered, "Speak to it."

Lucy smiled back and she turned toward the book again. What to ask? She took a small breath, leaned into the book's middle seal and whispered, "I need to find Nathaniel." The floor dropped away from beneath her and the air swirled hot and fast around her. Lucy gritted her teeth. Was she waking up? Was she too late? Suddenly, her feet touched solid ground, or sand rather.

It was hot and dark and a chemical odor tinged the air. Lucy looked around her at several camo tents and beige hummers. An explosion sounded nearby, lighting the night sky with streaks of red and orange, Lucy felt the ground shake and on instinct, ducked to a crouch. She knew where she was. She was somewhere in the Middle East and she was in the middle of a war. The explosion faded, its brightness replaced once again by an eerie silence. Lucy looked about, unsure of what to do next when she was unexpectedly bathed in light again, this time from above. The light was accompanied by the deep thumping of an approaching helicopter. Sand began to whip against Lucy's face and she dove behind a tent to avoid being landed upon.

The helicopter touched down and the blades slowed. Lucy peeked out from behind the tent wall and almost called out loud as she looked into the face of her father.

"I need a surgeon here!" he screamed almost into Lucy's face. She stood staring at him, completely aghast. She hadn't asked to see her father, why was she here? It was obvious, though, that

Lucy could not been seen, because Sargent Richard Bower had no reaction to a strange girl in jeans and sneakers. Soldiers burst from the tents all around, yelling and moving with a strong purpose.

"Who is it, Sarge?" someone hollered as they headed to the helicopter.

"It's Nate!" Lucy's father yelled back. There was a panic in his voice that Lucy had never heard before. It made her shiver in fear. Whatever had happened moments before had terrified him. The soldiers felt it too and froze in their tracks.

"What the hell are you asking for a surgeon for then?" someone said angrily, "It's the surgeon in there!"

"Move!" Richard Bower hollered and the entire unit snapped into action. Where they were hurried before, now they were full of fire. They moved twice as fast towards the craft's bay door. Lights appeared out of now where, brightening the camp. More voices came from the tents and more soldiers appeared, ready to help, in any way. Whoever was in that helicopter, he was important and Lucy's heart dropped when she realized the only logical option.

The stretcher appeared and Lucy cried out loud to see the bloody and broken body of Nathaniel being run by six soldiers to the closest tent and disappeared inside.

"We were in Section 39, blue level!" Richard Bower ordered to the camp. "We were trying to help injured children in a school when we came under attack! Nate took a bullet for me, the stupid ass. I got us out and took out three or four of the insurgents but there are more there. There are also survivors still in that school! Get there and go ballistic!"

"Sir yes Sir!" The camp replied and immediately armed up and began boarding the same helicopter to be taken back to the front lines for retribution. Richard Bower didn't stay to watch them go but headed to the medical tent where they had taken Nathaniel. Lucy followed close behind.

The medical tent was in full upheaval with everyone working around the main surgical table. Several nurses bustled around and soldiers worked too, fetching equipment and yelling orders to each other. It was chaos and Lucy couldn't even see Nathaniel. Suddenly there was a yell from the table and a single bloody hand rose up above all the shoulders. The room froze. Silence fell over the room.

"I need two nurses and Sargent Bower," said Nathaniel's voice from the table. He sounded tired but not beat. "Everyone else, thank you for your concern but I assure you that I will be fine. Please go out so I can save my own sorry ass."

There was a light chuckle though the room as the soldiers made a begrudging exit while mumbling words of encouragement. As they all left, Nathaniel's prone form slowly became clear in the center of the tent. He looked very much as Lucy knew him, his hair was cut shorter though and he wore the green army uniform with the vibrant white and red band and cross on his arm.

"Joan," he started kindly and a brunette nurse stepped forward, "start an IV, heavy on the fluids and morphine. I seem to be in a great deal of pain."

"Yes Doctor," Joan nodded and got to work.

"Mary," he called out and Mary moved so she was in his line of vision. "You finally get your wish. Get the scissors and cut off my uniform."

Mary smiled ruefully and immediately did as she was told. The nurses worked quickly and quietly. Lucy took this moment to take a good look at her father. It had been three years since she had seen him and, other than in pictures, she had never seen him looking this young.

Despite his haggard and panicked appearance, Lucy's Daddy looked just wonderful and tears came to her eyes as she slowly reached up to touch his cheek, but paused, inches away, instinctively knowing that her hand would pass through him. A beard had grown on his strong jaw and Lucy was reminded of the fact that he had shaved the beard because she hadn't liked it as a child. She smiled at her father, blissfully happy to be where she was at this particular moment.

Her happiness vanished when she heard one of the nurses gasp audibly. Directing her eyes back to the table, Lucy let out a scream. Mary had managed to cut through Nathaniel's uniform to reveal that the entire side of his body was completely savaged by gunfire.

"Yeah," he said sarcastically, "I know, I'm pretty hot. Calm down."

Marry started to cry.

"Hey hey hey, "Nathaniel said softly to her while reaching for her hand, "It's going to be okay. Don't worry about it." He winced and asked, "Hey Joan, let's not be stingy with that morphine now. I ordered extra last week."

No one else in the room seemed to enjoy the humor but he ignored that.

"Com'ere Dick," he grinned and shrugged at his own slurring. There was blood in his teeth. Lucy didn't know who he was talking about until her father stepped to the side of the bed. He had never liked being called Dick. Now she realized why. Richard pulled up a stool and sat beside Nathaniel. The nurses put dressings on the wounds and added more drugs but it was obvious where this was going.

"What do you want now, Doc?" Richard Bower said with a sad grin.

"I want you to shut up for once," Nathaniel grinned, "and listen."

Richard sighed and dropped his head. "Can I get someone else? Kapinski or Brown?" he offered. "I gotta be honest with you, my friend, I don't know if I can do this."

"Like I want Kapinski," Nathanel protested jovially. It sounded strained. "I love the guy, but really, he has a memory like a sieve and the bed side demeanor of Genghis Khan."

Richard smiled but didn't respond.

"Listen up Sargent," Nathaniel continued, "Right after all this, you need to call the switch board and get a new doctor in here because I don't know if you got the memo but you are going to be severely short-handed fairly soon."

"Enough joking around," Richard said seriously.

"There is never enough joking around, jackass," Nathaniel countered, "Dying man's rules. You have to ask for someone from the 56th Unit. They have seasoned docs there, no greenbacks, okay? Be firm on this because they are going to seriously try to jack you around and these soldiers *need* a solid. Got it?"

Richard nodded.

"Also, we need more sutures and erythromycin, okay? We needed that shit like yesterday."

Richard nodded again.

"Now, don't tell the men the details."

Richards head snapped up. "Of course I will!" he yelled. "I will tell them that you were supposed to stay behind the wall because you are medical. I will tell them that you for some goddamn reason decided to run out and jump in front of bullets made for me. I will tell them that you are the bravest man they have ever known."

Nathaniel smiled lightly. The nurses loaded more gauze

onto his dressings, for they were soaked already.

"Don't be dumb," Nathaniel muttered, "they don't want to hear that crap."

"They always want to hear the truth and that is what they will get."

Nathaniel closed his eyes for a second, "You have a wife with a kid on the way. There are a million single jackass soldier doctors in this world."

"You are the best doctor I have ever seen!" Richard yelled.

Nathaniel sighed, losing the energy to fight. "We will agree to disagree."

Richard nodded.

"A few more things." Nathaniel's voice became soft, "First, I want all my crap to go to the unit, okay? Don't send it back for some other guy to get a dead man's stuff. That's creepy."

Richard nodded again.

"Second, I want to be buried with other soldiers, I don't care where, just not alone."

Richard swallowed and began to cry but nodded his head.

"Last," Nathaniel's voice was a whisper now, he coughed and blood bubbled at the corners of his mouth. "As you know, I have never had a family. I hated being an orphan, I hated being a foster kid. I hated not having anywhere that I belonged. It wasn't until I joined the army that I found my family. I have you and the unit to thank for that."

Richard began to sob.

"Remember the time we got stuck off base after dark and you paid that idiot cab driver in Pez to take us back to base?" he grinned.

"Moron thought it was ecstasy," Richard laughed through his tears, "maybe because that's what you told him it was."

The two chuckled for a moment. Lucy thought back to the picture she had found when they were cleaning out the den before her mother's wedding. Was that Nathaniel's arm draped over her father's shoulder? Was he the figure cut out of the picture? Did he sit and look at a picture of his best friend and not realize it?

"I ask only one thing of you, Dick, for the years of freaking awesome friendship that I have given you," he grinned again.

Richard laughed and sniffed, "Anything, my friend, anything at all."

"If your wife has a daughter, could you name her Lucy?"

Richard didn't hesitate, "Yes."

"I don't know why, I have just always liked that name. I used to think that I would marry a Lucy one day, but clearly, that's not going to happen."

Richard nodded, the tears flowing again. "I promise."

"Good," Nathaniel whispered, "good."

He paused and laid his head back on the pillow. His face relaxed.

"I'm going to close my eyes now. I'm pretty bloody tired. Wake me at first light if I'm not up already. Thanks for being the best friend a guy could ask for. I don't know what I would have done without you."

Nathaniel closed his eyes and died.

Richard Bower laid his head down and sobbed over his friend's hand. Lucy could not choke back the sobs that emanated from her as well. She was still crying when she found herself standing in an airplane hangar, in front of an open casket. Nathaniel, in full dress uniform, was laid to rest with the flag folded and ready to be draped over the deep wood. She kept sobbing as the image changed again to show Arlington Cemetery, a cross with the name "Nathaniel Parish" and the dates. Then she found herself back in Purgatory at the Book of the Dead. She took a deep breath, and steadied herself by leaning against the stand. Slowly, her sobs decreased and Lucy looked around her.

Nothing much had changed. The line of people had moved and there were new people in the spots behind her. She ought to make some sort of effort to return back home but Lucy was hesitant. Despite the circumstances, Lucy had loved seeing her father one last time. She did not want to let him go quite yet. On impulse, Lucy leaned forward and whispered to the book, "I need to see Richard Bower."

Again the floor dropped away and the air swirled around her and Lucy found herself in a bar. It was dark and a twangy voice played from beer sodden speakers in the corner. Lucy looked around, it wasn't crowded and the few patrons that were in attendance sat pathetically at the bar. None of them were her father. Thinking that she had somehow gotten the wrong place, Lucy started to move to the door but then an all too familiar voice cut through the dimness.

"Have another one for the road, pal," the buttery voice cooed, "it won't kill ya." Lucy turned with surprise to see the chiseled features of Roman acting as barkeep. He looked identical to how Lucy knew him except he was wearing a tight black t-shirt with the name of a heavy metal band on the front. He was speaking to a young man at the bar who was resting his head on his hands.

"Why did she have to leave?" the young man sobbed into his hands. It was clear to Lucy that the guy had a reason to drink but had also had quite enough already. Roman didn't respond but just waited, the boy smacked his hand on the bar and Roman produced a shot of whiskey at the speed of light. The guy shot it down, emptied his wallet onto the bar and stumbled off the bar stool. He reached in his pocket for his keys.

"You shouldn't drive, kid," an older man called from a few seats down. "Call him a cab," he said to Roman, who ignored the request but stood watching, his face unreadable. The guy waved the old man off and stumbled towards the door. It dawned on Lucy what she was watching and she screamed out in horror.

"Don't!" she yelled at the young man as he passed her, "Don't do it! You will die and you are going to kill another man too!" She reached out to grab at him but her hands passed right through his arm.

"Have a good night, friend," Roman called in a pleasant tone and when Lucy looked back at him, she saw a grin pass over his face unlike any she had ever seen. It was the look of a man who was proud of a job well done.

"No!" Lucy screamed again but the floor fell away and suddenly she was in a car. Frantically, she looked around her. She knew this car, she knew it well. Looking into the drivers' seat she saw her father. He drove along, completely unaware of what was about to happen. He was whistling to himself.

"Dad!" Lucy screamed, "Dad no! Stop the car!" She knew that it would do no good, she knew that he couldn't hear her but she couldn't stop herself. Tears poured down her face as she snatched at the steering wheel, her hands passing right through it. She saw the approaching headlights, swerving in the distance.

"No!" Lucy screamed again. She couldn't do this. "Please, I want to go back!" She yelled into the air. "I want to wake up! I don't want to see Richard Bower!" the lights came closer. Lucy could now see the face of the boy from the bar. His eyes closed and his head lolled back in the car. She heard her Father curse and the car veer in an attempt to avoid the collision. "I want to leave the Book, I want to leave Purgatory. Please! I can't see this! Please help me!"

Lucy woke up.

Gavin's face was within inches of hers, he was screaming her name; panic pressed deep into his features.

"Gavin!" Lucy breathed and relief swept over his face. He gathered her in his arms and held her tight. She grasped him back, holding on to reality with everything she had.

"Oh thank God you are back!" he whispered into her shoulder. "Thank God!"

He let her go and looked at her, now his face was eager for confirmation. Had it worked? His eyes asked. Lucy nodded and grinned. He grinned back and hugged her again – his relief was tangible and Lucy was touched as she shook out her shaking hands.

"Ahem," came a pinched voice from the corner.

"Roger!" Lucy exclaimed. She quickly reminded herself to hide their true reasons for being there. "Did you get any of the information that you were looking for?"

Roger's face darkened even further and Lucy knew her answer.

"I got no readings whatsoever," Roger seethed. "Nothing. It appears that your brain does nothing during hypnosis." This was of course something Lucy had suspected would happen. All the same, she let her face fall.

"I'm so sorry Roger, I had hoped that you would be able to get some good info." He stood up and motioned to the equipment.

"It's like it was broken or something." He picked up a ribbon of the paper, it had nothing but a single black ink line. There were six or so of these long papers trailing over the carpet. Roger grabbed one, angrily balled it up and drove it into the ground.

"Nothing!" he yelled, "nothing!" The tension in the room rose. Without looking at her, Gavin reached over and quickly pulled the sensors from around Lucy's face and neck. Wordless, he stood up, pulling Lucy with him. He took her hand and led her slowly past the couch, away from Roger who was now in a red-faced rage. His hands were in fists at his sides, sweat beading on his brow, "What did you do?" He pointed an accusatory finger at them. "If my colleagues find out about this, I'll be a laughingstock!" He paused in thought, then raised his eyes to them again. They were in slits. "You came here simply to mock me! You are going to report back to Dr. Hannon so that you can all have a good laugh, aren't you?"

    Gavin moved them to the door, keeping himself between Lucy and Roger. Suddenly, Roger lunged at them, or at Lucy, hands outstretched reaching to strangle her throat. Lucy suppressed a scream as she pulled backward and to the side to avoid his reach. Gavin moved quickly, grabbing Roger's arms and simultaneously kicking his legs out from under him, tossing him to the ground. In one fluid move he secured one hand over Roger's throat as his knee held the enraged man's chest to the floor.

    "We would like to thank you for your hospitality, friend," Gavin said in his best societal voice as Roger choked out a gasp, "but we really must be going now. We won't tell anyone we were here if you won't." At this Roger nodded enthusiastically, his face turning bright red, "and we above all things, wish you a very merry Christmas." Gavin released him and pushed his body away from them in a roll. He half pulled, half carried Lucy out of the house with Roger coughing and sputtering behind them.

Chapter Ten
Temptation

"Tis one thing to be tempted, another to fall."
~ William Shakespeare

Lucy threw on her seatbelt while Gavin squealed the car down the street. They drove for a few moments before Gavin looked at Lucy and winked.

"That was hard-core," Lucy exclaimed, "very Rambo of you."

He shrugged. "I watch COPS, what can I say?"

Lucy laughed shortly but then blew out a gust of air.

"So?" Gavin prompted, "tell me everything!" While Lucy recounted every detail of her visit to Purgatory, he found a hotel, pulled in and got them a room. By the time she finished, they were sitting in a pub getting served their food.

Gavin whistled and leaned back in the booth. "That's a lot to take in, Red." Lucy just nodded. "So Nathaniel knew your father and that's why he named you Lucy?"

"Yup," Lucy said.

"Are we happy about this or totally weirded out?"

"Both."

"Good to know."

"I would like to ask you to do something for me if it comes down to me not being able to do it myself," Lucy asked.

"Anything," Gavin answered quickly.

"I would like you to kill Roman if I am unsuccessful and he kills me."

Gavin choked on his beer. "You're out of your mind, Lucy," he said while wiping his lips.

"He killed my father!" Lucy exclaimed.

"No," Gavin corrected, "no, he didn't. A drunk driver killed your father."

"But he's the one who got him drunk in the first place!"

Gavin shook his head. "Lucy, you yourself told me that there are no accidents, no mistakes, that everything happens for a reason,"

"My father's death was senseless!" Lucy almost yelled and received several strange looks from the other patrons. "And you heard what Turner said, if we can manage to kill Roman, he will return to the depths for a long time. He needs to be punished."

Gavin reached out and held both of her hands. He looked her dead in the eye and Lucy's heart slowed. "Isn't Hell enough?" he whispered. "Listen to me, Red. I know that this has all been a great shock to you, and to me too, but we can't go killing Demons. You are feeling your father's death all over again, paired with Nathaniel's death; it's a lot to take. Let's deal with what we can do for now. After this is all settled, we will deal with Roman. I promise I will deal with him as you see fit at the time."

Lucy nodded, slightly. "You promise?" she demanded.

"I promise," Gavin said seriously. Lucy relaxed, completely

trusting in his word. Roman would pay for his crimes, one way or another. Gavin continued, "Now eat something until we figure out what we are supposed to do next."

"Oh, I know where we have to go," Lucy said plainly. "I have had the feeling since waking up."

Gavin opened his hands and rolled his eyes. "Were you gonna share this info?"

"I don't think you are going to be happy," Lucy warned. "We have to go east."

"East?" Gavin asked incredulously, "East? How far east? For how long?"

Lucy shook her head. "I think it's far," she said vaguely, "but all I know is east."

"Awesome," Gavin replied, his voice dripping with sarcasm. "Well, since we are basically on the East Coast, I guess we have to cross an ocean to go any more east."

"Well then," Lucy said as she finished her dinner, "I guess tomorrow we have a plane to catch."

"This is very quickly becoming a crappy movie," Gavin replied with a smile and Lucy grinned back.

They flew to London, figuring that anything further East would have a connecting flight from there. The only thing of note was Gavin's constant sarcastic glares at Lucy while stating, "East, hey? Just east," and rolling his eyes. Upon arrival at Heathrow and much to her dismay, Lucy received no further feeling about what direction to go. Lucy considered continuing east until told otherwise, but Gavin argued that east could mean lower Russia or Iraq and guessing wrong could cost them valuable time. Once again they were stuck and the pair decided to wait until a new idea presented itself. They found a room in a dilapidated ancient hotel that looked fit to just fall in upon itself. It had two prim little twin beds though, and the sheets were clean. Lucy figured she couldn't ask for more. They called Gavin's parents to check in and his mother seemed thrilled with the fact that her son was taking a wild trip across Europe. So thrilled, that she offered to call and explain it all Lucy's mother for her when she arrived back home from the cruise. Lucy dreaded the day she would be forced to have that conversation with her mom.

Lucy had never been to London but Gavin had spent a great deal of time there with his family. Gavin became the tour guide and Lucy, despite her worries, found herself relaxing and enjoying herself through the streets of London as Gavin showed her all the sights. She and Gavin spent most of their time laughing and talking and were more than once mistaken for a couple. It got so tiring that they stopped correcting people, figuring that it didn't matter anyway. For days they walked hand in hand making each other laugh. Lucy realized one day that she hadn't had one of her sobbing fits in three days. It was both relieving and terrifying.

For New Year's Eve, Gavin rented a car and surprised Lucy with a trip to Stratford-upon-Avon and watched as she became teary eyed at Shakespeare's birthplace and gravesite. Lucy could not stop smiling as they drove back to London. They ended up in a pub called the Bok Bar in Covent Garden. There was an exhibition game on between the Springboks from South Africa and the All Blacks from New Zealand. Lucy and Gavin were welcomed to join a table with another couple. They introduced themselves as Jonathan and Kelly, Londoners and staunch Springbok fans.

"Sorry friends," Gavin shrugged, "I'm an All Black through and through."

"So you come to a bar filled with Springboks?" Jonathan laughed, "You are lucky it's only an exhibition game. You might be in trouble otherwise."

"I'm always in a little bit of trouble mate," Gavin grinned mischievously, "that's how I know I'm alive."

Jonathan laughed out loud as Kelly ordered them a round of drinks.

Within moments they were screaming and yelling along with the rest of the bar. Their new friends decided that Lucy and Gavin were to have the full rugby experience and ordered round after round for them. Lucy and Gavin shrugged and drank it all, figuring that it would be rude to refuse. The game finished in the Springboks' favor and the pub was so deafening that Lucy could only mouth words to Gavin to communicate.

"I'm drunk!" she said silently to him over the table.

"Me too!" Gavin mouthed back and grinned.

Apparently, the fun had just begun. The Bok Bar lit up with a traditional band and it was moments later that Gavin was pulling Lucy to the dance floor to attempt their own pathetic version of a jig. The next hours were spent with more drinking and more laughing and more dancing. Finally, the countdown began and a scream of HAPPY NEW YEAR radiated through the pub. Lucy hugged and kissed all her new friends, making her way around the circle until finally ending up at Gavin. She looked up at him with a slight sway to her stance.

"Happy New Year, Gavin," she smiled, "Thank you for everything you have done for me."

Gavin pulled her in for a tight hug and kissed her head. "I would do anything for you, Red. Anything at all. Happy New Year." Lucy closed her eyes and found herself smelling the now so familiar scent of Gavin's collar. The party was still going but Lucy was exhausted and motioned for Gavin to pull them out. They said goodbye to their new friends, promising to e-mail for future meetings and stumbled out onto the cobblestone street in the dark of midnight, still laughing. Gavin gave a light salute to the rental car and promised to see it in the morning. He pulled Lucy close to him as they walked arm in arm back to their hotel.

It started to drizzle but it was surprisingly warm out and with their bellies full of ale and pub food, the pair just giggled again and kept walking.

"This was one of the best days of my life," Lucy said to Gavin. He only hugged her tighter and grinned. The drizzle turned to a full on pour and Lucy let go of Gavin to step into the middle of the road and grin. She turned her face up to the sky and let the water pour over her. She opened her arms and spun in a circle, laughing out loud. Taking a deep breath she turned to see Gavin grinning at her. He reached out and grabbed her hand and pulled her into a nearby door way. It was small and they tucked tightly in between the stones. He said something but the rain was hitting the pavement so powerfully, Lucy could almost not hear him.

"What?" she laughed.

"You are beautiful in the rain, Lucy," he repeated. Water dripped down his face and he made no move to wipe it away. Then he smiled at her and suddenly Lucy seemed to see Gavin for the first time. His boyish good looks weren't diminished by the fact that he was soaking wet and Lucy was struck by how dashingly handsome he really was. On impulse, she reached up and brushed his sopping hair off his brow. She moved slowly and tilted her head to the side, gazing at him. Everything felt warm and fuzzy and Lucy sighed with contentment. Gavin put one hand on the side of her face, and studied her as he traced her cheek with his thumb.

Then Gavin leaned over and kissed Lucy, hard. She wasn't surprised by it; in fact, the kiss felt like the most natural thing in the world and Lucy found herself wrapping her arms around his neck and pulling him closer to her. She twined her fingers through his hair as he pulled her tightly to him. The kiss was strong and powerful and it felt so right, so comfortable, so safe that she let it continue far longer than she should have. Gavin pulled back and looked at her softly for a moment. With horror, Lucy realized what she had done. Her heart stopped and her stomach clenched in embarrassment as Nathaniel's face came to her mind. Suddenly terrified and ashamed of herself, Lucy instinctively bolted from the door back into the rain. She ran across the street and into a park before Gavin caught up with her.

"No! Lucy, no!" he yelled in her face as he grabbed her shoulders and forced her to face him. "I need to say this." Rain poured down his face and chest. His shirt was soaked and it clung to him. "I love you, Lucy Bower. I have loved you since the first day I saw you." She started to open her mouth to speak but Gavin just kept talking as the rain drenched them more. "I know I'm not an Angel and I know that I don't have magic powers and I know that I don't look like the cover of a magazine. I know those things, Lucy, but I love you and I would never put you in danger and I would never make you chase me. I know I am not as perfect as Nathaniel, but you need to know that I love you with all my heart and I would do anything for you." As he leaned forward and rested their foreheads together, he closed his eyes,

"I have nothing to give to you but my love. And I already know what you are going to say but I had to tell you." Lucy was panting, her heart pounding – she couldn't decide if she was terrified or thrilled. He paused and continued in a quieter voice. "So we are going to go on tomorrow as if nothing happened tonight." He put his hands on either side of her face and lifted his eyes to meet hers. Lucy's heart broke with the pain in them. "I love you." He kissed her again, softly, unbearably slowly and so sweetly that tears sprung to Lucy's closed eyes. And then suddenly it was over and he was gone. Lucy opened her eyes to see him walking off through the streets of London. She stood watching him go, her tears mixing with the rain as it poured over her.

Chapter Eleven
Train

*"One should always have something
sensational to read in the train."*
~ Oscar Wilde

Lucy headed back to the hotel alone and now completely sober. Gavin wasn't there when she let herself into the tiny room and took a warming shower. Lucy had no idea what she was doing and could not stop crying about the situation she now found herself in. Had she led Gavin on? She had to admit that she hadn't minded being mistaken for his girlfriend, in fact, she had liked it. What did that mean? Did it mean that she wasn't in love with Nathaniel? No, she certainly loved Nathaniel; he was her soul mate. She felt terrible for betraying him like this. Still though, Gavin was right, since she had been with Nathaniel, she had been in constant danger. Nothing had been normal or calm – Nathaniel's love for Lucy had always made up for the chaos. But now that he was gone, it was harder to rationalize.

Lucy shivered in the shower. Did she love Gavin too? She

thought about what Nathaniel had told her about the Hall of Souls and the fact that most people are not lucky enough to find their soul mates. Most people are completely happy for their entire lives with someone that was close to them in the Hall of Souls – not necessarily their soul mate. But now that Lucy knew her soul mate, could she be happy with Gavin? Thinking deeply, Lucy decided that in fact she could be very happy with Gavin. The last two weeks had proved that. Gavin was funny and charming and kind to her. He made her laugh harder than anyone else in the whole world, even Nathaniel. She had to admit that on some level, she had fallen in love with Gavin because he was very easy to fall in love with. But he wasn't Nathaniel and nothing could make him Nathaniel.

Lucy sighed. Gavin had been right when he had said that he knew what her answer would be. She would always choose Nathaniel, over everyone else, every time. She had not yet come to terms with why that made her sad. Once she found Nathaniel, she reassured herself, everything would be just as it should be. She and Gavin would be friends and she and Nathaniel would be together forever. She dressed in her pajamas and crawled into bed. Lucy fell asleep thinking that she was going to make everything work out even if it killed her.

She woke in the morning with a blazing headache and the sudden, desperate need to take a train. She assumed this was a sign that they should continue on their travels. Lucy was relieved that they would have a new purpose. Gavin had not returned and she was immediately fearful that something had happened to him. She got up quickly and dressed, intent on heading to the car to see if he had maybe decided to just sleep in there until he was able to drive safely. At the same time, she imagined him dead in a ditch or mugged and left bleeding at the side of the Thames. She was pulling on her sneakers when Gavin came into the room. He was clean and dry but looked weary and tired. He smiled when he saw her.

"Oh thank God you're okay," she exploded and leapt at him. She hugged him tightly. "I was worried about you." Gavin hugged her back.

"Sorry Red," he said with a remorseful smile. "I didn't mean to scare you."

They broke apart and Lucy bit her lip. "About last night..."

"I don't want to talk about it," he said sternly. "I apologize for the whole thing, I was drunk and sentimental and I just want to you pretend that nothing happened. I didn't mean it. Okay? I'm not kidding here," he added severely.

"Okay," Lucy agreed. She didn't acknowledge the slight pang of disappointment she felt. It was for the best anyway. Gavin smiled and Lucy smiled back.

"What's the plan?" Gavin prompted lightly.

"Breakfast, then a train," Lucy replied.

"What kind of train?" he asked while starting to pack their things.

"I don't know," Lucy replied, "just a train."

"Maybe you will get further instructions at the train station?" he said hopefully.

"I'm figuring." She shrugged. "At least this is a start."

"Then off we go!" Gavin said brightly.

They packed quickly and returned the rental car. Gavin didn't tell Lucy where he had spent the night and she didn't ask. They made their way to St. Pancras Station and tucked into a diner for a quick breakfast.

"Thoughts?" Gavin queried.

"Hmmm," Lucy said while looking around, "nothing yet."

"Okay," Gavin answered. "Keep me posted." They finished eating and wandered around the station for an hour. Lucy was starting to get frustrated. "Maybe it's like a subway. Maybe we are closer than we thought," Gavin offered.

"No," Lucy said vaguely, "I feel like we are in the right place but I don't have the feeling of what train to catch."

"Maybe they are here!" Gavin exclaimed.

"No," Lucy said dismally, "they are still far away."

"Okay," Gavin replied, ever the optimist, "let's keep walking then."

They wandered more and even visited an increasingly irritated ticket agent to see if a location would come to mind if Lucy started buying a ticket. That didn't work either and the ticket agent threatened to have them thrown out for fooling around. It was a full two hours later that they were sitting in the waiting area. Lucy was totally despondent and Gavin had started to doze in the chair beside her.

"Help me," Lucy whispered to the domed glass ceiling, "please, please help me."

Nothing.

She sighed and slumped back in the seat.

Suddenly she sat up and grabbed Gavin's arm.

"Wha?" he said, startled.

"Let's go!" Lucy yelled. She stood up and grabbed their bags and started running to the ticket booth. Gavin struggled behind her to catch up. She slammed into the wall below the wicket.

"You again?" The ticket lady rolled her eyes. "Look sweetheart, I don't have all day and I've had enough of your shenanigans so you buy a ticket right now, or I'm calling the police."

"Two tickets to Bulgaria please," Lucy panted while pulling out Nathaniel's Visa and slamming it on the counter.

The ticket agent blinked at her for a moment before checking her computer, "There is a train leaving in ten minutes," she said slowly.

"Two tickets please!" Lucy pressed and pushed the credit card closer under the glass.

The ticket lady rolled her eyes but printed the tickets and wordlessly passed them over with Nathaniel's charge card. Lucy took them and turned with Gavin toward the platform. She heard the ticket agent claim she needed a drink in a low tone. Lucy grabbed Gavin's hand and the two bolted for the platform, threw their tickets at the conductor, boarded the train and tossed themselves into a seat just as the train pulled out with a lurch.

"Nothing like cutting it close there, sweetheart," Gavin said sarcastically.

"Sorry man," Lucy replied, "don't shoot the messenger."

He smiled. "I'm glad we are on our way somewhere at least, but Bulgaria? Really? How lame could you get?"

Lucy smiled. "I can't even imagine why we have to go there but I can assure you that I'm right."

"Yeah, big shocker there, Red," Gavin said while settling himself into the seat. "You think you are right about everything."

Lucy grinned. "Someone has to lead this operation."

"Speaking of operation," Gavin replied, "what exactly is our plan when we find them? I mean, I can only assume this Malachi guy is pretty hardcore to be holding three people hostage, two of whom have supernatural powers. So, what the hell are we going to do to free them?"

"I don't know that yet," Lucy replied thoughtfully, "I have been so intent on getting there that I have no idea what the plan is once we arrive. I can only assume that we will figure it out as we go?" she added lamely.

"Well," Gavin said thoughtfully, "I have watched enough

Mission Impossible movies to tell you that the element of surprise is a good one. Also, the ability to blow crap up – that helps too."

"Duly noted," Lucy replied. "My thoughts are that Roman and Nathaniel had to have been incapacitated in some way. We get them free and everything will be okay."

"But Red, we are woefully unprepared for a battle with a Demon. You need to be prepared to maybe call in some backup at some point."

"Like who?" Lucy asked, confused.

Gavin smiled. "Like the police. You know those guys whose job it is to kill the bad guy and save the hostages? Them? My thought is that we figure out where everyone is, using your little soul finder there and call in a nice big Bulgarian SWAT team to nail this dude's ass. Okay?"

Lucy had to admit that Gavin was right; they had little or no way to fight Malachi, but she didn't think the police would be able to help either.

"Fine – that's the plan then," she agreed, but really had no intention of calling anyone when the time came.

Gavin, feeling somewhat placated, settled in for the ride. The train ride was three horrific days long and completely miserable. If they weren't beside a crying baby, they were beside someone with motion sickness. Food proved to be a challenge in the final leg, as it appeared there was none on board and everyone just knew to bring some for themselves. Lucy and Gavin, having no such thoughts, starved for the first few hours until Gavin shoved his jacket under Lucy's shirt and paraded her shamelessly about, talking about how hungry they were. A woman kindly offered them some sort of pudding that Gavin devoured and Lucy choked down. They slept sitting up and ate standing up, didn't shower and were generally wretched and outrageously cranky by the time they arrived at their destination.

They stood on a busy, chaotic street and winced at the bright lights. Lucy looked to the setting sun. Her heart quickened at the sight and she knew where they had to go.

"Nathaniel is in that mountain range," she smiled, "I know it."

"Awesome," Gavin said sharply, "that's super great."

"I'm so sorry, Gavin," Lucy said, "I can go the rest of the way alone, you don't have to come."

"Yeah," he snapped, "because I can just leave you to hike through a set of mountains on your own."

"I said I was sorry!" Lucy snapped back, her anger flaring. "What do you want me to do?"

Gavin sighed, suddenly deflated. "I know there's nothing you can do. I'm sorry I snapped at you. I'm just tired and cranky."

"I know," Lucy groaned, "I really wish there was another way. Thank you again for coming with me."

"Stop thanking me," he ordered with a weary smile. He looked about them. "I guess we should find somewhere that sells camping equipment. Those mountains look uninviting at best."

"I have no idea how to camp," Lucy offered with a deep tone of regret.

Gavin ran a hand over his now prickled chin and cheek, "Well, lucky for you I do know how to camp. I would however, like to take a day to rest and bleach that train off my skin if that's all right." He sounded very testy indeed and despite Lucy's eagerness to get going now that they had another destination, she agreed that they needed sleep and supplies and a shower. She knew that she had to smell horrible.

They found a clean and comfortable hotel and for once paid a reasonable price, since it was now past the holiday season. The hotel, however, did not have double rooms and were very confused with the pair when they implied that they did not want to sleep in the same bed. Their request was completely denied and they received a room with a queen sized bed. After showering and eating a huge meal, Lucy found the hotel laundry and while Gavin showered she washed, dried and folded all their clothes. Among the piles of clothes, she found the shirt that Gavin had been wearing in the rain that night in London. Before tucking it into the washing machine, she impulsively sniffed the collar. Gavin's cologne wafted to her nose and she found herself inhaling deeply. The image of his face in the rain came back to her in perfect clarity.

Lucy often didn't know if her photographic memory was a blessing or a curse, but never more so than at this moment. She brought back his exact words, the look in Gavin's eyes, the depth with which he spoke, and she felt her heart quicken at the thought. Maybe if the details had been hazy, especially considering how much she had had to drink, then she might not have the same feelings. But her memory allowed her to see every single moment. It shocked her that she was so happy at the memory. Lucy did not feel regret or guilt or even sadness. She felt great contentment with it, as if it had settled happily into her consciousness to live forever. Lucy quickly shoved the shirt into the washing machine and once again assured herself that once she was reunited with Nathaniel, everything would be fine. There would be no room for feelings for Gavin as long as Nathaniel was around.

She finished the laundry, folded it neatly and made her way up to their room. Gavin had showered and was completely passed out on his stomach, wearing only his boxers. Water still beaded upon his broad shoulders and Lucy again had to suppress the London rain memory. There was no couch in the room and Lucy was too exhausted to care, so she stripped down to her t-shirt and crawled quietly into bed beside Gavin. He seemed to sense her presence for he immediately rolled over and flung an arm over her in a tight embrace. Lucy again chastised herself for not tensing at his movements. Instead, her body instinctively relaxed completely and within seconds she was deep asleep in Gavin's arms.

Lucy awoke to the blinding sun. She groaned and rolled over, pulling her pillow with her. Beside her, she heard Gavin do the same.

"What time is it?" she mumbled.

"Half past go back to bloody sleep I think," Gavin slurred. "So let's go back to sleep, Red." He wiggled slightly and shifted further under the sheet and Lucy realized that their free hands were clasped tightly.

"Hmmm," Lucy mumbled. "We should get up."

"Sleep baby," Gavin babbled. He was already falling back to sleep.

With that, Lucy faded back into unconsciousness.

When Lucy woke again, it was dark and she felt like she had been asleep for days. Looking at the clock, she discovered that in fact they *had* been asleep for a full day and a half. She stretched. If their bodies wanted to sleep that long, they must have needed it. She slipped out of bed and padded over to the shower. Lucy took a long hot shower to wake herself up. When she had dried and dressed, she came out of the bathroom to find Gavin dressed and looking out the window.

"Look at this place, Red!" he exclaimed, "I hadn't noticed when we got here how gorgeous it is!"

Lucy joined him at the window and smiled. Bulgaria was in fact quite lovely, it was clearly old but well preserved. "It looks like a fairy tale." Lucy smiled.

"Beauty and the Beast," Gavin joked, poking her in the ribs, "and I'm the beauty."

"HA!" Lucy exploded.

"Look, I'm sorry I was such a bear when we got here," Gavin started.

"Do not apologize," Lucy chided him, "I am dragging you through chaos and you have been doing everything I have asked without question. You have a right to complain every once in a while."

Gavin shook his head. "Red, I have to tell you that this has been the most fun I have had in a long time; despite the Demons and the death and the chance that I could be skinned alive and all that, it's been a blast."

"Holy crap, do you ever have a low fun standard," Lucy laughed.

"Totally low," Gavin chuckled. Lucy looked back out over the mountain range. From here it looked picturesque but she knew that up close, it would not be so pretty.

Chapter Twelve
Betrayed

"Betrayal is the only truth that sticks."
~ Arthur Miller

They shopped the day away, spending more on Nathaniel's credit card. Lucy shuddered to think about how they were going to pay the whole thing off at the end of all this. Gavin proved to be an excellent resource when it came to all things camping. If it was summer this might be a pleasant trip, but in the cold of January, the threat of freezing to death was real. However, there had been a recent break in the weather and the snow levels and temperature were not deadly when they headed out on the newest part of their adventure.

They took a bus to a small town deep in the range and hitched a ride with a strange man and his dog until the road ended. He seemed convinced that Lucy and Gavin were in some sort of suicide pact. After his truck drove away, Lucy and Gavin stood with nothing but rock and snow around them.

"Navigator?" Gavin prompted, looking at Lucy. Her

memory kicked in and she brought up the last time someone had said that to her. It was when Nathaniel and Roman were flying them to Seaport, Gavin's vacation town, to cause a natural disaster and incite the anger of Force. Thinking of Nathaniel made Lucy warm inside and she smiled despite the dismal nature of their current situation. In addition, the closer she got to Nathaniel, the better she could feel him. She closed her eyes and felt a pull deep within her. Details of the path became clearer, like she was scanning through a map.

"It's not that far and I feel like there is a road or pathway to him," she said confidently. She opened her eyes. "Yes, not that far."

"Good then," Gavin smiled, "you lead the way." They hiked the day through and Lucy still had the feeling that they were getting much closer when Gavin set up camp and started a fire. He taught Lucy how to make a decent meal out of absolutely nothing and how to build the fire up to make sure they were safe overnight. Lucy sat, wrapped in her sleeping bag, watching Gavin kneeling beside the fire, cutting wood with a small hatchet. The firelight played off his handsome face and strong chest. Lucy smiled.

"What are you grinning at?" he caught her eye.

"I'm happy," Lucy replied.

"Oh," Gavin nodded, "that's good."

"We are closer to Nathaniel than ever," Lucy replied quickly. "It won't be long now."

Gavin's lips tightened for a second. "That is so great, Lucy." She knew he was feigning his enthusiasm and she hated both of them for it.

"You won't have to put up with me for much longer," she grinned, desperately trying to continue the façade.

He stood and put his hands in his pockets before looking at her sideways. "Oh I don't know about that." He was quiet for a minute before continuing. "I am about to say something, but I don't want you to get mad."

"That is the first way to make me mad," Lucy replied testily.

"I think we should turn back," he almost winced.

Lucy's mouth fell open. "Are you out of your mind?" she yelled.

"You went right to the yelling there, hey?" Gavin sat down calmly.

"Of course I'm yelling!" she hollered. "Do you have any idea how close we are? I can feel him, Gavin! Feel him! I know where he is! Why, after going all this way, would I now turn back?"

"Because you have common sense?" Gavin challenged. "Because you aren't an idiot? Because unlike every other heroine in the world, you know danger when you see it?" Lucy opened her mouth to counter but he kept going. "This guy is bad news, Lucy, really bad news and I think we, well, I have made a terrible mistake by taking you here. We need to go back to town and find the cops and you can lead them to Nathaniel. They can save our friends."

Lucy sat stunned for a moment. "You never had any intention of coming the whole way, did you?" she asked in almost a whisper.

"Lucy, I told you days ago that we should call the cops when we got close. That was always my intention," he stated plainly.

"And how are we going to kill Roman, hey?" Lucy yelled again. "How are we going to free Nathaniel and Anastasia? How, if there are a bunch of cops around, are we supposed to hide Nathaniel's powers? Do you have any idea what would happen to him if the world discovered he existed? Any idea?" she demanded. "Use your imagination, Gavin, and try not to be such a coward next time!"

Gavin sat quietly and nodded at Lucy's comment, as if confirming something for himself. Lucy rolled her eyes and opened her mouth to apologize.

"You should turn in." Gavin motioned to the tent. "You are exhausted."

"Oh, and you aren't exhausted?" Lucy shot back.

"I have some thinking to do."

"What about?" Lucy pushed.

Gavin didn't look at her before replying, "Nothing that you would want to worry about."

Lucy's anger flared again as she stomped into the tent and flopped down on the mat. She pulled off her boots and threw the sleeping bag around her. What did Gavin expect from her? Did he want her to stop loving Nathaniel? How would that even be possible? It wasn't her fault that he agreed to come on this trip with her! He knew that her intention always was to try to get everyone out themselves. He couldn't now change the plan and expect her to go along. She shouldn't have called him a coward though, that was wrong. Guilt and exhaustion overtook her. Lucy rolled over and once again reminded herself that everything would be just fine as soon as she found Nathaniel. She repeated this to herself until she finally fell asleep.

The next morning, Lucy awoke to the smell of coffee. Her mind drifted back to the dorms and any given Saturday morning. Any minute now, Anastasia would come barreling in the room to jump on her. Reality set in cold and hard, like the ground she was laying on. Lucy groaned as she rolled and felt every tree root and rock she had been sleeping on.

Lucy cocooned herself into the sleeping bag and stumbled out of the tent – she could feel the tension in the air. She flopped down on the ground in front of the fire.

"Did you even come to bed last night?" she demanded.

Gavin was looking at the fire and blinked slowly as he turned his head to look at her. The hurt and guilt in his eyes was beyond anything Lucy could ever imagine. Clearly, the events from last night were not forgotten and she sighed. Gavin was right, what was she thinking? They had to go to the police. They would figure out a way to explain everything once Nathaniel was safe. Trying to overtake a Demon was a foolish idea at best. She opened her mouth to recant every word she had said last night, apologize and agree to go to the police.

Before she got a word out, she felt something cold press up against the back of her skull. She froze in terror. A man appeared from the bushes behind Gavin dressed in some sort of stiff leather security uniform. Gavin didn't jump up in surprise but stood slowly and nodded at the men.

"You suck at navigation buddy," the guard said to Gavin in a heavy European accent, "we barely found you." He motioned to whoever was behind Lucy holding what felt like a gun to her head. "Get her taken care of, Malachi is expecting them." Lucy's mouth fell open as a shockwave ran through her. What had Gavin done and why?

The gun at the base of her skull pushed into her. "You heard him," a voice said into her ear, "behave yourself or all your perfect memories will be splattered all over the rocks." He found himself quite funny and cackled at his own joke. Lucy looked back at Gavin with pleading in her eyes. How could he do this to her? Why? She felt something sharp poking into her arm through the sleeve of her shirt. She looked down to discover that the guard was injecting her with something.

"No!" she screamed and tried to stand but the guard

restrained her with his other hand on her shoulder, pinning her to the ground. Blackness started to touch at the edges of her vision. She twisted and growled on the ground fighting against the hands holding her and the medication raging through her system. She looked again at Gavin. "Why?" she whispered as tears began to flow.

Gavin shook his head. "Because you are right, Lucy," he said sadly, "I am a coward."

Chapter Thirteen
Captivity

"To death do I hand them over, with the fetters of death they have been bound. To the evil messengers of death do I lead them captive."
~ The Atharva-Veda

His eyes snapped open and he leapt to a crouch, as the chains prevented him from standing upright. He growled lightly, like a fire had been lit in a furnace. His cell partner mirrored his actions in preparation for an unexpected assailant and grunted in query when none was found.

"She's here," was the explanation given.

"Here? In the castle?"

"Yes."

"Sorry."

"She's alive, that's all that matters now."

"I wonder what the plan is now that we are all here." Knowing there was no danger made him bored so he sat back down, being careful not to rest his back against the wall.

"Will it get worse?" He couldn't sit now, he might not sit

down again until he figured out a way to get her out. He had the feeling that he may never see the sun again. This was inconsequential. She needed to be safe.

"Most likely, that's the way we Demons work." His voice was rueful.

"Not all of you," was the quick reply.

They smiled weakly at each other.

"Rest," he ordered, "who knows, we might have to save our strength for something."

The Angel begrudgingly and gingerly sat back down.

Lucy slowly forced her eyes open. She didn't want to be awake. In fact, she could not remember a time that she had wanted to be conscious less. Her vision was blurry, seeing only that she was lying on a large bed maybe with a red or dark pink silk comforter. Her eyes burned and her head pounded so she closed them again. She clenched her eyes shut. Anything to not feel what she was feeling right now. Gavin had betrayed her. How? Why? This whole time she had been fooled into thinking that he actually cared about her. That he actually loved her. She tightened her hand into a fist around whatever fabric she was laying upon. The satin crumpled weakly in her palm. Tears squeezed out the corners of her clamped eyes. How could he?

Suddenly, Lucy heard a rustle of something and a door opening and closing. She was no longer alone. She forcibly pushed her eyelids up and urged her arms to straighten and bring herself somewhat upright. The person beside her was vaguely familiar but the form was more of a blur than anything. She blinked once, twice, not believing her eyes; praying that she wasn't in some sort of dream.

"Oh thank God, Lucy!" Anastasia yelled and threw herself

on top of Lucy on the bed.

Relief flooded through Lucy. Anastasia was alive and she was here, right here in Lucy's arms. She wept with gratitude. The friends held each other laughed with joy. Lucy's strength came back to her as whatever the guards had given her began to wear off. They broke apart and regarded each other as they knelt on the bed.

Anastasia looked almost better than she had the last time Lucy had seen her. She was wearing a full face of glamour makeup, her hair glossy and clean and swept up into a romantic twist at the nape of her neck. Her nails were done and her skin glowed. She wore a ball gown of bright blue silk that looked stunning on her frame. Lucy looked down at her own grubby hiking clothes, broken filthy nails, and pulled away from hugging Anastasia's crisp form.

Anastasia sensed the change and laughed. "Oh please, woman," she exclaimed, "don't you dare be stupid like that. Do you have any idea how many dresses I have? This thing can get totally ruined." She smiled but Lucy noticed that there was no happiness behind it.

"What's going on here?" Lucy asked "What happened?" She looked around her. They were in a huge bedroom chamber. The walls were stone but covered here and there with massive, ornate tapestries. They sat on the largest bed that Lucy had ever seen. It had four enormous posts that extended up ten feet in the air to a vast silk canopy. The room had several oak wardrobes and dressers, each more beautifully made than the next. There were two doors. One was much larger than the other but both were made of thick oak. Lucy assumed one was the bathroom and one was the exit. There was a rotund area on the left that had an ancient, beautiful table and chairs and a roomy sitting area that looked out through thick glass to the mountains beyond. They were very high up. She stopped and cocked her head to the side, she couldn't feel

Nathaniel. Not at all. Was he here? Had he been moved? No, then she would have felt the difference. She couldn't feel him at all.

Lucy stood up unsteadily and walked to the window. "Are we in a castle?"

Anastasia nodded. "Yup – somewhere in Bulgaria, I think, but I'm not sure." She bit her lip. "I don't know much of what is going on here." She stood up and joined Lucy at the window. She sighed as she gazed out. Lucy's heart sunk; despite her outward appearance, Anastasia had not been treated well here. They sat down on two chairs and Lucy waited to hear her friend's story.

"Let's see, when was the last time I saw you?" She sat back, thinking. She sighed again and looked out the window. "I know it looks pretty fairy tale like around here," she whispered to the windows, "but this place is Hell on Earth." Lucy sat and let her speak. "I was in my room, the night of my parents' Christmas party. When suddenly he just appeared. Like poof, out of nowhere, there was Alexander in a tux standing in my room. I screamed, of course, but no sound came out and I tried to run but I couldn't. It was like my muscles were frozen in place."

She shuddered with the memory. Lucy, remembering her own encounters with Demons, shuddered with her. "He grinned at me and I thought, There is something very very wrong here. And man was I right about that. He lifted a finger to his lips and said, 'You have to be quiet. There is no need to rouse the suspicions of your parents. We wouldn't want to hurt them, now would we?' and I knew right then that Alexander wasn't who he said he was and he wasn't *right*, you know?" Lucy nodded her understanding.

"So I stood there and stared at him, frozen, for what seemed like forever.

"'We are waiting,' he said finally, 'for your boyfriend.' And I thought, why would Roman come here? How does he know to come? 'Lucy will figure it all out, you see,' he explained. 'We can always rely on Lucy to get the answers, can't we? And then she will send Roman and hopefully Nathaniel too and then we will all have a little fun.' And I threw up in my mouth at that one because no horror film could have captured the look on his face. I started to cry and the tears just poured down my face.

"It felt like forever that we stood there. He told me that if I didn't agree to come with him that bad things would happen," she paused and swallowed, "to my parents. So I told him I would go with him where ever he wanted me to. I would do whatever he wanted me to just so he wouldn't hurt them. He smiled at that, and mumbled something about me exercising my 'free will'. He made me write a note to my parents about how we had fallen in love and were going on a trip to celebrate our engagement. I didn't think my parents would believe it but apparently they did. He made me call them a while ago and they were thrilled with it all." She shook her head. "So anyway, we just stood in my room waiting and waiting. Then suddenly, there was this small noise by the window. I barely heard it but Alexander, he grinned and just pointed at the window and the glass just vanished, part of the wall too, and there, standing, no floating, was Roman and Nathaniel." She gave Lucy a pointed look and Lucy hung her head. "You can imagine my shock seeing that my boyfriend and best friend's boyfriend could fly. You would think that if my best friend knew such a thing that she would have shared it with me," she added angrily.

"You wouldn't have believed me," Lucy defended.

"I would have if they had shown me!" Anastasia flashed. "You just left me in the dark like I was some child that needed protecting! Like I was stupid!"

"There wasn't a need to tell you," Lucy replied, knowing full well how Anastasia would respond.

"Apparently, there was!" Anastasia shot back, "Because look where we are now!" She gestured her arms around the room.

Lucy's shoulders fell forward. Anastasia was right. Just as Lucy had known back on the dock in the rain, this was all her fault. "I'm so sorry." She looked pleadingly at her friend. "I am so so sorry. If I could go back and do anything again, it would be that."

"I know," Anastasia tilted her head back and looked at the ceiling, "There was no way of any of you could predict what would happen." She looked at Lucy. "It's okay. I probably wouldn't have told you either, thinking I was protecting you." Lucy reached across the table and the two held hands for a moment before Anastasia continued. "So there they were and then absolute chaos ensued. Alexander grabbed me and threw me over his shoulder and suddenly, we were flying. Roman screamed in rage seeing us flying away. Alexander, though, doesn't have wings," she added hastily. "I don't know if that is important. They battled in the air beside my parent's house, he made fire out of his hands and threw it at them. Roman and Nathaniel were at a huge disadvantage because Alexander was holding me. They couldn't really do him any damage. I was terrified.

"It went on for a while and I couldn't see anything but I heard Roman and Nathaniel scream. Then everything went black and I woke up here."

"I'm so sorry," Lucy said again. She had a feeling that she would be saying this for a long, long time.

"Now it's your turn," Stasia demanded. "Spill it, Bower. And leave no detail out."

Lucy sat back, drew in a deep breath, and started talking. She told Anastasia everything from the first moment she met Nathaniel to the moment she awoke on the bed. She filled her in on Purgatory but omitted what she had learned about her father and

Roman – she would deal with Roman when the time was right. She did tell her about her discoveries about Malachi or Alexander, as Stasia knew him. She told her how Gavin had betrayed her but omitted all other Gavin information – it was still too painful to think of how he played her. She told her how much she had missed her and Nathaniel. By the end Lucy was sobbing but Anastasia sat still. She patted Lucy's hand for comfort but didn't shed one tear.

After Lucy composed herself, she looked about the room. "What happens here?"

Anastasia opened her mouth to reply but was interrupted by the door slamming open.

"You are about to find out," Anastasia whispered as she stood. Lucy could feel the terror radiate off her.

A man strode into the room. The entire tone of the room changed. It became colder, the lights even dimmed slightly, and Lucy shivered lightly. The atmosphere was in sharp contrast to the man's appearance. He wore a suit and a charming smile that highlighted his movie star façade. His bleach blond hair was slicked back off his sharp features and his piercing blue eyes. Lucy knew this was Malachi because she recognized him from Roman's murder scene in Hell. The last time she laid eyes on him he was bleeding to death in an alleyway. She liked him better that way. He could not look less like a powerful Demon and yet he was and Lucy felt her heart speed up.

"Ladies," he cooed as he approached, "I am so pleased to see that you have caught up." He looked at Lucy and her spine tightened in fear. "Lucy," he said, "I have been awaiting your arrival. I have always wanted to meet you."

Lucy was not interested in maintaining any sort of façade of niceties and she was about to tell Malachi precisely what she thought of him, but she changed her mind after glancing sideways at Anastasia. Stasia was so petrified of Malachi that she was visibly trembling. If the always confident and intrepid Stasia was shaken to the core, it was for good reason and it would be foolish for Lucy not to follow her lead.

"I hope that you weren't too upset about your, shall we say, hasty arrival?" he said smoothly. "My soldiers do become a tad overzealous at times. I assume you weren't injured at all?" He reached a hand out lightly and this small movement caused Stasia to whimper and cower back several inches. On instinct, Lucy flinched as well but Malachi kept his distance.

"I am fine," she replied quietly, "thank you." Malachi smiled. "I would like to see Nathaniel if possible though." And his smile mutated into a grimace.

"Has Nathaniel provided any comforts to you?" he demanded, his voice suddenly thick with anger. "Has Nathaniel reunited you with your best friend? Kept that best friend safe and alive awaiting you?" His eyes flashed red and Lucy's stomach clenched. "Answer me!" he raged, stepping closer.

"No," Lucy whispered – her own voice shaking.

"Then why would you request to see him?" he thundered. "Why? When it is I who have spared your life and the life of your friends! It is I," he continued, "who has gone to enormous trouble to bring you here unscathed and create a place for you to be safe! Be grateful for what you are given, girl, or you will suffer for it!"

He stepped closer to her and grabbed her wrist. The agony his touch produced was so powerful that Lucy instantly fell to her knees screaming. Fire raged from his hand up her arm and across her body, searing her from the inside out. Lucy felt her skin char and bubble on her bones and she could do nothing but scream as smoke poured from her mouth. As quickly as it started, Malachi let go of her and the burning stopped. Lucy slumped on the floor and saw that there was no damage to her at all, not her body anyway, the damage to her mental state felt permanent. The message had been received.

Malachi's mannerly behavior returned. "Oh I do hope you aren't upset, dear Lucy," he said as she stumbled back to her feet. He leaned in slightly. "Whenever something like that happens, do remember, little dove, that it is always your own doing. You have done it to yourself. Isn't that right, Anastasia darling?" he added, turning his head to regard her. Anastasia nodded emphatically and Malachi smiled. "Very good then," he said, straightening. "Let's move on to more pleasant matters." He looked Lucy up and down. "You do not look your best right now, my sweet. Let's get you cleaned up and the two of you can relax until dinner time." He started to move toward the door, "Extra guests for supper, Anastasia. Can you believe our good fortune? What a grand time we will have indeed." Anastasia nodded and offered a weak smile but a shiver ran through her. Malachi grinned and walked out the door. It shut and locked behind him.

Lucy slumped down in the chair, defeated. Stasia sat on the arm of Lucy's chair and rested her hand on Lucy's shoulder. She seemed incapable of offering any more comfort than that.

"Is that the way he always is?" Lucy demanded.

Anastasia paused, considering whether to lie or not. "Yes, and sometimes worse."

"This is all my fault," Lucy raged at the walls, "we are trapped in a Hell on Earth and it is all my fault!"

"Shhh," Stasia consoled, "no it isn't." She lifted Lucy's chin to look her in the eyes and Lucy saw Anastasia closely for the first time. She was not as radiant as Lucy first thought. Her skin under her makeup was grey and thin and dark circles resided under her now dull and empty eyes. She had been enduring this Hell for weeks alone and Lucy's heart broke for her. "We can't lose hope," Stasia whispered urgently and Lucy saw a small spark of light come back to her eyes. "I think that's what he wants, is for us to lose hope." Lucy nodded and sniffed back her tears. "Now," Stasia started to speak faster, "they are going to come for you. The girls won't hurt you but don't do anything weird or talk to them because they won't talk back. And don't look too close because I tried once and it isn't nice."

"What girls?" Lucy was confused. "Look too close at what?"

The door opened and Lucy and Anastasia stood.

"At their eyes," she whispered. Five blond girls in short black dresses walked into the room and toward them. They were stunningly beautiful except for the fact that their eyes were completely black.

Lucy had seen girls like this before; soulless creatures that served Demons in Hell. This apparently was her beauty team and Lucy shuddered with the thought of things so evil touching her.

"Just close your eyes and pretend you are at the spa," Stasia said with a sad smile. "They won't hurt you." Lucy nodded as she followed the girls into the bathroom.

The bathroom was an expansive tiled oasis. Lucy was washed and waxed, polished and primped. Lucy took Stasia's advice and didn't look the dead girls in the eyes and spent the time reflecting on the past few weeks. Why would Gavin betray her? Was he being controlled by Malachi the whole time or was he a master liar? How could Lucy have been so wrong? Where was Nathaniel? Was he here as she felt or was she wrong about that too? The strong pull she had felt in the mountains was dampened so much that she questioned ever having it.

Two hours later, she emerged wearing a stunning emerald green silk gown with her auburn locks cascading down her back.

The dead girls knew what they were doing for when Lucy finally looked in the mirror, she was breathtaking. She could not help smiling slightly – it had been a long time since she felt pretty. Anastasia had been sitting by the window, reading from an old book. They were equally shocked to see each other.

"You look so gorgeous!" Anastasia exclaimed.

"You can read?" Lucy laughed and Anastasia joined in. It felt good to laugh and they both embraced lightly, being sure not to rumple the other. Simultaneously, they both let out a light sigh, for they could pretend and play dress up all they wanted but the fact of the matter was that they were being held captive by a Demon. It was bizarre and terrifying. Both of them became teary eyed at that which was unspoken between them. Lucy thought of the fire that consumed her when Malachi touched her.

"Will he kill us?" she whispered.

Stasia shook her head and frowned to keep the tears back, "Sometimes I think it's inevitable and other times I am sure he would have done it by now."

Lucy nodded. They both sniffed and half laughed as they wiped each other's tears.

"It's better with you here," Stasia said quietly and Lucy smiled but Stasia didn't smile back, "I mean--"

She was cut off by the door opening. A soldier stood in the archway, dressed in the thick leather armor that the guards who had apprehended Lucy had worn.

"Dinner is served," he almost shouted while staring straight ahead. Stasia reached down and grabbed Lucy's hands tightly.

"I was hoping," she stammered, "that since Lucy just got here that we could just eat in our room today and do," she paused, "it, tomorrow."

"What happens at dinner?" Lucy whispered, suddenly

tense.

"Dinner is served," the soldier ordered again as if Anastasia had never spoken and her shoulders slumped slightly before she started walking to the door, pulling Lucy with her.

The wide stone hall was lined with ornate rugs and statues. At first, the pieces appeared to be from a classical age but as Lucy looked closer she realized that they were unlike any works of art she had ever seen. The statues were of figures twisted in agony or terror – naked woman writhing in fire, men with their heads partially severed, their faces morphed into different stages of suffering. The tapestries were worse – scenes depicting torture and abuse of the like Lucy had never imagined. As another guard fell in behind the girls, Lucy wondered what castle this was and how Malachi had completely taken it over. Anastasia glanced back and forth between the two guards.

"This is going to be horrible," she whispered urgently. "But I just remind myself that it will be over--"

"Quiet!" the back guard urged behind them and Anastasia fell silent.

They descended a grand staircase and approached a set of thick double doors that were guarded by more soldiers who moved aside when they approached. The doors swung open by themselves to reveal an immense room that had been, or still was, the throne room for the castle. In addition to the massive dining table laden with an opulent meal, there was a fireplace that was larger than Lucy's dorm room and a raised stone platform that held a main golden throne and two smaller ones.

Despite the splendor of the room, Lucy was terrified. She could not shake the feeling that wicked things happened there. Malachi appeared from a side door and swept towards them. He appeared the dashing host in his tuxedo. Stasia began to tremble again and Lucy too shied away.

"Ladies," he called, "please accept my warmest welcome. I feel it's such a treat to have two stunning women as my dinner guests." He came closer and the girls stumbled back slightly. Malachi froze and offered a soft smile. "I will keep my distance, dears." He placated, "I don't wish to hurt you. Let's just have a nice meal." He smiled and gestured to the table and the three place settings. Lucy and Anastasia carefully took their places on either side of the head of the table. They were now separated from each other and both within reaching distance of Malachi. They gave each other pleading looks across the table.

Black-eyed waitresses approached and began serving wine and piling their plates with every single sumptuous food imaginable. Malachi smiled kindly at each of them and motioned to the food in a grand gesture of thanksgiving. Anastasia went after her food like it was going to run away. Maybe this was the only meal they got each day, or for the week even. Lucy followed Anastasia's lead but could not read the looks of warning that Anastasia was shooting her. She had not eaten properly for days, weeks even, and Lucy dug in whole heartedly.

Malachi was quiet for a moment, he did not eat but watched the girls enjoy the meal. Lucy tried to ignore his staring look and enjoyed lobster and Kobe beef and escargot. It was all delicious and Lucy realized how very hungry she was. As soon as she truly began to enjoy the meal, Malachi started laughing.

It was a haunting, frightening laugh and Lucy froze in her tracks. Stasia moaned lightly as if to say, "Oh here it comes." Lucy looked around her as she finished chewing a particularly large piece of lobster. The table was no longer full of delicious food. It was full of rot. It was all the same food but it was decaying and putrid. Lucy's own plate emitted a rotten odor. Flies and maggots swarmed on the brown and black lumps that used to be her dinner. She spat her mouth out on the plate and suppressed her gag reflex. Across from her, Anastasia calmly laid her fork down and placed her hands in her lap. Malachi kept laughing.

That was what Stasia was trying to tell Lucy with her eyes, *eat before he ruins it*. Lucy bottled the rage bubbling up inside her – it would serve her no good to be angry right now. Malachi was very dangerous and had made his point clear. He was in charge. Stasia's eyes were cast down and conveyed no more information. With a flick of his wrist, Malachi caused the table to empty of the rotten food. He left only the wine bottle and glasses which lit through the air and served themselves. Again, Lucy followed Anastasia's lead as she picked up the glass and drank. She showed no fear of being poisoned but then again, maybe at this point, Anastasia didn't care anymore.

Lucy drank the wine and found that it tasted quite good, it cleaned her mouth of the rotten lobster and for that, Lucy was grateful.

"What is this place?" Lucy asked impulsively.

"My home, of course," Malachi explained, "well, for now anyway. Before me, it was in shambles and belonged to some dead count. Seeing how he is staying in my house right now," he gestured to the floor, "I imagine that I am welcome to make this my home." He smiled at Lucy and she forced a smile back. "Now that dinner is complete," he grinned knowingly, "shall we move on to the entertainment portion of our evening?"

Anastasia moaned lightly and then looked terrified that she had made an audible noise but Malachi found it amusing and laughed.

"Oh come now, Anastasia," he winked at her, "it won't be the same old program. I promise."

Anastasia offered a fragile smile as she stood and moved toward the thrones. Lucy followed. Again, Lucy and Anastasia were on either side of the Demon, offering them no ability to talk or for Anastasia to warn Lucy of what new horror was to come. Lucy sat carefully, not knowing what punishments might ensue if she crumpled this expensive dress.

"Ah, don't worry about crumpling the dress, my dear Lucy." Malachi again, read her actions well. "You will have as many beautiful dresses as you wish for as long as you are here." He again paused with his eye trained on her.

"It's the most beautiful dress I have ever worn." Lucy spoke the truth and Malachi beamed with the praised.

"You do it justice, dear Lucy. Before I laid eyes on you, I certainly questioned what at all the fuss was about, but now I see that it was warranted. You are a stunning beauty."

Lucy simply smiled as her insides raged against her. What fuss? He smiled back at her, waiting.

"Thank you," she said softly.

Nodding lightly, Malachi looked forward to the wide empty room.

"Bring in the Jester!" he called out and a small door on the right opened. Malachi grinned widely at Lucy's cry of horror.

Gavin was led in by four soldiers. He was shackled with heavy manacles and thick chains restraining his hands and feet, and a thick steel band was around his neck. He too had been cleaned up and put into a tuxedo. Lucy imagined that Malachi had been planning to have him as a dinner guest as well but Gavin had obviously refused his invitation. The manacles rumbled as he thrashed and fought against the chains. The soldiers looked as though they were trying to control a particularly rabid animal and were frankly having a hard time of it.

"Tell me where she is, you lying bastards!" he raged at no one. His brow was sweaty and his eyes wild as he pulled against the restraints. "I mean it! You tell me now!"

Despite the fact that this was clearly against Malachi's original plan, he seemed delighted with this new course of events. He sat back on his throne, had a sip of wine and watched Gavin's behavior with unwavering interest. Gavin was dragged under violent protest to the middle of the room where the chains were secured to rings that were imbedded in the floor. The guards took a few steps back, shaking out their arms to get the blood flowing again. It was at this point that Gavin looked up and saw the royal group in front of him.

"Oh Lucy!" he exclaimed. His face relaxed in complete relief and joy. He fell to his knees and the chains went slack. He knelt on the ground breathing heavily. His heavy head lifted and his eyes met Malachi's. "She's alive," he breathed. "You can kill me now."

"Oh Gavin, I have no intention of killing you," Malachi said. "It appears you are far more entertaining alive."

"Please, kill me." he pleaded softly and Lucy's heart broke.

"No," Malachi answered sharply before turning to Lucy. "You see, my dear, Gavin is riddled with the most useless emotion ever created, guilt. Foolishness." Gavin's head fell again and Malachi continued. "He and I struck a deal, you see. All he had to do was bring you here and get you to come here of your own free will."

"He approached me last semester, after Chem one day." Gavin's voice was so hoarse Lucy could barely recognize it. He kept his head down and spoke to the thick stone floor. "I thought he was nuts at first, I didn't believe him but then he knew so much about you and Nathaniel and," he shuddered, "oh Lucy, I don't know what I was thinking. I made the deal and then didn't see him again until the 21st when he told me I had to meet you at the cabin and get you to wherever you felt you should go. You had to go there of your own volition, you see."

"Free will." Lucy thought of the conversations she had had with Nathaniel and even Roman about free will. It was the overriding factor in all human decisions made. Angels and Demons could only give options; humans had to make their own choices in the end. That's why he had forced the choice upon Anastasia back at her parents' house. Stasia had to choose to go with him and therefore, force Roman and Nathaniel to use their free will to do the same. "But I didn't walk into the castle of my own free will," she countered.

Malachi waved his hand in a gesture of dismissal. "Details, Lucy." He grinned like a school boy who had been caught cheating on a math test. "I still had to follow the rules, somewhat. You had every intention of walking into the castle and I just hurried the process along." He leaned toward her as if bestowing a great secret. "I made great use of free will when I tried to kill Anastasia. I came so close time and time again by just encouraging those around her to make horrifically unsafe decisions."

Lucy thought of the many accidents. The maintenance man with the light bulbs, Tim and the hot oil, Nick and the football, and the security guard at the dress shop. Lucy had been right on the dock; Malachi was behind them all. "That didn't work because of you and your little body guards so I came up with the Wrath to kill all of you. As you know that didn't work. So I decided to make you all come to me. Anastasia was easy to convince but I knew, Lucy, that you would be a tougher puzzle to solve." He grinned. "Personally, I think using Gavin was a stroke of genius. It's really been so much fun."

Gavin hung his head. "I really had no idea what I was

getting myself into. I didn't know the danger that this would put you in. I didn't understand how strong your feelings for Nathaniel were. I didn't know what I was doing. I didn't realize he was a Demon. I thought," he reddened in embarrassment, "I thought he was some sort of guardian angel or something."

Malachi laughed with deep enjoyment and Gavin shot him a hateful stare.

"It's not like the movies, kiddies," the Demon all but giggled, "I don't have to tell you who I am or what I am. Nothing needs to be written in blood, no ceremony needed, you just have to use your free will and say yes." He tented his fingers under his chin. "No hocus pocus or pentagrams required."

Gavin struggled to explain. "I thought he was my friend, a confidante – someone who could give me the upper hand." Lucy thought of the night that Gavin thought Lucy was asleep and talked to his "friend." Lucy had assumed that he was talking about Nathaniel. Now she knew that was wrong. His eyes met Lucy's and he pleaded with her. "I didn't want him to alter your mind, I just wanted a chance to spend time with you without Nathaniel around. I thought he was going to send you and me somewhere." He shook his head at his own foolishness. "I didn't ever think that he was the same as that Turner or the Bael guy you told me about, even after I figured out he was a Demon. I started to get a bad feeling about the whole thing after London but by then it was too late, we were too close and I couldn't convince you to turn back. I never wanted Nathaniel to be hurt and I certainly never thought that all this was his plan." His voice cracked as he whispered, "I just wanted a fair shot at winning your heart, that's all."

Lucy blinked back tears. Gavin wasn't the enemy here. She knew herself how hard it was to turn down a Demon's deal.

"I'm so sorry," Gavin whispered into the stones. "This is all my fault."

Lucy spoke without thinking. "Oh Gavin, it's not your fault, of course I forgi--"

Malachi gripped her arm in his strong fingers, ripping her words from her throat. There was no fire this time, it felt like there were hundreds of thousands of bugs crawling on her skin. Lucy screamed and writhed as she instinctually tried to get away from Malachi but he held fast. Lucy felt millions of tiny legs scrabbling over her body, in her ears, and mouth. She could hear Gavin raging in the background but Malachi's voice cut through everything.

"You will never say that word here!" he screamed at Lucy. "On no occasion will you utter those syllables again! Do you comprehend what I am telling you? That word is useless! Do you understand?" His grip tightened to elicit a response and the creatures on her body sped up, their legs poking and pricking into each pore of her skin. Lucy bucked in her chair.

"Yes!" she screamed. "I understand!"

Malachi let go and immediately the sensation stopped. Lucy sat breathing heavily and shaking. Malachi resumed his previous posture as if nothing had happened and eyed Lucy to indicate she was to do the same. She forced herself to straighten her spine and readjust herself in the chair. Gavin sat silently, unable to hide his disdain for Malachi in his face. Anastasia had not moved nor spoken.

"Drink your wine, ladies," Malachi said lightly but it was an order. Robotically, Lucy and Anastasia picked up their glasses and drank. Malachi addressed the guard by the door, "I think we need to complete our party."

The guard nodded and headed out the door.

"Let them go," Gavin pleaded to Malachi, "I will do anything. Anything at all. You can have my soul, all the money I will ever earn, you may take anything from me you want."

Malachi gestured to the soldier beside the throne dais who without question walked over to Gavin and started beating him with his staff. Gavin grunted but made no move to try to protect himself. Lucy started to cry out but with a warning look from Malachi, she silenced herself. Malachi stood slowly and sauntered down the steps where he knelt neatly beside Gavin. With a flick of the wrist the soldier paused mid-swing.

"I don't need you, little boy," Malachi hissed in his ear. "I already get to take whatever I want from you because, you see, I can do whatever I want. I will treat her however I see fit because you all belong to me now."

Gavin spat blood onto the stone floor in response.

Malachi smiled and returned smoothly to his throne.

There was a knock at the door and Malachi broke into a wide smile as he winked at Lucy. Her skin went cold.

"This is the best part!" he exclaimed as he settled into his throne and waved at the soldiers to admit the new additions.

The door opened and Lucy's reaction was immediate. She cried out in delight, stood, hiked up her skirts and started to sprint.

Chapter Fourteen
Games

"You have to learn the rules of the game.
And then you have to play better than anyone else."
~ Albert Einstein

He wore shackles on his bloodied wrists and on his ankles below his shredded pant legs – he had no shirt. His entire body was covered in a layer of filth that blended with his dark hair and his grey eyes were sunken and dark. Despite his disheveled appearance, he stood tall and straight. Lucy didn't care either way as she raced toward him. He was alive and breathing and standing and right here, oh God right here. She had done it, somehow she had found him and everything was going to be okay. She craved his touch, his smell, his breath on her skin. If she could have that, everything would turn out exactly as she wanted it to. She raced towards him without a care of anything else.

Nathaniel's eyes lit up when he saw her but his manacled hands raised in a warning gesture. Lucy was only feet from him and didn't have time to try to interpret his movements before she found herself airborne. All the oxygen exploded out of her and it felt like someone had punched her in the stomach as she flew backwards across the space to her throne as if being pulled by an invisible rope around her middle.

Screaming in protest, Lucy stretched her hands forward in a futile gesture of rage. Nathaniel's eyes betrayed his pain and disappointment. They had been so close.

Over it all, Lucy could hear Malachi's laugh. His maniacal, gleeful laugh cascaded over the space, leaving nothing but hate and pain in its wake. Lucy was plopped painfully back into her seat, where several leather ropes appeared out of thin air to restrain her to it. Tears poured from her eyes as she choked on her own frustration.

Lucy hadn't even noticed Roman before now. He appeared the same as Nathaniel, as equally as disheveled and dirty with only ratty pants to cover his substantial frame. His blond hair looked darker, but it was only the dirt that made it appear as such. He didn't acknowledge Lucy, having eyes only for Anastasia. The two were silent but stared uncompromisingly at each other across the space. Was this how it had been for Anastasia? Every day having the love of her life paraded in front of her without the ability to speak or be with him? Malachi had devised a unique and deeply horrific torture. Lucy could not imagine it could get any worse, but then again, she could have never imagined this either.

The soldiers urged Roman and Nathaniel forward until they were standing beside Gavin. Roman glanced at Gavin but seemed completely uninterested. Nathaniel offered his friend a kind smile and received one in return. Lucy wondered why Roman and Nathaniel weren't fighting. She didn't know if Nathaniel was strong enough to break those chains but he certainly was strong enough to knock about four of those soldiers down in one hit. With he and

Roman together, why had they not taken this castle?

"You would not smile so if you knew Gavin's intentions, Angel," Malachi suggested cruelly.

"I know his intentions," Nathaniel replied while locking eyes with Lucy. Her heart skipped a beat with both panic and excitement. "And as far as I can tell, they are true to those of a perfect gentleman." Malachi laughed but didn't add any more.

Lucy took a moment to take in Nathaniel's form again. She silently thanked God for keeping him alive and safe. Then Lucy's attention was drawn to how he moved; something was off and she leaned forward to examine him closer. When she saw the small pool of blood at his heels, her mouth fell open in shock. Malachi, again picking up on the gesture, smiled.

"Ah Lucy," he grinned, "How clever you are. Angel, do turn around and show Lucy your new, shall we say, unique physique?"

Nathaniel's steel eyes narrowed in hate but he made no motion to comply. A wave from Malachi's hand elicited a raining of blows from the nearest soldiers' baton. Nathaniel didn't cower but stood completely still, causing the soldier to increase the frequency and power of his blows, but Nathaniel did not move. He stood, staring at Malachi, completely calm. The soldier began to tire and paused to catch his breath.

Nathaniel was bleeding from cuts around his eyes and there were huge welts swelling upon his chest.

"Don't stop!" Malachi screamed his face red with rage. He motioned at the next soldier who took up the beating to the same effect. When this one tired he motioned for them both to step back.

There was silence.

"You," Malachi pointed at the first soldier. "Beat her," he quipped while pointing at Lucy. The soldier, showing an ounce of ethics, hesitated. "NOW!" Malachi shrieked and the soldier rushed at Lucy, who shied back and raised her tied hands up in a pathetic defense gesture. His bat was inches from her when he froze in mid swing. Lucy creaked her eyes open to see Nathaniel had turned around.

"We have finally found your currency," Malachi hissed at Nathaniel's back. Lucy stared, horrified at the bloody white feathery shards sticking out of his spine. Blood dripped in a slow but steady stream down his back and legs.

Malachi had cut off his wings. Lucy started to cry.

"It's really the only way for me to control them, you see." Malachi explained as if this was a job interview. "They gave me no other choice."

Lucy saw the pool at Roman's feet and knew he had suffered the same fate. She swallowed the bile rising in her throat.

"It doesn't hurt that badly, now does it boys?" Malachi smiled at his own joke.

"Tickles really," Roman offered drolly and Malachi laughed.

"What should we do tonight boys?" Malachi asked as if they were picking a movie to see. "The rack, the pit and the pendulum, the garrote, water torture or just a good old flaying? What would you prefer?"

The men were silent.

"You are going to torture them?" Lucy couldn't stop herself but Malachi didn't seem to mind the inquiry this time.

"Well," he explained, "that's what we've been doing because they heal so quickly you see. I mean, even the wings keep trying to come back and we have to keep cutting those off, don't we? And it's been fun hasn't it, Stasia?" he asked and Stasia cowered at his eyes but managed to mutter a non-committal noise. "But," Malachi continued like he was at a cocktail party, "I have to say it's getting a little boring." Lucy knew that torturing Roman and Nathaniel would not have the desired effect; there would be nothing that would make them cry for mercy, nothing at all. "So I think we should change it up a bit," he finished, training his eyes on Lucy. He smiled.

"How?" she whispered.

"Well, by torturing you and Anastasia of course."

Lucy opened her mouth to speak but the roar that erupted from the men on the floor in front of them was deafening. Nathaniel, Roman and Gavin raged simultaneously, thrashing and pulling against their chains. More and more soldiers came closer to restrain them. Anastasia began to weep. Lucy wanted to cry but she knew it wouldn't help matters and that was what Malachi wanted. She made a vow to do as little that pleased him as possible while still keeping her life. Only then could she maintain hope and some semblance of herself at the end of the day. She swallowed her tears, bit the insides of her cheeks to stop more from coming, and jerked her chin to the sky.

"Fine," she said quietly. "But not Stasia, she's been through enough."

The room went silent.

Malachi turned to look at her and regarded her with a new sense of awe.

"If I were more of a man and less of a Demon, I would think your attitude noble, Lucy. But as it is, I think you are a complete fool."

"What do you want from us?" Nathaniel asked. Lucy heard the small break in his voice and hoped that Malachi had not heard it. "You have us all here of our own free will. Now what? Do you think you can keep us here forever? The mortals are going to start to wonder how five University students went missing and they are going to start asking questions. People will start looking for us.

What do you want to happen, Demon? What do we have to exchange for freedom for Lucy and Stasia?"

Malachi smiled but did not respond.

"You have won," Nathaniel added fervently, "you have won. Now name your prize and let our women live."

"I want your soul to rot here," Malachi whispered while gripping the arms of his throne, "I want you to wish you were dead, not just while you are here but for the rest of your sad sorry lives. I want your hearts and minds to be so broken and so ravaged that you will pray to die every day. I want to annihilate any chance you ever have at enjoyment for the rest of time. I don't want to steal your souls, I want to stomp on them until they vanish to nothingness."

"Sir," Roman began, his voice was shaking and he swallowed to steady it. "It was I that offended. It was I that caused your death. It is my fault." He spoke deliberately, carefully. "It does not follow the order of the Devil for you to punish innocents in this matter. I am to blame. Punish me, forever if you wish. I am at your command but release the mortals and the Angel."

"You are quite correct," Malachi agreed amiably, "it was you that caused the offence in the first place. You were a fool of a boy with more temper than you had sense and you managed to catch me off guard. For that foolishness I vowed that you would pay. I had to wait though, you see, for to simply burn your body for hundreds of years would not only become boring, it wouldn't get to the root of you. So Roman, I waited and waited and waited for almost a century until I was released from the depths. It was a fortunate circumstance that you had also found people to love. I knew it would happen eventually and for most Demons it isn't a problem as long as you are fulfilling your duties. But for you, Roman, it meant so much more. Now I had the ammunition I needed to truly punish your soul."

The air exploded out of Roman in a gust and he stumbled slightly where he stood as the impact of what Malachi just said struck him to the bone. They now all knew that there was no way out, there was no negotiating, Malachi would punish them forever without pause and without remorse.

And it was Roman's fault. Lucy's heart softened for him. Maybe Hell was enough of a punishment for losing her father. She didn't want Roman dead anymore. She didn't know if she could ever forgive him, but she didn't want him to suffer any longer.

"I am bored of this conversation," Malachi announced. He looked at the head guard, "make them all go away, I am bored."

It was clear the soldiers didn't want any more to do with Malachi either for they moved quickly to shuffle the men out one door and the women out another. Lucy strained her neck to keep Nathaniel in her sights for as long as possible. He did the same and just as the guard pushed her through the door she saw it.

Nathaniel smiled.

He grinned really - a wonderful smile that he seemed to only have for Lucy and her heart leapt in response. In that moment, Lucy recalled every time she had seen that smile; the night they met and thousands of other times since flashed through her mind at a breakneck speed. Then his face vanished from sight and she was tossed through the door in a bustle of silk skirts.

Lucy grinned to herself as they were ushered back down the grand hallway. Nathaniel did that on purpose. He knew Lucy could replay that moment over and over with her photographic memory. He knew she would need that from him. It was a gift that would be perfect for Lucy alone and only Nathaniel knew to give that to her. Tears sprang to her eyes and she was truly, deeply grateful.

Lucy was relieved to see that she and Anastasia were to

share a room. They were undressed and prepared for bed by the female servants. Meanwhile, Anastasia was borderline catatonic – staring with empty eyes off in the distance as though she were somewhere far away.

Within moments, the women silently left the room. Lucy heard the heavy lock clunk into place after the door closed. The pair quietly climbed into bed and lay side by side.

"Well," Lucy tried to sound bright, "this is certainly different than our sleepovers in the dorm. At least the bed is bigger and you can't kick me with those dancer legs."

Anastasia didn't respond but rolled away from her.

Lucy sighed. Where was her friend? She understood that so much had happened here and Stasia had been alone through it all. Her heart broke for her friend, but surely cutting Lucy out wasn't the right answer. Was Stasia just so broken that she couldn't see the way out? Lucy needed to devise a plan. There had to be a weak spot out of this castle and given enough time and charm, Lucy would find it.

With that thought, she rolled over, shut the horrors of the day out of her mind and fell fast asleep. She woke up much later. The black sky still pushed through the paneled windows. Lucy sat up to discover that Anastasia was sobbing. Lucy immediately wrapped her arms around her friend. She was secretly relieved to see some emotion out of her friend and was shocked when Stasia pushed her away.

"No!" Stasia yelled as she sat up. "Get away from me!"

"What have I done?" Lucy pleaded. "What the hell is wrong with you?"

"I was so happy you were here," Stasia said through her sobs.

"Well, I was happy to see--"

"Shut up!" Stasia cut her off. She cried a moment more. "I was happy to see you because, because," she faltered and Lucy just froze, hoping to get to the bottom of this all. "Because now he had someone else to pick on," Stasia finished quietly. Lucy swallowed as the truth struck her. Anastasia had been withdrawn because she was riddled with guilt. "It's been only me that he could bully. He would beat the boys but that did no good. He only figured out to cut off their wings a few weeks ago. It was just me. At first he would make me dance for him for hours, but then I accidentally smiled for him and that wouldn't do. He couldn't have me enjoy my life for a second, now could he? I was grateful that you came so that he would leave me alone for a minute. I am a horrible person, Lucy, and no friend to you."

"Don't be so stupid," Lucy exploded at her and Stasia looked up wearily. "Seriously!" Lucy exclaimed, "Stop being an idiot. You and I are here together and if I had told you about Roman in the first place you might not even *be* here. I didn't trust you with that information and for that I am truly sorry. I will take the punishment for you every single time because I love you!"

"You don't hate me?" Stasia asked as she used the sheet to wipe her eyes. "Because I hate myself a little. I feel like a selfish cow."

"I could never hate you! I will take a hundred beatings for you! We are in this mess because of me. I," Lucy's voice chocked, "I made a mess of everything and it's all my fault."

The friends fell into each other's arms and wept until their tears were exhausted.

"What are we going to do?" Stasia finally whispered.

"We are going to find a way to get us and our boyfriends out of this bloody castle." Stasia raised an eyebrow, "I don't know how yet but we will figure it out." She reached for her friend's hand.

"But you can't shut me out like that again. I need you and you need me and together, we will fight this."

Stasia nodded and sighed as if a weight had been lifted. Lucy finally saw a small twinkle come back to her friend's eye.

"Which boyfriend are you going to save?" she asked with a sly smile. "Tell me about Gavin."

"Nothing to tell," Lucy tried to sound flippant but one look at Anastasia's disbelieving face and she knew she was beat. "I don't know!" she exploded. "I just don't know! He was so super great during this whole thing and he's funny and charming and saved my ass on more than one occasion and when we kissed--"

"You *kissed him*?"

"Yes," Lucy conceded, "yes I did. Well, he kissed me and I kind of kissed him back because," she paused, "because, I don't know why. It's not that I don't love Nathaniel, he's my soul mate! It just feels so easy to be around Gavin, you know? When we got here I thought he had totally sold me out but now I know that he didn't and he is just as much a victim of Malachi's actions as we are. But when I just saw Nathaniel," she started to tear up, "I know where my heart belongs."

Stasia nodded. "Okay then," she half smiled, "we won't mention it again. Let's go back to sleep, we have no idea what is coming tomorrow."

They lay down side by side.

"What usually comes?" Lucy whispered.

Anastasia shook her head and Lucy didn't press. She needed to get everyone out of here. Stasia fell fast asleep, now relieved of the burden of her guilt. Lucy rolled onto her side and looked out the window. The mountain range, black and slate grey, could just be seen in the moonlight. Lucy squinted her eyes at the sky.

"Where are you guys?" she whispered to no one. "Why

aren't you coming for him? I know he's not tied to Heaven anymore, but surely this kind of stuff can't possibly be allowed? Why aren't you all busting in the door and stopping this Demon in his tracks?" She sighed, "I don't get it."

Lucy rolled back and stared at the ornate bed hanging. She brought up the image of Nathaniel smiling at her and immediately, her heart softened. With Nathaniel's face in her mind's eye, Lucy drifted off to sleep again.

Chapter Fifteen
Dig

"You load sixteen tons, what do you get
Another day older and deeper in debt
Saint Peter don't you call me 'cause I can't go
I owe my soul to the company store."
~ Tennessee Ernie Ford

Lucy was awakened the next morning by light streaming through the thick windows. She was alone in the bed and was concerned until Stasia appeared from the bathroom. She sat up, her white sleeping gown billowing about her.

"Morning," she tried to sound bright but her tone was off.

"The girls will be in soon," Stasia said quietly.

"The 'girls?'" Lucy said, trying to evoke a grin from Stasia. She succeeded.

"The dead facers," Stasia half giggled.

"Dude!" Lucy exclaimed while leaping off the bed, "they are Fem-bots!"

"Dead face Fem-bots," Stasia nodded appreciatively, "I like

it!" They laughed for a minute. "I'm so happy you are here," Stasia said, "I missed you."

"Missed you too loser," Lucy said, "let's try our best to make the most of this. I don't want either of us getting out of here and being lunatics because of it."

The door opened and the "Fem-Bots" paraded in. Lucy was expecting them to be holding more gowns for the girls to wear but they seemed to be carrying a uniform of some sort. Lucy looked inquiringly at Stasia who looked as curious as Lucy was. The outfits were tank tops and shorts with a set of light beige coveralls overtop. The coveralls were made of a thin material and overall, Lucy was pleased with the comfort level. For Lucy, who spent more time in sneakers than anything else, it was a good change from the ball gown.

There were no shoes.

Lucy looked out the window at the purple mountain range.

"It's beautiful here," she mused.

Stasia smiled, "Yeah, it really is. I always imagined that we would travel Europe together one day."

Lucy grinned, "You and I would have so much fun in London. I didn't feel right about shopping, but man, Gavin and I walked past Harrods, and seriously….." she trailed off as they giggled to each other.

"Gavin was fun though, hey?" Stasia asked.

"Yeah," Lucy smiled, "we had a riot really." Her throat tensed lightly. "I felt bad though. For having fun while you guys were," she looked around, "here."

"Luc," Stasia grabbed her hand across the table, "you went to freaking Purgatory to find us. You deserved to have a little break."

"Thanks," Lucy smiled weakly.

"Plus," Stasia grinned, "when we get out of here, we are going to rip it up and all this will be a distant memory."

"Speaking of getting out of here," Lucy started but she was cut off by a rap at the door. Both girls jumped as one of the guards opened the door.

"Follow," he said shortly and Lucy studied his face. He was the same guard that had escorted Nathaniel back to his "accommodations" the night before. Lucy and Anastasia quietly padded barefoot after him down the hall. Immediately after Lucy's feet left the soft plush of the carpet and hit the cold stone of the grand hallway, she emitted a shudder as a chill carried up her legs.

Quickly, she engaged her mind and reviewed every guard she had ever seen at the castle and began to file them. To anyone else, their identical uniforms and postures would make them seem like a blur; to Lucy, her new challenge was born. A small smile emitted from her mouth. She would keep track of where they all went and when. They were human, not dead like the women, so they had to have some kind of shifts. Lucy would figure it all out. She didn't know why she needed this information but her gut told her it was important. Plus, it was something to occupy her very demanding mind.

They travelled through the castle and took stairway after stairway down, a floor across and down again, over and over. Lucy's feet became colder and colder. Finally, they came to what could only be described as the catacombs of the castle. Lucy tried but she could not "feel" where Nathaniel was. She suspected though that he was close. The air was cold and moist and water could be heard from far off. They walked further, deeper, darker into it all -- until they came to the hole. The neat and somewhat orderly stones that made up the walls, floors and ceiling of the tombs changed at one corner, to a jagged, raw opening.

"What is that?" Staisa asked.

"Dig," the soldier stated blankly. He stood beside the entrance, his back to the wall and stared out with soldier eyes.

"What are we, the freaking Seven Dwarves?" Lucy demanded to his empty visage. "We are college students, we can't dig through this!"

The guard snapped his head sharply to regard her. The movement and his sudden eye contact caught her off guard and she bumped back into Stasia, who was doing nothing but staring into the dank tunnel.

"Then I suggest you figure it out!" he hollered at Lucy. "I am instructed with making you dig. And you don't want me to *make* you do anything." The coldness in his eyes cut into Lucy and she froze as he snapped his chin back to face forward again.

Lucy and Anastasia gazed blankly into the tunnel for a moment.

"The castle must be built into the mountain. A lot of medieval castles were built like that, for fortification. I am not totally up on my Bulgarian history but there is one in Montsegur, France that was built in 1204..." Lucy started but immediately shut her mouth and stopped her memory from 'helping' her right now. They stared silently into the frightening chasm, shuddering to think of what was in there.

"No shoes," Stasia whispered, looking at the jagged stone protruding from the ground. "No shoes."

It struck Lucy. This would be a very painful process in bare feet. She watched as a single tear leaked out of Stasia's eye. Malachi did this to hurt her. A dancer's feet are her life. Stasia could ruin the rest of her days by stepping into that tunnel.

Lucy wrapped an arm around her friend, "I'm so sorry."

Stasia leaned her forehead against Lucy's. "The bastard," She whispered in Lucy's hair so quietly that the guard couldn't even hear. She took in a sharp breath and shook out her shoulders. "Little does he know though," she said loudly, "that I could dance without my feet. I'm that bloody good."

Lucy grinned, "Let's do this." She reached down and hand in hand they stepped into the dark.

Dark didn't describe it. Within seconds of stepping into the tunnel, Lucy couldn't see anything. The blackness covered them completely, settling heavily like a blanket on them both. Lucy felt Stasia's hand in hers give an involuntary tremble. The tunnel was wide enough for the pair to walk side by side but as they moved cautiously forward, Lucy could feel the ceiling brush against the top of her red curls. They walked slowly, trying to preserve their bare feet for as long as possible but it was hopeless, within ten steps, Lucy could feel the serrated stones beginning to rip into her skin. She forced herself to ignore the pain and keep moving.

They walked for several minutes with the tunnel descending rapidly underfoot. It became so steep that Lucy's ears popped. Eventually, a dim light could be seen far ahead and the girls made their way carefully toward it. A scraping sound resonated to them and Lucy concluded that someone or, knowing Malachi, something else was already digging. When they came to the end of the tunnel, Lucy's heart lightened and a smile broke across her face.

"Well," Gavin drawled, looking up from his shovel, "it's about time you two princesses decide to join the party."

"Gavin!" Stasia grinned and hobbled carefully toward him for a hug. Three weak lights had been placed around him with picks and shovels littering in between. Despite the chill in the air, Gavin was sweating with exertion and had pulled off the top part of his coveralls and was working in just the tank top. He had been blessed with boots and Lucy was relieved. He would most certainly give his boots to Stasia.

Gavin looked shockingly at Stasia's feet as she approached.

"Where the hell are your boots?" he demanded, "you are going to cut your feet to bits!"

"We weren't given any," Lucy said.

"Well here," Gavin said as he dropped his shovel and, as Lucy knew he would, he sat down and starting unlacing his.

"No," a heavy male voice came out of the dark and Lucy jumped as a guard stepped forward into the light. "The boots aren't for them."

Gavin looked at him pleadingly. "Surely I can't wear boots while these two lovely ladies suffer?"

"The boots aren't for them," the guard repeated. Lucy filed his face away; she had never seen him before. "Those are the orders." To make his point he pulled a whip off of his belt and began winding it around his hand. Gavin, being more than willing to take the whipping but not willing to watch Lucy get whipped, stood quickly.

"Well, let's do something about it shall we?" he reached up and pulled off his tank top. He glanced at the guard who said nothing so, assuming he broke no rules, Gavin ripped the cotton in two and after some knot tying, fashioned two white slippers around Stasia's feet. "Don't know if that will do any good for our dancer here but it might help a little." He looked at Lucy, his eyes full of apology and she simply shook her head. There was no need.

"You are so kind, Gavin." Stasia smiled.

"Dig," the guard ordered and again they all jumped, having somewhat forgotten that he was there.

"What do we do?"

"Well," Gavin explained, "we just dig and dig and dig. Since you two are here, I will use the pick on the rock and maybe, Stasia, you could shovel it into the buckets and, Lucy, you could carry it out."

"Out to where?" Lucy asked, "back to the castle?" She didn't see any big piles of rock anywhere and this would produce a lot of rock.

"To the hole in the side of the mountain. You walked past it when you came in, you just didn't see it because it is so dark."

"How long have you been at this?"

Gavin shrugged. "I was awakened in the night and dragged down here. I assume that it's morning now?"

Lucy nodded. "Why are we digging?" Lucy wondered aloud.

"I dunno," he replied, "I was told to dig down as far as we can, but it doesn't have to be as wide as this. It only has to be wide enough for us to get through."

"Huh," Lucy replied.

"Dude," Stasia said while picking up a shovel and starting to throw rock into one of the buckets. "Nothing here makes any sense and it is all designed to make us nuts. There is no purpose for the hole in the mountain. It is just a project to make our lives suck as much as possible. Don't over think it."

"This reaches a very high level of suckage very quickly," Gavin replied, "but the whip comes out if you stop for more than three minutes." He nodded his chin toward the guard. "I've named my friend here, Ben."

The guard gave him a warning look.

"Then tell me your real name, friend!" Gavin countered and the guard rolled his eyes. "Ben's really a softie but his Dad was a drunk, his mother a saint and he basically raised his siblings. He likes cotton candy and Tom Cruise movies."

Lucy started to laugh. "Ignore him, Ben," she said to the guard, "he was dropped on his head as a child and has no social skills." Gavin and Anastasia laughed out loud.

"Dig," Ben replied, but there was certainly a softer tone to his voice than before.

"Yes Ben," Gavin replied and hoisted the pick axe over his head. "You heard him gals, work or someone is going to beat the crap out of you and it ain't gonna be Ben." He winked as he threw the pick into the solid rock. It broke away easily and Lucy realized that the entire mountain was made of shale not solid stone. This would not be impossible; it would be back breaking work, but it was possible.

So the process began where Gavin would break the rock, Stasia would shovel the rock and Lucy would carry the rock back up the tunnel and up a small slope to a different hole. This one did open to the outside but a heavy outcrop prevented her from seeing anything but the lower half of the mountain. She would have been faster if she could have carried two buckets but with the blackness of the tunnel, she had to carry one of the lanterns in her other hand. Her bare feet were getting ravaged on the rocks, every nerve lighting up in pain with every step, but Lucy kept going. She could only assume that the first day would be the worst.

They worked in silence for quite a while before Gavin spoke again.

"Where are you guys staying in Chateau Creepville?"

"We have a pretty nice big room upstairs somewhere. We are surrounded by the dead girls," Stasia replied.

"Ah yes, they are charming, aren't they? Well, my accommodations are less than enjoyable. I am sharing a cell with an Angel and a Demon who enjoy bickering like an old married couple."

"What?" Lucy exclaimed while heading back for another bucket. "Why didn't you say so? Are they okay?"

"Yeah," Gavin replied, "they are fine. They are angry and cranky and upset to not be with you two but they are alive."

Lucy and Anastasia didn't know what to say so they just fell silent.

"It's more proof that Malachi doesn't actually need this hole dug," Lucy offered later. "Roman and Nathaniel could pound this off in twenty minutes."

No one answered so they just kept working. They were not offered water or a break for hours. The trio worked mainly in silence, saving their energy for the task and as the hours dragged on, the only sounds they made were grunts or pants of exertion. To Lucy, it felt like they had been down there for days. She started slipping and thought at first that water must have gotten on the rocks, but when she shone her lantern down on the ground, she was horrified to see that she was sliding on her own blood.

Just when she was about to sit down and cry, Ben spoke.

"That's enough for today. More tomorrow. Return to your rooms. You will be expected for dinner shortly."

Stasia started to cry lightly. "I can't do it." She slumped against the shovel. "I can't put on a pretty dress and watch him beat Roman again, I can't!"

Gavin laid a hand on her shoulder. "This isn't forever and Roman can take it even if you can't. I myself beat him up all the time." He winked at her and she offered a weak smile. "He can take it, don't worry. It isn't forever."

"Let's get out of the dark," Lucy said, dropping her bucket and hobbling toward the exit. Stasia, Gavin and Ben followed. They got back to the dungeons and even the weak light coming from the lanterns there burned Lucy's eyes. The same guard that escorted

Lucy and Anastasia down was still standing at the entrance. Lucy mentally named him Jim. He stepped in front of them to lead them back to their room, and had the wherewithal to slow his pace when he saw the bloody footprints Lucy was leaving. She winced with every step.

Ben turned and walked Gavin down an alternate hallway. Gavin offered Lucy a grin before disappearing from view. "You look lovely in grime, Red," he called down the hall and Lucy couldn't help but smile before wincing at her next step.

They were met in their room by the dead girls, who once again and with some level of care cleaned and fluffed them into looking like proper princesses. The only things that gave them away were the blisters on Stasia's hands and the gauze wrapped around Lucy's feet before they were tucked into the satin shoes. Tonight, Lucy was put in a deep burgundy gown that cascaded into a series of roses toward the ground. Her hair was tied up with only a few tendrils hanging about her ivory skin. Stasia was placed in a teal green tight dress that had more sequins than fabric.

"Well, at least we look pretty," Stasia said, looking at herself in the mirror. "Those dead girls know their stuff."

"That they do," Lucy said, standing beside her.

There was a rap at the door. Jim opened it and stood to the side to escort them to dinner.

Lucy sighed, "Let's go look pretty with a creepy Demon!"

"I don't even care, I'm starving. I thought for sure that I was going to pass out a few times today. We can't keep this level of output with no food all day." Anastasia stalked out the door, forcing Lucy to hobble after her.

Chapter Sixteen
Let's Make a Deal

"Will you take the box or go for what's behind the curtain?"
~ Monty Hall

They were again seated at the massively ornate table. Lucy could barely see Anastasia over the pile of food between them. Her mouth was watering and her hands had started to shake from the lack of nutrients in her body. The side door opened and Nathaniel, Gavin and Roman were led in. Gavin was still wearing his coveralls, and Roman and Nathaniel were still shirtless, still bleeding. They sat at the other end of the table, far from the food. Lucy wondered when the last time they had eaten was.

Lucy counted seven guards in the room and noted their position and faces, including Ben and Jim from the day. She gave them each a generic name to keep track of them, for if there were only seven in total, they might have a shot of fighting their way out of this castle one day.

Nathaniel's eyes lit up at seeing Lucy and he smiled lightly at her as he mouthed the words, "So beautiful." Lucy's heart leapt in response and she held back tears of joy at once again getting to see him. Roman only had eyes for Anastasia and inquired silently with his eyes after her health. A light nod reassured him that everything was all right.

The main door opened and Malachi sauntered into the room. He wore a tuxedo, a different one from last night Lucy recognized. His easy gait and the twinkle in his eye certainly gave the impression of a man of greatness. They all knew better.

"Good evening!" Malachi called as he greeted them from the head of the table. "I'm sure you are all wondering why I have called you all here."

"Is it the weirdest murder mystery dinner party ever?" Gavin offered from the opposite end of the huge table. Everyone turned and glared at him. Was he crazy?

Malachi surprised everyone by laughing out loud. "I like that Gavin, no, no, that would be fun though, maybe another night." He reached down and plucked a grape off the display on the table and popped it into his mouth. "But I'm sure ladies that you are hungry. Do help yourselves."

Not having to be told twice and knowing that the magic wouldn't last long, Lucy and Anastasia attacked the food while offering apologetic stares down the table to the equally hungry men.

"I think we ought to have some fun tonight though," Malachi explained as he sat down.

"Well, this is really my definition of fun," Roman shot back sarcastically. "How about you two?"

"Love it," Gavin added slyly.

"It's like Disneyland, only with Demons," Nathaniel quipped.

"Good one." Roman nodded his approval and Nathaniel

shrugged.

"Are you unhappy, gentlemen?" Malachi challenged. He stood back up and Lucy could almost feel the rage coming off him in waves. "Because I assure you, I can make you far more uncomfortable."

Dread shot through Lucy as she instinctively ducked her head and winced. She looked down at the other end of the table, planning on silently pleading with the men to stop antagonizing Malachi. Nathaniel met her eyes and quickly darted his gaze toward her heavily laden plate of food. If he could point, he would have. They were distracting Malachi so Lucy and Stasia could eat. Bless them. Lucy shot Nathaniel a pleading glance before going back to eating.

"We're just saying that this isn't the worst all-inclusive resort we have ever stayed at, but it really doesn't deserve the five stars it got on Trip Advisor," Roman drawled, "for one thing, it's run by a complete lunatic." He barely got the last syllable out before he was yanked in the air by unseen hands. Roman did not scream out but writhed in the air, silently enduring whatever particular pain Malachi was inflicting upon him.

"You have the foolishness to mock me!" Malachi howled at Roman's thrashing frame. "Do you not know the depth of my abilities? I have been torturing Demons for two thousand years, you disgusting little pup! I will annihilate you!"

Anastasia stopped eating and pushed her plate away.

"My Goodness," she gasped in her best society voice. Lucy could hear the tremor beneath the surface. "I am just so full, I couldn't eat another bite. Could you Lucy?"

Lucy had completely lost her appetite but had certainly eaten more than she had gotten the day before. The plan had worked, as foolish as it was.

"No," she said, trying to sound light, "I just couldn't cram more in if I tried. Thank you, for the lovely dinner. It was exquisite."

Malachi had seemingly forgotten that they were there. His tone changed back to one of kindness. "Well, that's excellent." The food vanished and Roman was dropped back into his seat. He winced when what was left of his wings hit the back of the chair but was silent. "I was going to say before I was so rudely interrupted that we could--" he cut himself off and glared again at the other end of the table.

"Stop looking at her like that!" he screamed at Nathaniel. Lucy looked over to see Nathaniel staring at her and grinning. She instinctively smiled back, but paid for her lack of caution with a sharp slap across the face. "Stop!" Malachi screamed. Lucy rocked back in her chair, cradling her stinging face. The inside of her mouth tasted of blood. She heard a chair scrape as Nathaniel shot out of his seat to lunge at Malachi and two more as Gavin and Roman jumped up. Suddenly she was being pulled from her seat by her hair. Malachi gripped her curls tightly in his massive fist, his other hand clutched at her throat and his fingers dug into her skin on either side of her trachea. There was no need to explain the threat. He could rip out her throat before they even got close.

The three men froze in mid leap and allowed the guards to drag them back to their chairs, leaving trails of dirt on the mirrored table's surface. Malachi let go of Lucy's throat but kept a handle on her hair as he tilted her face to look at him.

"What is it about you two?" he wondered while studying her. "I can *feel* it between you." He lightly touched the back of his fingers to the side of Lucy's face, tracing over his own red hand print. She winced in preparation for some new horror when his skin touched hers but none came. "You are so beautiful, it's true, and I can understand his drive, but," he looked around, "there is something more there, isn't there? I mean, all five of you are connected in some way that is beyond what is normal. It's strange." He looked back at Lucy with awe in his face. "But something between you and the Angel is quite unique indeed and I wonder, my fiercely striking Lucy, if it is you?"

"No," Lucy stammered, feeling a change in how he was holding her. Something new was pulsing from his hands. She didn't like it. "No, I'm just a normal girl. Fairly boring really."

"I don't like the feeling you two evoke in each other." Malachi said thoughtfully, "I don't think you should be in the same room anymore."

"No please," Lucy pleaded, but she knew the stronger she reacted, the worse Malachi's reaction would be.

"So then," Malachi addressed Nathaniel directly with a loathsome challenge in his eye, all the while tracing the contours of Lucy's face under his well-manicured fingers. "What shall I do to entertain myself? Hmmm, what do you think, Angel? Is there anything that you would recommend? Something, I don't know, something to keep me busy for a long, long while?" His finger glided down Lucy's cheek, neck and flittered across her collar bone. Lucy whimpered.

Nathaniel growled, his silver eyes shooting daggers at the Demon.

"Oh, that is a *much* better vibe," Malachi grinned, "that makes me feel all warm and gushy inside. Hate is always better than love Angel. Always. Come Lucy, let's go have some fun." He let go of Lucy's hair only to scoop her up in his arms and carry her toward the door. "We aren't to be disturbed," he called to the guards over his shoulder. Take them all back, except, give Gavin a room, he was entertaining and shouldn't stay in the dungeons. Beat the other two if you get bored."

"NO!" raged Nathaniel as he tried to dive after them, clawing at the table to get grounding, his fingers clawing at the wood as two guards held fast to his chains. Lucy watched helplessly over Malachi's shoulder as he strode confidently toward the door. The last thing Lucy heard before they left the grand room was Nathaniel scream, "Do anything you want to me, please, I'm begging you! Just don't touch her!"

Lucy was devastated. She wouldn't see Nathaniel again and she could not imagine what Malachi was going to do to her. She shuddered to think of what the night would bring. Malachi strode easily past the main hall of the castle to another door across the way. A huge door was open and he sauntered in to what appeared to be a den or sitting room with Lucy still in his arms. The room was huge but still held the feeling of being cozy. Four huge plush chairs surrounded a roaring fire and a desk sat off against the far wall surrounded by book shelves. On the walls were various animal heads and trophies for different sports. Malachi walked Lucy in and sat her quite gently on one of the chairs. She sunk in and curled up defensively, allowing her long skirts to act as both a shield and a comfort.

"Don't be afraid," Malachi said reassuringly, his strong jaw softening, "I am no rapist." Yet Lucy brought up, clear as day, the images she had seen in Hell of Malachi in the beginning stages of raping Roman's sister. As if he could read her mind, he added, "Not anymore anyway."

Lucy wasn't reassured.

As if to make his point more clear, he walked away from her and over to the bar in the corner. He poured himself a large glass of amber spirits in a heavy crystal tumbler.

"What would you like?" he asked smiling.

Lucy didn't think before spouting, "Holy crap would I love a beer right now."

Malachi threw his head back and laughed heartily before looking at her with a sense of delight. "Then a beer you shall have, Lucy." He opened the small fridge under the counter and produced a bottle.

Lucy drank deeply before saying a light, "Thank you."

Malachi simply nodded.

He sat in the chair next to her and gazed into the huge fire for a few minutes.

"You fascinate me, Lucy Bower," he said while training his bright blue eyes on her. "How did you get your photographic memory? And don't bother lying," he added, not without kindness.

"I was born with it," Lucy answered. "When I was a toddler, my parents started to figure out that something was different about me. By the time I was reading, they really figured something was different."

"And when did you meet Nathaniel?"

"March 20th last year."

"Liar," he said with a smirk.

Lucy sighed, "I was told by the Angel Gabriel that we met on June 21, 1992, when I fell in a pool and drowned. They believe my soul travelled to Heaven where it met Nathaniel."

"And?" he prompted.

Lucy didn't feel like games. "And you know," she said wearily. She expected another slap but got silence instead.

"I'm not able to say it…" he finally said quietly.

"Not able or allowed?" Lucy risked a look at him. He was staring at the flames of the fire.

"Both," he answered quickly as if getting it over with; the ripping of a verbal Band-Aid.

Lucy paused for a moment. Where was this going? Certainly, developing a relationship with their captor might not be a huge mistake but what it might cost her was what gave her pause. At the end of the day, she had no choice.

"And he was my soul mate," she finished.

"I have heard of such things," he said quietly. "I have yet to see it."

"No?" Lucy asked, still terrified that she was overstepping.

"I do not work for the guild. What time I spend on the surface is in fulfillment of my own interests. I pay little attention to human ties."

Lucy didn't know what to say so she just sat quietly.

"I assume, Lucy," Malachi said softly, "that you are a very smart woman."

"I do okay," Lucy answered.

"There are very few people on the planet that are as smart as I am," Malachi offered. Lucy was surprised that he could not sound less conceited. "Not to drop names, but I haven't lost a chess match since Professor Moriarti walked the Earth."

"He was real?" Lucy could not stop herself from leaning forward with interest.

"He was indeed, although he was no professor." Malachi smiled and Lucy carefully smiled back. This would be a nice conversation if it wasn't with a demented Demon.

"So you want to play chess?" Lucy asked slowly, she didn't want to get it wrong and have Malachi's temper flare.

"Yes," he said with gusto, "well, I want to have the chance to lose at chess. I want to have a conversation with someone who might know more than I do."

Oh God, Lucy thought, *I've become the teacher's pet.*

"And I believe, Lucy," he continued, "that you are that

person." It was obvious that Lucy didn't have a choice in the matter, but she had another idea; it might get her killed, but she had to take the risk.

"Are we going to be digging for a while?" she asked.

Malachi raised his eyebrows. "Yes," he replied deliberately. His tone warned that caution was needed.

"Then I will play chess with you tonight, but could you please give Anastasia boots for tomorrow?"

"Anastasia?" he answered, "Not yourself?"

"No." Lucy didn't want to explain. "Just her."

"See," Malachi threw his hands up, "that is precisely what I was talking about. You all have this strange connection. You, Lucy, ask for the boots and have no thought whatsoever for yourself. It's quite strange behavior." Lucy didn't say anything, she just sat and waited. He could either grant her request or he could beat her with a broken bottle, she had no idea. His volatility was the worst element of the torture. "Tell you what, you get boots for playing that you may *not* give to Anastasia, but you will get boots for Anastasia if you win."

"It's a deal," Lucy spurted before she chose her words. She winced at her choice.

Malachi chuckled, "Don't worry Lucy, not all deals with the Devil are bad."

Lucy shuddered.

Suddenly, a chess set appeared on a table between them. It was solid marble and the pieces were so ornate that Lucy had to take a moment to admire their detail and craftsmanship.

"It's a gorgeous set, isn't it?" Malachi offered.

"I've never seen anything like it," Lucy replied, not trying to hide her admiration.

"I got it as a gift from King James the First," he explained.

"As in the King James Bible?" Lucy prompted with a small smile.

Malachi shrugged affably. "I tried my best, the man refused to listen to reason."

Lucy laughed lightly as she stood to turn her massive chair to better face the table. "Excuse me, my lady," Malachi exclaimed as he jumped out of his own seat to come over and adjust Lucy's. "Please allow me."

"Thank you," Lucy said quietly as she adjusted her skirts and sat back down. Was she seeing the real Malachi or was this persona all an act? She didn't know what to believe. Lucy had been put on the white side of the board, which she preferred anyway. Malachi poured himself another drink and without asking brought Lucy another beer. She took it gratefully. If anything, it would keep much needed calories in her.

"A beautiful lady in a five thousand dollar gown drinking a bottle of beer," Malachi mused as he sat back down, "never have I seen such a sight."

"Well, I kind of do things my own way," Lucy shrugged. She regarded the game board. Lucy tried not to use her memory for chess, not if she wanted to make it fair anyway. She had studied every famous game ever played, she could recreate any master move she wanted. She knew every game Bobby Fischer, David Edmonds and countless others had ever played. She could replay every move in her mind, which usually made games quite short. She was hoping that's what this would be. "I am ordered to win," Lucy looked directly at Malachi, "is that right?"

Malachi laughed. "Well Lucy, you can certainly try to win, but I warn you, I have been playing this game since its inception so I might just surprise you."

"But if I win," she countered, "Anastasia gets proper work

boots for digging from now on?"

"Yes Lucy," he conceded kindly, "no tricks. You might be shocked to discover that I never break my word."

"No," Lucy countered as she looked him in the eye, "I don't find that surprising at all."

He cocked his head and regarded her for a moment before saying, "Ladies first."

What Lucy thought would be a short game became the toughest game of her life. Malachi almost had her a couple times by somehow catching her completely off guard. It was clear that he knew just as much about chess as Lucy did, if not more, and she found it difficult to predict more than a couple moves ahead. They did not speak other than to hmmm or ahhh or even mutter a quiet, "interesting move." The quiet was nice for Lucy, who had not had peace in many weeks. Indeed, exhaustion leaked at the corners of her mind, causing her to almost drift off at times while waiting for Malachi to move. She roused herself and several times asked for coffee, which was brought by one of the dead girls. In the end, though, and just as the sun was casting a rosy hue from behind the purple mountains, Lucy uttered a weary, "Checkmate."

Then she looked at Malachi for his reaction. Would he be irate? Sulky? Hateful?

He grinned.

"That, Lucy Bower," he exclaimed, "was the best game of chess I have ever played. Well done! Well deserved. Good game." He did not reach out to shake her hand and Lucy was grateful. "Did you have fun?"

"Yes," Lucy said truthfully, "despite my exhaustion and the fact that this dress is cutting into my ribs, I actually had a very fun time."

Malachi laughed. "Well, good then."

There was a quiet pause. Lucy bit her lip as Malachi stared into the fire, his face almost sad.

"May I be excused to get some sleep?"

He roused at her question.

"Yes, you may. I need to go anyway." He waved and two dead girls came to escort her. "You and Anastasia will have boots from now on."

"Thank you, very much" Lucy said automatically as she stood. If this is how she earned their boots, then maybe there was a chance she could win them a way out of here. She would have to trick Malachi though, which, judging from the chess match, would not be an easy thing to do.

Malachi looked surprised. "You are very welcome." He went back to staring at the fire and Lucy slipped out the door.

Chapter Seventeen
Best Laid Plans

"It wasn't raining when Noah built the Ark."
~ Howard Duff

Lucy tried to slip quietly back into bed, but Anastasia sat bolt upright the moment she laid her head on the pillow.

"Oh Lucy!" Stasia cried while throwing herself against her, "Are you okay? Do you want to talk about it?"

"I'm fine," Lucy explained, "just tired. We played chess."

"Chess?" Stasia stared at her. "Are you screwing with me?"

"No," Lucy shook her head, "not at all. We literally just played chess."

"I was sitting up all night worried sick that you were being tortured and raped!" Anastasia said angrily.

Lucy looked at her. "Well, sorry babe, he didn't give me the option to text you and fill you in on the details!"

Stasia hung her head. "Sorry," she mumbled, "I was just so worried."

"As was I. Don't worry about it, I'm just really tired." She rubbed her face and laid back down, "I just need to get some sleep before we have to get up and dig again."

"Of course," Stasia replied as she lay down as well.

Lucy closed her eyes and did fade off for what was only a few minutes until the dead-girls arrived to dress them for the tunnels. Lucy wearily crawled off the bed and stood swaying while she let the girls dress her. As promised, two shiny pairs of boots were brought out and placed on Lucy and Anastasia's feet.

"Why the boots today?" Stasia asked.

"I won them," Lucy explained, "in the chess match. My plan is to eventually win us our freedom."

"Holy crap," Stasia said, tearing up, "that's hard core. You are the best friend a girl could ever ask for."

"Shut up," Lucy said with a weary smile. "Let's go dig a stupid tunnel."

Gavin was equally thrilled to see that Lucy was alive and seemingly un-traumatized. He was just as confused about the explanation for the evening activities though.

"He must have thousands of people that can play chess with him," he pounded the pick-axe into the slate, the loose shale shattered and piled around his feet. "Why you?"

"I don't know," Lucy replied, "he said that he hadn't lost at chess since Professor Moriarti walked the Earth."

"He was real?" Gavin countered and Lucy shrugged. "Well Lucy, keep it up. I know spending time with an evil Demon isn't a picnic, but it might benefit us in the end." He cast a sideways glance. "Ben," he said into the shadows, "how's it goin'?"

There was, of course, no response from the guard, but Gavin smiled anyway and kept digging. The day continued on, and Gavin, Lucy and Anastasia talked lightly and shared stories to pass the time. The weariness of their muscles told them that the time was up and they were escorted back to their rooms. Gavin's new chambers were down the hall from the girls.

They were once again cleaned and dazzled and put into gorgeous dresses to be presented for dinner. Lucy was so tired she felt nauseous and closed her eyes several times while the girls were doing her hair. An hour later, Gavin joined them again in the hall, this time in a tux to walk with them to dinner. Two guards, Ben and Jim, were in front of them and two more, John and Peter, were behind.

"Please say there is food," Gavin muttered under his breath.

"If you eat today," Lucy whispered to him, "try to see if you can sneak some down the table to Nathaniel, not if it will get you hurt though."

"Nice!" Stasia shot Lucy a bitter look. "So I guess Roman doesn't matter?"

"Roman isn't alive," Lucy countered sharply in a whisper, "he doesn't need to eat. Nathaniel will die if he doesn't get food soon!"

"Still," Stasia said sulkily, "it's not all about Nathaniel all the time."

Lucy rolled her eyes and was about to fire something back when Gavin interrupted them.

"Hello hungry people," he said quietly, "pay attention to me here. You are starving and you are tired and us fighting amongst ourselves is exactly what the bad guy wants so knock it off."

Lucy sighed. "You're right. I'm sorry Stasia. I, of course, hope Roman gets some food too."

"I forgive you," Anastasia said loftily and flipped her hair.

Lucy looked at Gavin. "Seriously? Do you see this?"

"Stasia," Gavin hissed, "quit being a snot."

"Piss off Gavin!" Stasia hissed back.

Lucy threw her hands in the air as they approached the ballroom.

They were once again sat at one end of the table but Nathaniel and Roman were not brought in. As Malachi promised, Lucy would not be put in the same room as Nathaniel again. Her heart broke a little with the realization that Malachi indeed stayed true to his word. He arrived shortly after they were seated. The meal tonight was lobster, a favorite of Lucy's but certainly not of Anastasia's. Lucy imagined that Anastasia would fault her for that too.

Malachi was again a gracious host and they were delighted when the food did not rot, but stayed fresh and delicious while they filled themselves fit to burst. They all ate heartily and timidly enjoyed each other's company. Malachi sat quietly, not eating but sipping his wine and listening intently. Anastasia's mood improved significantly over the meal, even casting an apologetic glance toward Lucy to which she received one in return. Gavin had been right; hunger was not their friend.

After the meal, Malachi stood and addressed them, "I hope you all had a good dinner and I will see you tomorrow."

"Thank you for dinner," Gavin said sincerely, "it was delicious."

"I'm glad you enjoyed it, we may now all retire for the evening," he stepped back from the table and extended out his hand, "Lucy? Shall we?"

She had no choice but to reach up and slip her palm into his. Terror gripped her as she prepared for fire to rip through her body but no such sensation came. Malachi instead gripped her hand securely yet gently as he guided her out of her chair and toward the far door. She cast one glance over her shoulder at her two best friends. Malachi might be kind right now, but there was no limit to the cruelty of his nature. Lucy would be in constant fear for her friends' lives as long as they were in this castle.

Gavin offered a soft smile but his eyes were pained. Lucy watched them until the door closed behind her and the Demon. The moment they left, Stasia slumped down on the table.

"Hey hey hey," Gavin put a protective arm over her shoulders. "She's going to be okay. I don't think he will hurt her."

"This is Hell," Stasia said into her forearms, "this is Hell. Dig all day, no food except for one meal that might rot away at any moment, surrounded by creepy guards and even creepier dead girls, Roman being tortured, Nathaniel being tortured and, and and…now Lucy stuck…." She trailed away and sobbed.

"Listen to me carefully," Gavin said sharply. "We are going to get out of here. I don't know how and I don't know when, but this is not forever and if you know something has an end to it, it is easier to endure. Roman is tough, much tougher than you think he is, and he will not die here. Neither will Nathaniel. We just have to stay strong and be ready to get out when the time is right. Lucy is the smartest person on the planet and she will survive these little visits with Malachi. She will." His voice wavered, "She's going to be okay."

Stasia sat up and regarded him. "You really are in love with her, aren't you?"

"I am," Gavin nodded, not embarrassed at all, "very much so."

"I'm sorry," Stasia sniffed back her tears and used her napkin to wipe her eyes, "this must extra suck for you."

"To know that I am going through all this and no matter what I do, there is no way that I am going to get the girl at the end of it? Yep, sucks a bunch," Gavin said but then smiled. "But that's my gig, not yours, you just keep your chin up and we will get out of here, somehow."

"I was really rude before," Stasia said, sitting back in her chair. "I was a total jerk."

"You can't help it," Gavin said with a smirk. This earned him a smack on the arm but a laugh as well. "Come on you," he said, pulling Stasia to standing, "let's get you up to your room for some sleep. More fun is to be had tomorrow." They walked to the door that the two guards opened for them.

Gavin saw Stasia safely to her room before heading to his.

"Nighty night Ben," he said jovially to his guard in the hall. "Thanks for making me feel like the president's mistress every single day." As he closed the door, he could have sworn he saw Ben's mouth crinkle in the faintest of smiles. Gavin grinned; they each had their own plan for escape.

Meanwhile, Lucy was being served coffee in the same room as last night. Malachi sat in the same chair, sipping tea from a delicate cup. He had decided that tonight would be a match of wits and debate. They discussed the historical validity of euthanasia. A hefty topic and Malachi was starting his points against it (even though he assured her that he could not care less on the matter) when Lucy stopped him.

"Will a winner be declared?" she asked, trying to sound light; she didn't want to poke the bear.

Malachi locked eyes with her and his read nothing but amusement.

"I don't know if a winner can be declared in a debate."

"Really?" Lucy countered, "I think President Ford would disagree."

Malachi laughed out loud. "Fair enough. I think I am...Demon enough to admit when I have been beat. What is your wager, Lucy?"

"If I win the debate, Nathaniel and Roman get a proper steak dinner for a week."

"A week?" Malachi bellowed, "Who am I, Walt Disney? Are you out of your mind? No."

Lucy started to smile at the Disney reference but she caught herself. "Three days," she countered.

"Not consecutive."

"Deal."

"Why Roman, though?" he asked thoughtfully. "You must understand that he is in fact quite dead and does not need to eat to survive or even to thrive. The Angel may need to eat, but the Demon, does not."

"Because I know he enjoys eating," Lucy replied smoothly.

"That was a lie," Malachi countered quickly. His eyes narrowed. "Do not lie to me, Lucy, it is not wise."

Terror ripped through her. She had overstepped and had to be very vigilant to not do that. Tears pricked at her eyes when she thought of what he might do to her.

"Nathaniel would just give Roman half, if not most of his and I want him to get a full meal," she blurted.

Malachi sat with this for a moment.

"So," he shifted in his seat to eye her more carefully, "you are telling me that you know for a fact that if I give Nathaniel food, he will share it with Roman, even though they both know that Roman doesn't really need it and Nathaniel does?"

"Nathaniel will insist upon it. I promise you that. If you give Nathaniel a loaf of bread, he will, without hesitation, hand half or more of that piece over to Roman or anyone else in the room for that matter."

Malachi beckoned one of the dead girls. "Bring a loaf of

bread to the dungeon and offer it only to the Angel, watch exactly what happens and report back." The girl walked away, her blond hair swinging down her back. He turned his attention back to Lucy. "But why would he do that?"

Lucy suppressed a smile. If she lost the debate, at least Nathaniel would get bread today. She had managed to trick Malachi with this one little thing. Her heart rejoiced. What more could she convince him to do?

"Because that is who he is," Lucy explained. She swallowed the heavy knot that began to settle in her throat as she thought about Nathaniel's kind-heartedness. "That's what he is made of; he would give you the shirt off his back and be happy that you are happy."

Malachi shook his head in thought. "Angels are baffling, really."

"I believe he was made that way before he even became an Angel." Lucy tread lightly, "I think that's his…way."

The dead girl returned and whispered something in Malachi's ear. He nodded and waved her away. "He took the bread, immediately split it and gave the larger portion to the Demon. They are currently bickering about it."

Lucy smiled and could almost hear the two of them half arguing and half joking about it. She felt the tear slip down her cheek before she even knew it was there. Malachi just watched her.

"What did he do to make you love him so?" he wondered almost to himself.

"Nothing," Lucy sniffed and wiped away the tear. It would not do to have Malachi see her weep. "He didn't have to do anything. We are soul mates."

"I wouldn't know anything about that," he countered thoughtfully.

"Everyone has one," Lucy said as if this was a dating show. She winced at her own tone.

"Not me m'dear," Malachi answered, "for I did not come from the Hall of Souls."

"What do you mean?" she countered. "You have a soul and therefore..." Malachi batted his hand in the air, dismissing her logic and Lucy sat silently, the rest of the sentence hanging heavily between them.

"Shall we begin the debate and see if you can win three non-consecutive meals for my prisoners?" Malachi asked. Lucy nodded and retrieved the volumes of information in her memory on the topic of euthanasia. Newspapers, magazines, books and videos lined up in her mind, ready to be used. She sighed; she was so tired. She rejoiced though in the fact that she had one small victory today. "Of course, I won't allow the meals to start for several days." Malachi added lightly while taking a sip of his tea, "after all, they had a half loaf of bread today." Lucy glanced over to see that he was staring at her with his piercing blue eyes. "Or did you think you fooled me into doing that, Lucy?"

Dammit.

"Not at all," she shook her head vehemently. Malachi smiled good-naturedly but something lurked beneath it. Lucy had to be cautious if she wanted everyone to get out of there alive. "I'm sorry," she admitted, "I just want him to live. I will do anything so he can live."

Malachi shook his head. "Anything?" he countered.

"Anything," Lucy whispered, terror gripping at her spine. What had she just revealed? Whatever it was, Malachi was sure to use it against her.

"Perplexing behavior. You may present your opening argument."

Lucy and Malachi debated late into the night. Several times Malachi stood and paced in front of the fireplace in frustration at making his point heard but Lucy noted that despite the heated nature of the discussion, he never once raised his voice. Lucy's temper of course almost got the better of her a couple times and she had to censor herself while cursing her red hair and matching irritability.

It wasn't quite as late as the night before. The sun had yet to rise when Malachi called it a draw. Lucy had to concede. She was exhausted and losing focus rapidly. Malachi showed no signs of fatigue and yet allowed it to be a tie so Lucy could sleep. She knew his compassion would come with a price.

"Since you did not win the debate so to speak," Malachi concluded, "you win no food for the prisoners."

Lucy sighed. "Can they at least get one or two meals?"

"I do feed them, you know," Malachi added, "the Angel would be dead if I hadn't."

"Please?" Lucy hated to beg.

"One meal," Malachi said with a smirk.

"Thank you," Lucy said sincerely. "May I be excused?"

"Yes, excellent debate Lucy, think of a topic for tomorrow."

"You can choose," Lucy said wearily as she trudged toward the door, dragging her heavy skirts with her. "I can debate about anything."

"You are the most self-assured nineteen-year-old I have ever encountered in all my years," Malachi observed, looking at her with something akin to admiration. Lucy hid the shudder that shot up her back. "I promise you that Marie Antoinette was not so confident in who she was as a person as you are."

"When you spend your whole life answering the question, 'what *are* you?'" Lucy almost slurred in exhaustion, "you have no choice but to come up with an answer." Being too tired to see his reaction, Lucy walked out the door and did not observe the raised eyebrows or small smile touch his lips.

Chapter Eighteen
The Great Debate

"I love argument, I love debate. I don't expect anyone just to sit there and agree with me, that's not their job."
~ Margaret Thatcher

The next weeks passed much the same. Lucy, Gavin and Anastasia would dig all day, eat a hearty meal with Malachi and then Lucy was drawn into the den for a debate or a chess game or any match of wits. One day, Malachi even had a game of scrabble set out on the table, he beat Lucy soundly only because he ignored the "only in English" rule and ended up with an ancient word that apparently meant "mosaic." Lucy spent her time trying to unravel Malachi. He was charming and charismatic, intelligent and even kind. Lucy often struggled to remind herself that he was a powerful Demon and no friend to her. The food stopped rotting on the table, he did not hurt any of his human companions and to her knowledge, he had not whipped the supernatural ones either. Breakfast had even shown up a few times for Lucy and Anastasia and the guard Jim looked the other way when they snuck a bagel to

Gavin during the walk down to the tunnels.

Lucy had acquired other privileges for her friends. Meals for Nathaniel and Roman were commonplace, they were even given proper beds and blankets to sleep under. Malachi would not budge on the wing trimming and adamantly refused to even accept it as a bargaining tool. She and Anastasia were permitted to wear loose comfortable gowns at off times and torches were installed at regular intervals through the tunnel to make the job much safer. He also eased up on their security detail. Guards watched them through the day and whenever Gavin was with them but if it was just Lucy or she and Anastasia, dead girls escorted them around the castle.

The tunnel itself was getting very deep indeed and the trio had no idea where it was designed to go. Lucy started to suspect that Anastasia had been right that it was a make work project, and they would get to a certain depth only to be directed to fill it all back in. Digging was becoming easier as their muscles developed and strengthened. Gavin looked more like a lumberjack and Lucy's legs were becoming powerful and muscular. Anastasia was already very athletic so her body just maintained the same level of perfection. The tunnel was starting to get deeper even when they weren't digging and the consensus was that Nathaniel and Roman were being made to dig through the night. It became clear though that Malachi was somehow not in the castle during the day. This discovery came from Gavin, who had finally began a tentative and shaky relationship with Ben the guard.

Turned out that Ben (who never did reveal his real name so they continued to call him Ben) was an avid soccer fan. Gavin was not an avid soccer fan but was an avid liar and finally broke through with talk of the Bulgarian Soccer Team. Ben would cautiously speak to Gavin throughout the day about soccer and eventually other topics, but the moment the sun went down at night, he would shut up like a clam. Gavin finally asked him outright and Ben had quietly admitted that his boss was not present in the castle when the sun was up. He then made it very clear with a cuff upside the head who was in charge when Malachi was not present.

Lucy found this fascinating. Where did Malachi go all day? It's not like he had a desk job and had told Lucy that he did not have to perform regular Demon duties. Where did he go and why? She was determined to find out one night and was concocting a strategy in her mind as they approached the den when Malachi cut through her thoughts.

"There is someone I would like you to meet," he said as he opened the door.

Lucy entered the room, terrified at what she would find. A tall gorgeous blond woman in a striking black dress stood beside the mantle. The fire illuminated her flawless skin and perfect body as she regarded them and took a sip from the crystal champagne glass in her hand. Lucy's heart stopped in fear.

This was *the* Demon. The one that had been in Hell at the exclusive club where Roman had allowed them a reprieve during their visit last winter and she was the one that had been watching Lucy and Gavin at the nativity play on Christmas Day. Although Malachi was a dangerous creature, this woman felt far more unnerving to Lucy and she didn't know why. She seemed deceptive in some way, like she was putting on a show. Although all Demons lied every day in order to do their job, there was something distinctively different about this one.

"Oh, the Lucy you always speak of," the woman mused as if in answer to an unasked question. Lucy disliked her instantly.

"Lucy," Malachi motioned graciously with his hands, "this is Octavia. She is a very old friend of mine."

Lucy didn't know what the protocol with meeting a new Demon was. Should she shake hands with her? Nod? High five? What? She settled with a small nod and a wave and was rewarded with a tight and unkind smile in return. If Octavia remembered seeing Lucy before, she made no sign of it.

"Hello," Lucy said, "it's nice to meet you." She began to walk to her usual chair and whether by coincidence or petty cruelty, Octavia sauntered over and sat in it as if that was her intention the whole time. Lucy paused in her steps, now unsure of where to go. Octavia shot Lucy an innocently wide eyed look.

"Lucy, sit here," Malachi offered a new chair on the other side of his and she accepted it and sat down. "I have told Tavia all about you." He offered and Lucy smiled politely. In her experience, Octavia would respond in one of two ways; she could extol how happy she was to meet Lucy and hear all about her memory or she could choose to say some sort of insult hidden as a compliment.

Octavia chose the latter.

"Yes, and I have to compliment you, it is rare that a common human can hold his attention so completely."

Well done, Lucy thought and at the same time, *I do not need you to like me, just don't stop my heart from beating.*

So she smiled and said, "No one is more surprised than plain old me." Malachi's eyes crinkled at the edges as she continued, "As a matter of fact, I am certainly out of my element here and as such request that I be excused."

Octavia did not look impressed but one perfectly formed eyebrow raised slightly.

"You may not be excused," Malachi replied, "we haven't even started our debate."

"What is the topic this evening?" Lucy asked.

"The usefulness of God."

Octavia broke out laughing – it sounded like bells on a sleigh. Lucy began to panic. This was not a good topic to get into with two Demons. It wasn't a good topic to get into with a pack of University students at a party. She was in dangerous waters here and she had little idea as to how to get herself out.

"I don't even know the arguments for something like that," she countered lightly, "I don't think I have any reference manuals in my head that support or counter that topic."

"Exactly," Malachi added, "it will be a debate of belief systems."

"Oh goodie," Octavia said, her voice dripping with sarcasm. "Couldn't we torture her instead? And by that I mean we watch others torture her because we are too lazy to do so?" Lucy paled.

"No," Malachi said sternly, "I think this is a viable topic and we are going to debate it."

"Well really," Lucy said cautiously, "this is not a topic that humans often discuss."

"It's the most debated topic in all human history," Octavia shot at her.

"No," Lucy's brain fired on all cylinders, "the debate of the *existence* of God is the most debated topic in human history. We will be discussing God's *usefulness*. Because we all know beyond a shadow of a doubt that God exists, the debate is not in his actuality but in his functionality in the human world."

"Yes!" Malachi exploded, "Didn't I tell you? She is so extraordinary!"

Octavia just glared and Lucy's stomach clenched. She would have to be very careful. She got the impression that Malachi was the one in charge and Octavia was expected to toe the line, but she got a stronger impression that Octavia didn't care what she was expected to do.

"So," Octavia retorted, "what is God's functionality in the human world then?"

Lucy thought. "Well, he created the world, so that was a fairly big function."

"No, *now*." Octavia looked interested for the first time. "What do you think he does for a regular human *now*?"

Lucy wished that Nathaniel was there, she wished she knew what he would say. She had little idea of the answer. Which was most likely Malachi's intention; he wanted information and yet he also wanted to stump Lucy and force her to struggle.

"I think what he did create continues to function in its design with a beauty that is unmatched. I believe that the system which God shaped was so perfectly ordered that it has run for millions of years without the need for intervention on his part."

"Give me an example," Malachi replied.

"The Arctic Woolly-Bear Caterpillar," Lucy replied. "It spends the majority of the year in a stasis cocoon where it produces glycol to prevent it from freezing to death. It feeds only one month out of the year in the spring and goes back into hibernation. There have been reports of this creature living up to fourteen years to get the nutrients it needs to turn into a moth."

Octavia laughed. "And what good does that do? What a waste of a resource! A silly caterpillar in Tuktoyaktuk provides what to the human race exactly? That's precisely the problem with God's design; he added scores of useless items that provide nothing to the system itself."

"I disagree," Lucy replied and Octavia bristled. "That caterpillar provides vital pollination in a region that has an incredibly short spring season. Without its specific evolution, the plants in that area would suffer and that would lead to the larger animals in the area having less foliage to eat and the humans therefore having less meat available to them. Without the caterpillar, the entire ecosystem would be negatively affected and that trickles to the rest of the country and the world." Lucy sat forward in her seat, feeling the roll of her own mind. It was as if she was racing downhill and could not stop herself, even if she wanted to.

"That is the beauty of God's design; every single aspect of it is connected to everything else. The entire system is perfect in its own reliance upon itself. Much like the human race. No human can survive without other humans. It is our connection with each other that feeds our innermost selves and in essence is the cause of the success of the human race. When we learn lessons and rely upon the existence of something as insignificant as the Arctic Woolly moth, we secure our own existence. That is God's function."

There was silence.

Malachi slowly turned to Octavia, his face flushed, his eyes vibrant. "She's perfect," he breathed.

Lucy could have sworn that Octavia paled and Lucy began to sweat. She did not like Malachi praising her so much in front of someone who clearly saw Lucy as an adversary. Malachi looked back at Lucy.

"Excellent debate, Lucy," he said with a smile. "You may be excused."

She felt like she had done something wrong and suppressed the urge to backtrack verbally. She had no idea if Malachi would protect her if Octavia attacked her, but she doubted it. As she rose and moved to the door, Malachi stood with her and held her arm to escort her to the waiting dead girls.

"Excellent work," he whispered to her and Lucy hated herself for the surge of pride she felt. "No digging for you tomorrow. Sleep all day and your meals will be brought to you."

"Everyone," Lucy whispered back, "no digging for anyone. Even those in the dungeon," she added.

Malachi's mouth tightened but his eyes sparkled. "You are making me soft, Lucy. Fine. Everyone gets tonight and tomorrow off."

Lucy flashed him her biggest smile. Everyone would be thrilled. "Thank you so much."

Malachi smiled back as he closed the door on her, leaving her in the front hallway with her escorts. It had been about a week since the guards had stopped escorting them around. Lucy could not wait to get back to their rooms and tell Stasia and Gavin that they had a full 24 hours off from duties. She picked up her pace and all but skipped up the stairs and down the expansive hallway to their rooms.

Lucy was so lost in thought that she didn't even realize that the two dead girls had vanished. She didn't even hear him coming nor feel a presence close to her; especially one as noteworthy as this one. She didn't know anyone was there until a hand wrapped around her neck and pressed against her mouth, preventing her from screaming.

Every nerve in Lucy's body came alive as she twisted to free herself from whoever held her. She kicked and tried to scream and writhe under his arms. It was for nothing, though, for within a second the man had her off her feet and into the blackness of one of the massive ornate guest suites and had closed the heavy oak door. A fire appeared in the hearth and every candle in the room ignited, illuminating her captor's face and Lucy's legs buckled at the sight.

Chapter Nineteen
Just Breathe

"Life is not measured by the number of breaths we take but by the moments that take our breath away."
~ Hilary Cooper

Nathaniel didn't speak but grabbed Lucy's face and pressed his mouth to hers, preventing her from speaking. Not that she could if she wanted to. There was nothing to be said. She fell back against the door, bringing Nathaniel with her. Heat pulsed from his lips onto hers and Lucy's entire body turned to water as she wrapped her arms around his neck and she held on for dear life. All her thoughts left her mind, all her worries left her consciousness, everything she had ever known vanished from her thoughts and were replaced only by peace and deep unabashed love.

She didn't know how Nathaniel had gotten there and she didn't care. She needed him so badly right now; she needed him close to her. It was only by Nathaniel's presence that Lucy could ever feel that everything would be okay again, that anything in her world would be happy again. She clutched at him with everything she had left. Tears poured down her cheeks as she ran her hands over his face, through his hair and down his bare chest to confirm that somehow, someway, this was real, that Nathaniel was here and he was hers and always would be. All she could think to do was breathe.

Suddenly, her dress felt cumbersome and she began to reach behind her to pull violently at the buttons. Nathaniel reached and within seconds the soft navy silk was piled at their feet. Lucy stepped out of it and her shoes, never taking her lips or eyes away from Nathaniel. He grabbed at her roughly, clutching at her red curls and kissing down her neck and across her collarbone. Lucy's head swam as he reached down and picked her up to cradle her in his arms. He carried her over to the deep, ornate four poster bed. He laid her down and regarded her for a moment, his piercing crystal eyes cutting straight through her.

"God I love you," he whispered huskily and he went at her, hungry with passion.

The next morning, Lucy awoke wrapped in Nathaniel's arms. For a moment she forgot where she was; it was like they were in their bed at the cabin and the ivy was twisted above their heads. As she cracked her eyes open she took in the stained glass window and the dark wood of the castle and her heart sunk at the realization of the truth. She could not fathom the punishment that would fall upon them if Malachi had discovered that they were missing. She glanced over at Nathaniel's gorgeous face, asleep on the pillow and smiled. *It was worth it*, she thought.

His eyes opened slowly and he grinned at her. Lucy's heart fluttered and she leaned in and kissed him lightly on the lips.

"Good morning, my Lucy," he said drowsily at her.

Lucy started to laugh, "How did you…"

"The guards have been very slack lately and I simply

knocked one unconscious while Roman and I were being led back from the tunnel. We went there to dig but suddenly, the guards turned us around and said we had the night off. They made the mistake of walking in front of us. Two seconds later, Roman and I were free."

Lucy sat up quickly, "What the hell were you thinking?" Lucy almost yelled, "Get out of here, go! Out the window! Out the door! Go get help!" She shoved at his leg.

"There is no point Lucy," he said while grabbing onto her hands, "there is something around the castle that I can't get through. Roman and I tried several times before you got here and it's like there is a black blanket draped over the whole castle. I could barely even feel you until you got here, I can't feel anything and we can't get out. I wish I could."

"Tell me everything you know," Lucy demanded, "everything. I have been spending a lot of time with Malachi and I am going to figure out a way to get us all out of here."

"Oh my Lucy," he grinned at her, "so brave and clever. He is planning something but we can't figure out what. I don't know why we are digging. There seems to be no purpose to it."

"That is Anastasia's argument," Lucy laid her head on his arm. She would normally rest upon his chest but Nathaniel could not lay on his back with his wings in such a state. "She thinks that it is just a make work project. He is going to have us dig to a certain depth and then just fill it all back in." She tucked her legs around his, entwining them as close as possible.

"Makes sense," he said twisting his fingers through her auburn curls. "Actually, it makes no sense and it is the most illogical thing I have ever heard of, which means it is a perfect explanation for *his* actions."

Lucy noted that Nathaniel didn't use Malachi's name and

his voice dripped with venom. "He hasn't hurt me," she blurted quickly and Nathaniel eyed her carefully. "He hasn't," she continued, "I wouldn't lie to you. He has been nothing but a gentleman. In fact, it feels like he is trying desperately to please me and I don't know why."

"To make me hate him more," Nathaniel was suddenly tense, and his voice seethed. "He knows that you will remember his kindnesses forever and I will spend my life despising him."

"Hate? Despise?" Lucy queried, "Those are strong words."

"And ones that are deeply deserved," Nathaniel retorted sharply. He paused. "I don't want to hear about you spending time with him, please."

"He told me he didn't come from the Hall of Souls, what does that mean?"

"He was never human," Nathaniel seethed, "he wasn't like Roman, where he lived a life and then was banished to Hell. I don't know what he is, but I know that he is no common everyday Demon."

Lucy did not discuss the privileges that she had acquired for everyone as a result of her interactions with Malachi. She also left out her visit to Purgatory. She would fill Nathaniel in on all that later. They had such a short time together and she didn't want to waste it on the past.

"How are we going to get out of here?" she asked and tried not to hide the fear in her voice.

"I don't know," Nathaniel said, gazing around them and up at the damask running over the top of the bed. "I don't understand why anything isn't happening from up above. They should be doing something about this. Demons keeping humans and Angels in captivity is expressly against everything that the agreement states between the two Guilds. It doesn't make any sense. It must have something to do with whatever he has around this place." He mused.

"Malachi isn't here during the day," Lucy replied, and Nathaniel winced at the use of his name. "The guards said something to Gavin."

"I agree, I don't know where he goes. Maybe he has another main base in Europe."

Lucy sighed. "Then what do we do?"

"I will get you out of here," Nathaniel grabbed her hair and pulled her head to lock eyes with her. "I swear to you Lucy, I will get you out of here if it kills me."

Tears sprang to her eyes. "Don't say that," she begged, "please, I will figure this out and we will all be fine."

"Ah my Lucy," he kissed her forehead fiercely, "I love you so much."

"How long can we stay here?" she asked.

"Not much longer," she heard his voice crack.

"I can't be without you," she began to sob against his shoulder, "I can't do this anymore. I need you. I love you so much and it's agony not being with you."

"Shh," he said, stroking her hair, "everything will be okay. Somehow."

"I love you," she whispered against him and she let the tears come. With Nathaniel, she could let down her guard and release anything that she had been holding and he could take it. He would take anything she could give him and weather it with love and grace. She cried for her lost University and her lost dorm room and lost friends. She cried because she was so exhausted at keeping this all up that she would rather die than do it for another day. She cried because Anastasia was trapped and Gavin adored her and she could do nothing about either. She cried because she had gotten them all into this disastrous mess and she had no clue how to get them out. She cried because the one thing in her life that was perfect was Nathaniel and she could only see him for these few hours and she was ruining it because she was crying.

"Shh," he said again, "I will make this right. I promise."

"How though," she demanded through her tears, "how? What are we going to do Nathaniel? What?"

"I don't know," he sighed. "I don't know. But I do know that if I tell you to do something, you need to unquestioningly do it, Lucy."

Lucy sniffed as her crying subsided.

"What are you talking about?"

"I know you don't like being commanded and I know you don't like being told what to do, but this might come down to something very ugly indeed, so please, I beg of you, do not cause trouble, do not draw more attention to yourself and if I tell you to do something, it is for a reason and you should do as I say."

Lucy smiled as she sniffed away the last of her tears. "You are so bossy!" she exclaimed and Nathaniel laughed.

"I have missed you so, Lucy," he grinned at her. "And I love you more than anyone could ever love another person."

"Why didn't our souls connect?" she asked impulsively, "Last night?"

"I don't think they can find their way out," Nathaniel said with sadness, "I think they know not to come out here. I think they understand that it isn't safe here."

There was a noise in the hallway and they both sat bolt upright in bed.

"We have to go," Nathaniel blurted, "I have to get back to my cell, it's not safe."

Lucy's heart sunk. Their time together had been more than

twelve hours but felt so much shorter. Surely, it couldn't be time already, could it? Nathaniel gently pulled her out of bed and helped dress her back in her silk gown. He took a moment to glance at what was left of his wings in the mirror.

"They will grow back," Lucy offered lamely.

"They already started to," Nathaniel said with a smile. "Just being with you…" he trailed off as he crossed to her in two strides, grabbed her face and kissed her. There was another sound in the hallway, men's voices, doors opening. The guards were looking for them. Nathaniel looked to the door and back at Lucy. He held her face and pressed his forehead against hers.

"Don't cause trouble, don't anger him and I will get you out." He whispered ferociously into her hair, "I will get to you again if I can. No matter how it all turns out Lucy, know that you are loved beyond the understanding of most humans."

"Don't talk like that," Lucy pleaded as tears came to her eyes again, "I am going to get us out of here. I will figure out his plan."

"I know you will. You will save us all, Lucy." Nathaniel squeezed his eyes shut and muttered something that Lucy could not hear. "You will save us all." There were more bangs, from the hall, and they were getting closer. Nathaniel opened his eyes. "I am hoping the guards are so embarrassed that we haven't even been reported missing. Wait for ten minutes then go back to your room. If you get caught, tell them you lost your way last night so just slept here." He kissed her lips softly, "I love you so deeply. Stay safe. I will see you soon."

With that, he backed away from her, and even had the audacity to saunter and grin at her. Lucy smiled back and shook her head. "My Lucy," he whispered as he opened the door a crack and slipped out.

Lucy fell to her knees and sobbed.

Her tears finally subsided again. Enough tears Lucy, she chastised herself, there will be no more crying in this place. She dried her face, breathed deeply and forced her mind to settle. Gently, she slipped into the hall to see that it was abandoned. Barely breathing, Lucy tiptoed down the passageway to her door and slipped inside.

Chapter Twenty
Spoiled

"And when thou art spoiled, what wilt thou do?"
Jeremiah 4:30

The room was empty and although Lucy was emotionally and physically spent, she was wide awake; every nerve in her body and mind was alive and buzzing. She sat at the window and began to think. Now that she had seen Nathaniel, her desire to escape had multiplied tenfold. It was clear that Nathaniel and Roman weren't getting any information. Indeed, Lucy was the only one who had the tools at her disposal to unravel the mystery and get them all out.

Lucy made a list in her head of things she needed to find out. She needed to know where Malachi went every day and why. She needed to know what the plan was for the hole, for although a torturous make work project was likely, Lucy was getting to know Malachi well and he was opposed to waste. If they were digging, her instincts told her it was for a reason. The problem that plagued Lucy the most was why them?

Why would a powerful Demon of the netherworld kidnap

and hold hostage three university students from Illinois? Lucy understood why Malachi wanted to torture Roman and maybe Nathaniel was just a bonus, but, if he wasn't torturing the girls, why keep them? Lucy and Anastasia were only brought to further punish Roman and Nathaniel, if they weren't allowed in the same room, why not let them go? Why keep Gavin at all? She had learned that Malachi did little without a cause, no matter how insane the reason, so why? Sheer entertainment? That seemed so pedestrian considering what Malachi was capable of. And what did Malachi mean when he said, "she's perfect"? Perfect for what?

There was a knock at the door and Lucy jumped as a guard appeared. It was Ben and he looked relieved to see her.

"You did not come to your room last night!" he exclaimed. "I checked!"

"Did you check the washroom?" Lucy shot back, and Ben shook his head. "Well, that's where I was!" She lied easily, "You need to have a serious conversation with the chef about the quality of the meat he serves! Look at me, I haven't even changed out of my clothes from last night! I thought I was going to die I was so sick!"

"Oh," he looked relieved and Lucy had to stifle a smile. "Are you better?"

"Yes, thank you." Lucy was sure to sound grateful for his kindness. "Why are you looking for me anyway?"

"There is no digging anymore," Ben began.

"What?" Lucy demanded, "Why?"

"Well, not for you anyway," Ben explained. "The orders are that everyone gets last night and today off and you never dig again. You are to sleep all day and spend your nights with Him. The others will continue to dig." He continued in a quieter tone. "We are also to follow your orders for anything you want at all. Food, gowns, anything within reason we are to get for you. You are also to be moved to your own private quarters."

"I want the others to stop digging too," Lucy said quickly, and Ben almost smiled.

"Nice try. I said, within reason." He started out the door. "Follow me."

"Where is Anastasia and Gavin? I want to explain if I am not going to see them anymore."

"We will explain to them," he replied as he walked into the hall. Lucy had no choice but to follow. They walked the length of the hall and Lucy simply assumed that she would be given a larger guest room, but she was led up a second stairway and down another hall. This hall had only two sets of double doors.

"That one," Ben motioned down the hall, "is his room, and this one is yours." He opened the doors and Lucy gasped.

The ceilings were much higher than the ceilings in Lucy's previous room, and the room itself was huge. Lucy was fairly sure that this one room was the size of the main floor of her mother's home back in Kansas. The walls were not exposed stone but were covered in bright white and gold ornate wall paper. They were in a sitting room filled with luxurious powder blue colored chairs and a chaise lounge. Lucy's feet sunk into the deep carpet. On the far wall were massive glass doors draped in thick blue curtains that were pulled back with gold ties, revealing a stunning view of the mountains.

There was gold fireplace with bunches of flowers draped on top. To the left was a large door that opened to an exquisite bed chamber in the same gold and blue and white with buckets of pink roses strewn everywhere. Lucy wandered through the bed chamber where she found two more doors, one to a closet that was as large as her dorm room at home. It had more period type dresses like the one she was wearing but along one wall was modern dress clothes and, more thrillingly, along the last wall were stacks and stacks of modern more casual clothes. Lucy could have sworn she spotted a pair of sweatpants and her heart rejoiced. She wandered back out to the sitting room where Ben was still standing guard. He pointed with his chin to the right wall, it was covered in blue velvet curtains, in the middle was a white and gold door.

"Is that his room?" Lucy whispered. Ben nodded. Lucy tightened her lips – she didn't like the look of this and seeing that the door had no lock on it, didn't like the feel of it either. She did not welcome the idea of becoming a personal slave to Malachi. She walked to the door to find that it was actually locked, although from the other side, and Lucy found that to be somewhat comforting. Then she spotted something under the curtain and with a shaking hand, she reached up and pulled on the silky velvet edge. The blue fabric pushed away, folding upon itself to reveal one of Lucy's favorite things, books. The entire wall was covered end to end in stacks and stacks of books.

She laughed out loud as she ran the length of the room drawing the curtain as she went. When she reached the end she stopped and looked back. She gently fanned her hand over the spines as she slowly paced back down the shelves. There had to have been five hundred books there. Some she knew and knew well: Shakespeare, Bronte, Sawyer. Some, she had never seen before and indeed some she didn't even know if they were books, items that looked like pamphlets or stacks of letters hid amongst the spines. She sighed in contentment. Malachi was certainly trying to be generous to her, and although his reasons were not clear, she had to take them at face value at this point.

"Is he here?" she asked.

"No," Ben shook his head, "gone, but you are instructed to rest for you are now expected to keep his hours." Lucy nodded and her eyes carried back to the rich library before her. Her heart skipped a beat again. She picked up a volume of Vanity Fair, and though she had read it and had the entire contents in her mind, she felt the deep desire to read it again.

"I will take a bath and go to bed." The thought of reading in a luxurious bath was an indulgence Lucy could not pass up.

"Very good, my lady," Ben said as he bowed to her and left the room. Six of the dead girls entered and escorted her to the opulent bathroom where they poured her a bath in a tub that could have passed for a swimming pool. Lucy relaxed in the water, and thought of Nathaniel. She felt like a horrible person for being in such luxury while Nathaniel and the others would toil in the tunnel and live in comparative squalor. She required this time though. She needed Malachi to trust her more, and though his trust was increasing, she needed it to expand tenfold. Lucy had to become his ally to discover out his plan and find a way out. If she got to read a few books on the way, so be it.

After her bath, she settled into the majestic bed and slept deeply under the dense comforters. Lucy was awakened hours later by the dead girls turning on the lights. She had no idea what time it was but assumed that it was time for dinner and another performance with Malachi. Stretching, Lucy forced herself to put the others out of her mind. Guilt right now would not benefit her. She had to throw herself completely into this role or Malachi wouldn't have confidence in her. As long as he maintained his gentlemanly behavior, Lucy could keep it all up and try to get as much information from him as possible. If Malachi turned back into a monster, she was dead meat.

The dead girls let her pick her outfit and she chose a soft flowing burgundy dress. Devoid of a corset or garters, Lucy felt like she had never been so comfortable; still, she eyed the sweats on her way to the bathroom. She insisted that the girls bypass the Gone with the Wind up-do and pulled her hair into a low side pony with some tendrils falling out around her face. She allowed them to do her makeup, but stayed their hands when they reached the glamour stage. They listened to her and after slipping on a matching pair of heels, stepped back to allow her to leave her bedroom unattended. Lucy found Ben in the hall and, although he was still in uniform, he was unarmed.

"No need for a billy-bat anymore?" she asked while eyeing his empty belt.

"Orders," Ben replied.

"Hmm," Lucy replied and he motioned for her to lead the way down the stairs to the dining room. The room had been transformed from the vast and bare medieval dining hall Lucy knew so well. One corner of the chamber had been set with an intimate table and chairs, lit by candles and surrounded with flowers. Malachi was already there. This too, deviated from their normal routine where they had to wait on his presence; he was waiting for her instead. He stood beside the table wearing a suit with his collar open and a bright smile on his face. Lucy was struck by how handsome he truly was. He had the same coloring as Roman but with softer features. He looked like a movie star. She sucked in a sharp breath and with it the scent of all those flowers and forced herself to smile as she crossed the room to him.

"Lucy!" Malachi said as she approached him, "may I say you look beautiful."

"Thank you," she replied as she sat down in the chair he was pulling out for her. "I had a great deal of help. My new closet is stunning, as is my new room. Thank you very much."

He waved her away. "It's nothing, really, but did you like the library? I had it added for you."

"Love it," she grinned widely, no need to lie, "thank you so much."

"Excellent!" He waved at the servants who presented them with a stunning meal.

"Are the others not joining us?" she asked hesitantly. Lucy had to tread carefully, she couldn't look like she was too concerned.

"No longer," Malachi explained, "but have no fear, they are in no danger and will be fed regularly."

"Wonderful," Lucy acted thrilled with him, "thank you."

"I just thought that since you and I got along so well, there was no need to have others about."

"I see," Lucy replied and smiled again.

"You may move about the castle as you see fit now, Lucy." Malachi continued, "A guard will always escort you, but it is for your own safety only. I feel as though I can trust you a little more than the others. Am I right?"

"Yes," Lucy answered quickly.

"You may also have anything that you wish, anything at all. Within reason, of course."

"Of course."

"I just want you to like it here." He put down his fork and knife and reached for her hands. Lucy could not help but hesitate. "I won't hurt you," he reassured, "I have come to respect you greatly, Lucy, and I hope you respect me."

"Oh I do," Lucy replied and slyly added, "It's just the first time you ever touched me was a very painful experience and my memory does not allow that thought to fade, so it's difficult."

"Allow me to make you new memories," Malachi answered slowly, avoiding an apology.

"I can try," Lucy said sweetly and reached her hands forward and suppressed a shudder as he held them tightly in his.

"Let's start over, shall we?" Malachi asked hopefully.

"Oh yes." Lucy grinned. With a squeeze of her fingers, he let her go and went back to his dinner. Lucy did the same and gritted her teeth – this was not going to be easy. There was a new tone in the air, an intimate one that had somehow replaced the amicable one that had existed just a day before. Was a Demon trying to woo her? And why? She decided to change the subject again and she thought maybe she should change it to something more on Malachi's turf.

"I was curious to know," she asked as coffee and a chocolate mousse were put in front of her, "if you ever met Hitler?"

Malachi's eyes lit up. "Oh yes!" he exclaimed and Lucy had to swallow her distaste again and force a smile. "I was one of his chief advisors!"

"Really?" Lucy encouraged, "That's fascinating." The evening continued with Malachi and Lucy discussing and debating the merits or lack thereof of Hilter's regime. Lucy often took the opposite stance on issues than Malachi did, not only because that was how she actually felt but also because he seemed to enjoy arguing. Indeed, Lucy enjoyed the debate as much as Malachi did. After dinner they moved again to the den where they continued their discussions on various topics. Lucy at times forgot where she was and did enjoy herself. Malachi seemed focused on what Lucy felt philosophically or morally about something and tried to interpret her feelings about it. He seemed, Lucy noticed, to have no moral compass. He had no way to determine if something was right or wrong based on beliefs. He seemed only to use human behavior as a guide. If the average human thought that murder was wrong, then it must be wrong, though he could not understand why. Lucy had to admit that she found Malachi as fascinating as he seemed to find her.

The night passed quickly, and soon Lucy saw the pink hue of the sun rising over the mountains.

"That is my cue," Lucy smiled wearily. "Bed time."

"Yes, mine too," Malachi said. They stood and moved toward the door side by side.

"Do you leave here during the day?" Lucy asked impulsively and then immediately chastised herself. It might be too soon to pry.

Malachi, however, didn't seem offended at all. In fact, he seemed touched that Lucy cared where he was. "I do, but you are in safe hands. I won't let the others get to you."

"What others?" Lucy was baffled. How many people were in this castle, anyway?

"You know, the ones from your other life. They have become resentful of you and hateful."

"Stasia? Gavin?" Lucy shook her head. "I don't think so."

"Oh, but they have," Malachi said sadly. "I have to protect you from them."

"Thank you," Lucy replied, "but if I would be able to talk to them, maybe...."

Malachi shook his head. "No, that would not be wise." His eyes narrowed at her and she knew she had pushed it too far. "Neither one of us will have anything to do with any of them anymore."

Lucy smiled and nodded. "I am starting to realize that you know best." She swallowed. "I hope you have a good day and I will see you tonight." She smiled her very best smile at him. To her surprise, Malachi reached out and tucked a tendril of her hair behind her ear. Lucy forced every muscle not to move or flinch and to keep the same brilliant smile on her face.

"Oh Lucy," he said softly, "you have no idea how special

you are."

Lucy could think of nothing to say so she kept smiling as he motioned for her to leave the room. She pulled the door closed and found Ben waiting for her on the other side. They started walking toward the stairs and Lucy glanced back to see an orange glow emanating from under the door. Malachi had started a fire.

Lucy was exhausted as the girls prepared her for bed. She was pleased though. She had made good progress tonight. Malachi was starting to trust her more and seemed to think that she was something special. He had kept his word too. Nathaniel was still alive and well in the castle, and if he was alive, the others were too. Lucy knew this beyond a shadow of a doubt. She knew that Nathaniel was alive because the dining room had been filled with compact amazon lilies. Those were the first flowers that Nathaniel had ever made for her after they met and Lucy knew he had made these as well. There is no way Malachi would be able to ship this many in to such a remote location and he certainly couldn't create them himself. He must have had Nathaniel make them all. With a rose in her hand and a look of peace on her face, Lucy fell into a deep sleep and wished she could dream of her love.

Chapter Twenty-One
Nature

"Maybe there is a beast... maybe it's only us."
~ *William Golding,* Lord of the Flies

The next few weeks passed exactly the same. Lucy again set into a kind of routine and rapidly became completely nocturnal. She didn't see anyone but Malachi and started to feel very isolated and lonely. She found herself looking forward to their conversations if only to feed the simple human need for companionship. She read obsessively, and discussed any new things she learned with Malachi. One night though, Malachi seemed out of sorts and did not have the same level of charm he usually maintained. When Lucy asked after his health he snapped at her to inform her that of course he was feeling well. Lucy stopped asking and fell silent. Malachi continued to be moody and when Lucy suggested a game of chess he refused and tossed the set aside. He seemed very much like a pouty child that had not gotten his way.

"Is there anything I can do to cheer you up?" Lucy finally asked, hoping he would say no and she might be able to excuse herself.

He was standing by the fire staring into the flames. He turned and trained his eyes on her. They narrowed sharply and darkened. Lucy's blood quickened. "Yes, yes there is," he seethed through clenched teeth. "You may tell me the fable of 'The Frog and The Scorpion.'" Lucy did know the story and, hoping that the tale might be her ticket out for the night, she relayed it word for word.

"One day, a scorpion looked around at the mountain where he lived and decided that he wanted a change. So he set out on a journey through the forests and hills. He climbed over rocks and under vines and kept going until he reached a river.

The river was wide and swift, and the scorpion stopped to reconsider the situation. He couldn't see any way across. So he ran upriver and then checked downriver, all the while thinking that he might have to turn back.

"Suddenly, he saw a frog sitting in the rushes by the bank of the stream on the other side of the river. He decided to ask the frog for help getting across the stream.

'Hellooo Mr. Frog!' called the scorpion across the water, 'Would you be so kind as to give me a ride on your back across the river?'

'"Well now, Mr. Scorpion! How do I know that if I try to help you, you won't try to kill me?' asked the frog hesitantly.

'"Because,' the scorpion replied, 'If I try to kill you, then I would die too, for you see, I cannot swim!'

"Now this seemed to make sense to the frog. But he asked. 'What about when I get close to the bank? You could still try to kill me and get back to the shore!'

'"This is true,' agreed the scorpion, 'But then I wouldn't be able to get to the other side of the river!'

'"All right then...how do I know you won't just wait till we get to the other side and *then* kill me?' said the frog.

"'Ahh...,' crooned the scorpion, 'Because you see, once you've taken me to the other side of this river, I will be so grateful for your help, that it would hardly be fair to reward you with death, now would it?!'

"So the frog agreed to take the scorpion across the river. He swam over to the bank and settled himself near the mud to pick up his passenger. The scorpion crawled onto the frog's back, his sharp claws prickling into the frog's soft hide, and the frog slid into the river. The muddy water swirled around them, but the frog stayed near the surface so the scorpion would not drown. He kicked strongly through the first half of the stream, his flippers paddling wildly against the current.

"Halfway across the river, the frog suddenly felt a sharp sting in his back and, out of the corner of his eye, saw the scorpion remove his stinger from the frog's back. A deadening numbness began to creep into his limbs.

"'You fool!' croaked the frog, 'Now we shall both die! Why on earth did you do that?'"

"The scorpion shrugged, and did a little jig on the drowning frog's back.

"'I could not help myself. It is my nature.'

"Then they both sank into the muddy waters of the swiftly flowing river."

"Very good, Lucy," Malachi said sharply. "So I'm sure you will understand now."

"Understand what?" Terror gripped her. Malachi lunged, grabbed her throat and punched her in the face. Lucy felt his fist slam into her cheek and was sure her eye would pop out of the socket with the force of it. The blow was so strong that the chair

Lucy was sitting in toppled over, throwing her to the carpet. She scrambled on her hands and knees to get away as blood ran down her face and dripped off her chin to splatter on her hands. Lucy screamed when he grabbed her ankle to pull her back toward him. She kicked at Malachi as he pulled her under him and punched her again and again and again. Lucy's eye swelled shut immediately and she felt the skin around her jaw tighten as it, too, swelled. She screamed again as he grabbed for her chin and pulled it close to his.

"I could not help myself. It is my nature," he hissed into her face before standing and vanishing, leaving Lucy to curl up in a ball on the floor.

Deep in the bowels of the mountain, Nathaniel stopped digging. "Did you hear that?"

"Was it the sound of shovel hitting rock?" Roman countered dryly, "Because that is all I hear."

"Lucy just screamed." He looked at the guard, calculating.

"Don't even think about it," the guard snapped as he held his bat high.

"At least send a guard for her!" Nathaniel pleaded, "She's hurt. She's in danger."

"We are all in danger, pal," the guard countered, "or haven't you figured that out?

Nathaniel looked down the tunnel, up, down and saw only rock and darkness. There was nothing alive, nothing he could use to his advantage. He was helpless. Frustration and rage overtook him and Nathaniel could not contain it any longer. His arms fell back, his fists clenched, he opened his mouth and roared to where the sky should be. He screamed until he had no breath left, then collapsed forward, spent.

"Feel better?" The guard sounded bored. Nathaniel didn't respond but looked slowly at the guard, his eyes narrowed.

"Do you miss your Grannie, son?" he asked and the guard suddenly began to pay attention. "Do you? That lovely lady with the silver hair that pushed you on the swing? What did you call her?" Nathaniel stood up, stepped closer to the guard and lowered his voice as he stared deeply at the man. "It was an odd name, wasn't it?"

"Maimey," the guard whispered. His eyes were wide with shock.

"That's right," Nathaniel cooed, "Maimey, of course. She's in Heaven, you know. She is, because I played crib with her there. She beat me solid. Fine card player, your Maimey, isn't she?"

"Yeah," the guard whispered as he shoved a tear from his eye with his shoulder. "Yeah, she was."

"Go find Lucy some help, okay? Get Gavin to help her." Nathaniel whispered, "And make Maimey proud."

The guard nodded and sprinted up the tunnel presumably to alert another guard.

They were silent, waiting for him to go.

Then Roman spoke. "You knew his Grandma?"

"Of course not," Nathaniel replied while picking his shovel back up, "but everyone has one and chances are she's dead and chances are she can play crib."

There was a pause before Roman spoke. "That was some serious manipulation there Angel. I'm impressed." Roman showed no sign of his usual sarcasm. "Lucy's going to be fine. She's tough, Angel."

"I'm counting on it."

Lucy coughed up more blood onto the carpet. Two of her back teeth were loose and although her jaw felt like it was broken, it had good movement so she was hopeful. She needed to get out of the room before Malachi came back, but she had no strength left at all. She lay back down on the carpet and started to sob, leaving globs of bloody drool in a puddle below her head. The door to the den opened, and Lucy, assuming it was Malachi, began to shuffle away from the door whimpering. A set of hands grabbed at her and she began to writhe to get them off of her.

"I've got you Red," came Gavin's voice. It cut through her fear and Lucy sobbed with relief. "I've got you."

He lifted her easily and carried her back up to her room, escorted by Ben. He laid her down on the bed and began ordering for things from the dead girls: ice, bandages, towels. With as much gentleness as he could muster, Gavin began cleaning her up.

"Did a guard do this?" he demanded of Ben as he wiped away layer after layer of blood, revealing the mottled, swollen mess of Lucy's face.

"No, it was *him*," Ben explained, "he just went at her by the sounds of it."

"And you just thought you would sit outside and let him beat her senseless?" Gavin's voice was quivering with rage. "We had an agreement."

"Whaaa?" Lucy tried to speak but her face was so swollen she couldn't. Gavin understood what she was asking though.

"I have promised good Ben here a great deal of money if he keeps you safe while you are here."

"You said alive," Ben countered sharply. "She looks alive to me."

Gavin leapt at him and grabbed the front of Ben's tunic as he pulled him over to Lucy. "Does she look okay to you?" Gavin raged at the guard. "You stupid, thoughtless, mindless oaf of a human! Does she look alive? I ought to kill you myself." He threw the guard on the ground but Ben popped back up to standing right away and straightened his tunic.

"I'm sorry, pal, but we all take a few licks around here now and then. He's not going to kill her."

"How do you know that?" Gavin countered.

"Because he told me to keep her alive no matter what happens!" Ben hollered at Gavin. "So you all want the same thing."

Gavin sighed and sat back down beside the bed to continue his attention to Lucy's face. Ben stepped back into the shadows.

"Well," Gavin smiled at her, "you could still win Miss America."

"I out it," Lucy mumbled.

"Don't doubt it," he grinned, "you are still terribly beautiful."

"A uooo okay?" she garbled.

"You sound like Rocky." Gavin grinned and Lucy laughed a little but winced when it hurt. "I'm fine, Stasia's fine, the guys are fine. Just digging that's all."

"ood," Lucy murmured. "I iss ooo."

"Oh God, Lucy, we miss you too." He leaned forward and brushed her hair out of her face. "I miss you." She tried to smile but couldn't move her facial muscles. Gavin's eyes hardened again and he glared at Ben. "Is he going to do this again?"

"Are you kidding me, man?" Ben challenged, "How the Hell should I know? This whole 'personal security' gig is getting way too heavy for me. It appears though that a resignation isn't an option. It actually appears that options aren't an option."

Gavin sighed. "Lucy, I have no idea what to do. I would be more than happy to go and try to rip that guy's head off, but I have to admit that I don't know if it would do any good."

"I'm onna et us out of ere," Lucy mumbled. "I ave a plan."

"Oh good," Gavin drawled, "because one of Lucy's plans often include her getting killed."

"It ill be otay." She tried to smile again and managed a weak sneer. Her eyelids began to sink and Gavin smiled at her.

"You are so tough Red," he touched her curls lightly, "sleep now, I will stay as long as I can."

When Lucy awoke, it was pitch black and she could vaguely sense that another person was in the room with her. Finally the figure stepped in front of the window and the moon cast light upon them. It was Malachi. She forced herself to sitting position and tried to shuffle away from him to the other side of the bed while making a moaning sound. Her face felt tight and achy, but it had stopped bleeding. She felt more movement in her jaw and could see partially out of her swollen eye. This was the side she turned to him and raised a hand in caution.

"Lucy please, please hear me when I tell you I hate that I hurt you." He sounded distraught.

He moved closer to the bed. "Stay away from me," Lucy warned in her garbled voice. This was a completely empty threat. She had no idea how she would stop him.

He lit a candle beside the bed and when he saw her bashed up cheek he fell to his knees, horrified. "What have I done?" Malachi said into his hands and it sounded to Lucy like he was weeping. She stayed silent. "Lucy," he pleaded while looking up at her, "I can't heal you, I can't make it better, I can't take it away, but please believe me when I say that I wish I could."

"Why?" she pleaded. "Why would you do such a thing?"

"I can't explain, Lucy." He reached across the thick comforter for her hand and slowly she gave it. "I can't explain why I do some of the things I do. Please know that you are the only human that I have ever cared for, at all." He choked on his words. "I cannot help my actions sometimes. Please be patient with me, I am trying." He never said sorry or asked for forgiveness; she didn't think she could forgive him anyway. "Can we go back to the way we were and forget this ever happened?"

"Don't ever hurt me again," she said, another empty threat. There was nothing she could do about it if he wanted to beat her to death. Defeat sank into her bones.

"Never," he agreed quickly and Lucy nodded. He rose. "I will let you sleep and heal and will see you in a few days." Lucy nodded again and watched him carefully as he left the room, head hung in embarrassment. Lucy laid still for a while, making sure he was gone. When it was all quiet, she sat up in bed. She was jittery and unable to rest. Tension creaked through her muscles as she forced herself to stand and stretch to get her muscles moving. She moved about the room in an awkward shuffle, trying to pace until a sharp cracking sound at the window startled her. Lucy padded over to the huge pane of colored glass that was now splintered with thick lines.

"Stress fracture," she whispered to no one. The window had shifted in its frame, causing the glass to crack; glass that had been in place for over five hundred years. The castle was sinking. Lucy looked over at her closed door and whispered, "How far are you digging? And why?"

Chapter Twenty-Two
Hell Hath No Fury

"Go to Heaven for the climate, Hell for the company."
~ Mark Twain

Days passed and Lucy was left to recover on her own. The girls attended to her every need and she spent hours sitting by the huge windows reading. Springtime had arrived in the mountains and Lucy could see green poking through the cracks in the stone. Ben, possibly feeling guilty for his lack of supervision, gave regular reports from the rest of the castle. Stasia and Gavin were fine, as were Roman and Nathaniel. Everyone was being fed regularly but the digging had increased and Malachi had begun using the guards for extra digging shifts. Finally, when Lucy's face showed only spots of greenish bruising, she was summoned for dinner. The girls loaded on the makeup to make her look normal and she dressed in a comfortable but flattering emerald green silk wrap dress. Lucy bit down on her anger and fear as she finished dressing and descended the stairs to the main hall.

Malachi greeted her in the dining hall as if nothing had

happened – making a point to compliment her on her appearance more than once. After dinner, they again retired to the den where Malachi pulled out the chess board and gave his opening move. They played in silence for a while.

"May I ask you a question?" Lucy tried to slow her breathing. She was terrified to even be near him.

"Of course, Lucy, anything," he replied pleasantly.

"How old are you?"

"Twenty one," he said quickly.

"Really," she pushed, "how old?"

He let go of the bishop he was holding and regarded her. "I am about two thousand years old."

"And what was your best day?"

Malachi was taken aback; he leaned back in his chair as if smacked in the face. "No one has ever asked me that question before, never, in all my years."

"So what is the answer?" Lucy prodded.

He thought for a moment. "I have two," he announced. "The first was in May of 1213. The world was so different back then, so quiet. These days there is always a constant hum about the world. There is no way to escape the noise of the world humans have built. But back then, Lucy," he said wistfully, "it was terribly quiet. I took an entire day and sat beside a river and read a book. Just me and my horse, and the light trickle of the water. It was so warm that day that I ended up taking a swim. It was the most delightful day I have ever had." He looked off out the window and smiled at the memory.

"And the second?" Lucy prompted.

"Ah," he snapped out of his reverie and picked the bishop back up, "the second is yet to come."

"That's cheating!" Lucy challenged good-naturedly, "You can't predict the future."

"Oh yes, Lucy, I can," he leaned forward, "and I promise you that my very best day will come and soon. Check."

Lucy looked down at the board to see that indeed her king was in check. She moved him and they continued the game. Lucy played well and did not give Malachi one bit of leeway in her game. The match stretched on far longer than usual. Lucy did not mention when she saw the rose glow of the sun coming up over the mountains as she normally would have. This could be her chance. She waited for Malachi to notice and it wasn't until the sun hit him directly in the eyes that he realized how late they were.

"Oh!" he exclaimed, "Out, Lucy! I am late and must go. Run out now."

Lucy followed his instructions and rushed to the door and even flashed him a bright smile before slipping sway. To Lucy's relief, Ben was fast asleep in the chair in the hall. She wouldn't have to convince him to go along with her newly forming plan. Lucy snuck the door open the smallest crack to see Malachi point at the hearth and a fire ignite within it. He then stepped hastily into the fire and vanished.

"He is going to Hell!" Lucy whispered to herself. She dashed back into the room and stood in front of the fire. Malachi had a great deal of power, but Lucy knew that when he was in human form, he was subject to the same injuries that a human would suffer. Stepping into a fire should have killed him, unless of course this fire was some sort of portal. Lucy shook her head at her own foolishness but could not stop herself from sticking her foot into the hearth and let the flames lick at her toes. She winced, prepared to be burned to a crisp, but instead her leg felt quite cool. She stepped further and further in until one foot rested inside the flaming fireplace and one on the outside. Mustering as much determination and bravery as she could, Lucy lifted her other foot, shifted her weight and was soon standing fully in the massive hearth.

The floor vanished beneath her and for a moment she felt like she was falling. She pinwheeled her arms in an effort to stay in an upright position, but seconds later still landed flat on her back on a soft surface. Lucy pulled herself up immediately, but she was completely alone in some sort of sitting room. She had landed on the carpet in front of the fireplace. Did she just move to another part of the castle? To a different castle? The room was windowless and made of stone but was completely lavish with plush red and golden chairs, and tables carved out of gold and set with thousands of glittering gems.

This place reminded her of the bar that Roman took her and Nathaniel to during their visit to Hell in the winter. She thought back to that day and she remembered that Roman had explained that the man who was chasing them that day – the man they knew now was Malachi – had much nicer places to go. This must be what he meant. Lucy's lips tightened in fear; Demons would be close. She had to get out of there and fast.

A gold inlaid mirror on the opposite wall reflected her image but something about the likeness seemed off. Looking closer, Lucy realized that it wasn't her refection at all; the image in the mirror was wearing a blood red off the shoulder corseted dress, not the green wrap she wore now. She spun around to see that above the fireplace was a monarch sized portrait of herself staring back at her. In the painting, she sat peacefully and regally gazing at the painter without a care in the world. Lucy swallowed the bile rising in her throat. "What is this place?" she whispered.

Lucy scanned the room for an exit. She had to get into the streets right away where she would not be noticed. Obviously, from the portrait, she would be recognized if anyone found her in this room and it was vital she find out what Malachi was up to. Hidden in the corner and covered with the same gold paneling was a tiny door knob. Saying a silent prayer, she crossed the room and turned the knob. Relief washed through her as the stench and overwhelming heat of Hell crept through the crack in the door. She crept out into the darkness and found herself on top of a hill. This felt strange to Lucy considering she had wandered Hell for days a few months ago and had seen no such thing. The entirety of Hell was a flat never-ending repetitive landscape stretched out before her as far as her eyes could see. The slate black roads and oppressively leaning buildings were visible through the yellow haze of toxic air.

She turned to see that she had just emerged from an equally oppressive building.

It was a house, really, but massive in structure and black as night. Huge turrets raised into the sky, disappearing in the smog. It was windowless and apparently door-less, but Lucy made a point to memorize where she had exited, for with any luck she would be able to get back in. She looked about and did not see Malachi or anyone for that matter. She decided to head towards the streets in the hope of possibly finding Random who might help her find out what Malachi was up to.

Lucy took several steps towards the streets and a recognizable fear gripped her insides. Sweat sprung to her forehead and she whimpered in terror at an unseen assailant. Her memory kicked in and she recalled that the last time Roman had told her to control the fear, as it was a by-product of Hell. Lucy slowed her breathing and forced herself to calm down. This is temporary…this shall pass, she thought to herself and she urged her body toward the streets, and the citizens, of Hell.

Immediately upon entering the city streets, Lucy saw the souls of Hell, rambling and shuffling in the same mindless pace that she knew well, their clothing hanging off their frames. However, after several steps, Lucy knew something was different. Something was wrong. The last time she had come, the people of Hell had paid no attention to her or Nathaniel. They had paid no attention to each other. Now though, they were noticing her, responding to her movements. The scuffling bodies turned toward her and although they walked right past, they walked past while staring at her. Lucy cautiously moved forward and scanned the growing crowd for Malachi or anyone that looked like a Demon. At this point, she might be able to convince the Demons that she had stumbled into Hell by accident. Hopefully they wouldn't kill her.

She walked farther, becoming more and more convinced that this was a terrible idea. How could she think that she would be able to find anyone in this mess? Meanwhile, her presence was garnering more attention, far more. People had begun to follow her. When she looked back there was a crowd of over a hundred stumbling after her, bumping into each other and staring wide eyed at Lucy. This was not the clandestine observation mission she had been hoping for. Finally, she decided to turn around and head back to what she could only assume was Malachi's house and leave. This had been a bad idea and Lucy needed to be rid of the whole scenario. She made a wide turn in the street, not wanting to try to navigate through the mob, and headed back in the direction she came.

It felt like forever before Lucy finally spotted the house looming above her. She quickened her pace and began to climb the hill but the mob followed and began closing in on her. Lucy began running up the steep stone road to the house, praying that she could make it before anything happened. The mob came closer, nearing with every step, they moved in front of her, trapping her in a circle of bodies. She had no idea what to do. She would have to call out for help. Malachi must be here somewhere, she would have to scream for his help and hope that he heard her.

She would think of some story to tell him later, right now, she was surrounded and terrified. Suddenly, an arm reached out of the crowd and grabbed her wrist. Twisting, Lucy flung her hand hard to try to dislodge the grip of the unseen assailant, but the grip held fast. Lucy saw it was a woman's hand with painted nails and tanned skin. She pulled back again, yanking her arm until the woman finally emerged from the mob and pulled away her black hood. It was Octavia.

"What are you doing here?" Octavia hissed, her blue eyes blazing. Lucy was too petrified to respond, and let Octavia pull her through the mob, that parted like a wave in front of them. They headed toward the house and in through the same door Lucy had left. Once they were back in the lavish sitting room, Octavia flung Lucy into one of the chairs. She tossed off the heavy black cloak she had been wearing to reveal a bright red leather corset and pantsuit. It could not look more like a Demon costume, but somehow it made total sense. All it was missing was a little tail. Octavia stalked over to the drink cart in the corner and poured herself a tumbler of amber liquid. She downed it in one gulp and poured another. She grabbed a second glass and did the same before carrying it over and holding out to Lucy.

"No thank you," Lucy shook her head; she wanted to keep her wits about her.

"Drink it now or I will rip out your larynx." The Demon sneered and pushed the glass toward her again. Lucy took the glass and drained it before handing it back to Octavia. The liquor burned down her throat and settled into a ball of fire in her stomach.

Octavia filled Lucy's glass again, handed it back to her and flopped into the closest chair and eyed the human. She seemed to be making a decision. Lucy tried to look innocent and meek. "You will need the drink to handle what I am about to tell you," Octavia said while crossing her long legs.

"I need to get out of here," Lucy said carefully. "If he catches me here…" she trailed off. She didn't know which Demon she was more afraid of right now.

"He won't be back for hours and it isn't safe to talk at the castle. Here is safe," Octavia explained. She took a sip of her drink. "I will get you back in time. He will never know you were here. Well, he might, but I hope by then it will be too late."

"What's going on?" Lucy asked as she eyed the painting over the mantle. It was unsettling to see her own image like that.

"That?" Octavia motioned to the painting. "That is the least of our worries, sweetheart."

"Then what is the most of my worries?" Lucy asked and took another sip of her drink. She had no idea what it was but it was actually making her feel much better.

Octavia stood and paced over to the mantle. "How much do you know about how the world works?"

"I know that the world is run on a specific balance between right and wrong. I know that humans have free will that allows them to determine their own fate. I know that Demons and Angels can only make a human look at an opportunity for good or evil but it is up to the human to make their own decision. I know that Demons walk the Earth in specific predetermined areas but Angels work from Heaven. I know that the Guilds made this agreement before the beginning of time and no one has ever violated it."

"Very good," Octavia nodded, sounding like a tutor. "Do you know who Malachi is?"

"As a human, he goes by Alexander but he is actually Malachi, a very old and powerful Demon. He was never human and didn't come from the Hall of Souls."

"He's the Antichrist, Lucy. The son of the Devil. Created from the fires of Hell in preparation for the coming of Jesus Christ. He is, by far, the most dangerous creature that has ever walked the Earth."

"He can't be," Lucy countered, "Roman would have told us back on the dock."

"Roman doesn't know," Octavia replied sharply. "Most Demon's don't know who Malachi really is. That is part of his power. Some even think that the antichrist is a myth of sorts." Octavia was quiet for a moment as she let this information sink in. Lucy just breathed. "Now, do you know why the most powerful Demon in the realm of the living or the dead has kidnapped three humans, an Angel and a Demon to hold them captive in a castle in Bulgaria for months and makes them dig a hole into the mountain?"

"No." Lucy tensed, in preparation of saying her least favorite words. "I don't know."

Octavia nodded. "I am about to tell you something that no one on Earth, in Heaven or in Hell know except for me and a small handful of conscientious other Demons. I tell you these things only because you are the only one who can stop it. You need to understand…" she stopped as the door suddenly opened and a waft of the hateful stench of Hell sailed in. Lucy tensed and Octavia stood sharply. But someone else equally as unexpected came through the door and ripped a cloak off her small frail form.

"Are you out of your mind bringing her here?" Mrs. Turner demanded of Octavia. "Those zombies out there are all but clawing at the walls. They know she's here." Lucy normally saw Mrs. Turner looking tired in a simple powder blue suit. No such person stood before her, for Mrs. Turner still looked older but was in a stunning, well-fitted beige suit with a bright blue scarf cascading over her neck. Her face looked lighter and less worn and her hair had a bright glow to it.

"She snuck in on her own," Octavia replied while sitting back down and motioning to the bar.

"Figures," Turner replied as she crossed the room quickly and poured herself a drink. She lit a cigarette and sat ladylike on one of chaise lounges. "What does she know?"

"Nothing," Lucy replied, "and if there was something that I should have known, maybe back in December, you could have given me a heads up."

"I didn't know any details back then. I was only following orders. I felt like things were strange since your mother's wedding day." She sipped her drink.

"Her wedding day?" Lucy challenged, "I thought you were just protesting Nathaniel's presence."

"That was annoying, yes, but I knew that Malachi was about, I could sense his presence and later I saw him." She looked at Octavia. "He was prancing about as a cat with blue eyes, don't you know." Octavia rolled her eyes as if this was expected.

Lucy thought back to that day and the blue-eyed black cat that had been clinging to the window sill while she and Anastasia were getting ready.

"That was Malachi?" she queried. "So when you said you didn't like what we were up to…"

"I thought that you had made some stupid agreement with Malachi, not smart at all. Turns out none of you knew even he was there, not even your Angel."

"No," Lucy replied, "what was he doing there?"

"Falling in love with you," Octavia cut in.

"What?" Lucy challenged. "What are you talking about?"

Octavia drained her glass and indicated Lucy should do the same. She followed orders and gulped her drink; it helped chase away the coldness that was settling in.

"The plan was originally to just kill Anastasia to torture Roman. Malachi came out of the depths after his death at Roman's hands in 1910 and in true Demon fashion, went after the poor soul that put him there. Roman, being the unlucky sap that he is, not only was executed for a death that was totally deserved, he was condemned to Hell for the death of the Antichrist. Malachi wanted nothing more than revenge. He quickly found out that Roman was dating this human dancer and a simple accidental death was planned."

"Why accidental?" Lucy asked, "Why didn't he just show up and kill her?"

"Because we technically aren't allowed to do that, although many Demons ignore the rules now and then," Turner picked up the tale as she got up to refresh her drink, "We must always respect the codes of the Guilds, and Malachi was breaking the rules by trying to kill whatsherface."

"Anastasia," Lucy cut in.

"Inconsequential," Turner waved her away with her smoking hand. "Anyway – he had to give the humans around her the choice to behave in such a way as to cause her untimely death." Lucy already knew that but it appeared that her theories on Malachi barely scratched the surface. "The Angel and the Demon," Turner continued, "and even you protected her so fiercely that trying to kill her accidentally became impossible. He began to watch the four of you and even that handsome unlucky boy Gavin, and quickly realized how important you in particular were to the dynamics of the group. Still, he could not talk to you or engage Roman or the

Angel for that matter, because it would violate the agreements between the Guilds. It infuriated Malachi that he could not violate the Guild codes and he began to question the codes themselves."

"He pushed the envelope even further by turning himself into the fictitious Wrath to come and kill you all, but still that did not work," Octavia continued, "Thwarted, he retreated back to Hell to think of a new plan. What he came up with was terrifying even to us." Octavia looked at Turner, who finished the thought for her.

"He has decided to plan a coup to take over Hell and then Earth itself."

Lucy scoffed, "Surely he can't think that he would get away with that. He won't be able to."

"What do you think he is doing?" Turner shouted at her. "Do you think Octavia and I are skulking around here for fun? We and a small group of sensible Demons are trying to stop him!"

"Wait," Lucy shook her head, "What about the Devil? Why isn't he doing anything?"

"Lucifer doesn't know anything, or else he would have stopped it. He is no fool and would not allow even his own son to disturb the balance between good and evil on Earth." Octavia explained.

"Then why don't you just tell him?"

"You don't book appointments with Lucifer you idiot, it's not a union." Octavia snapped. "Our only option is to stop him. Malachi has been confiding in small groups of us and spreading his ideas. He thinks we can allow Hell to rise up and take over Earth, annihilate the Angels and have all of Earth to himself to rule as he sees fit, basically taking over his 'fathers' power. He wants to remove free will from a human's abilities; any that don't fall in line will be killed and replaced."

"Replaced with whom?" Lucy whispered.

"With the citizens of Hell," Turner said quietly, "those mindless, zombie, creatures wandering aimlessly outside these walls will explode up to ground level and their evil will spread like an epidemic. It will be the end of mankind as we know it."

"But then he will have no live humans to control," Lucy prompted.

"He is going to create new humans."

"How?"

Octavia didn't answer, but looked up at the huge painting of Lucy over the fireplace. Revolt seared through Lucy as the truth stabbed her heart.

"He thinks you are the perfect human," Turner explained with a hint of softness to her voice. "That you are the new mother, the next Eve. The masses will follow you as their leader – they already know your face out there. He has been showing them your image." Lucy thought of the citizens following her mindlessly and shuddered. "He is going to make you immortal, and make you the face and the mind of the new humanity. You will be his partner, his wife, his lover. You and Malachi will repopulate the planet with his demon spawn."

There was silence from the Demons as Lucy vomited into the ice bucket beside her. Neither of them moved to help her, either because they couldn't or because they didn't want to. Within a few moments, Lucy's retching subsided, she wiped her face, calmed her breathing and sat back up.

"He is going to start calling you Lilith soon," Octavia continued as if nothing had happened.

Lucy's brain engaged automatically. "Lilith – the first female Demon, believed to be made from the same earth as Adam. It is an ancient name, a name of power."

"Yes," Turner said.

The door opened again and once more the women tensed. It was not Malachi who entered but a Demon that Lucy had never seen before. He was the largest man Lucy had ever seen. He had to have been at least seven feet tall with dark ebony skin and sharp features. He was striking, but the signature gemstone blue demon eyes made him even more so. He tossed off his cloak and, seeing Lucy, immediately rushed to her and kneeled at her feet.

"My beautiful and powerful Queen," he said, his voice as thick as molasses, "I did not know you were coming so soon. Let me introduce myself as your most humble servant and follower of the Antichrist."

"Abraxas," Octavia cut in drolly, "stop sucking up. The human knows everything and is on board."

Abraxas' face turned to stone as he stood and turned his back on Lucy. Apparently, there was no need to suck up any more.

"Why don't we just kill her?" he questioned the other two as if Lucy wasn't there. He too went to the sideboard to pour himself a drink. "Then Malachi will have to start his search again. Might buy us some time."

"We thought of that," Octavia answered. "Random seems to think she is key to the whole thing falling apart. He says she has to stay alive."

Abraxas rolled his eyes and regarded Lucy from the other side of the room.

"I don't see what's so special about her and I don't think we should believe Random about anything."

"If your plan fails and Malachi's plan works, I will make sure you are the first to suffer his wrath if you lay one finger on me," Lucy hissed at him.

Abraxas' eyebrows shot up. "Oh," he said, not without admiration, "I see now." He raised his glass to her in salute.

"Impressive."

Lucy nodded at him and turned to Octavia. "Why did Malachi try to kill me if he fell in love with me at the wedding?"

"Well, he fell in love with the idea of you. You intrigued him." Octavia corrected, "And he didn't try to kill you, he tried to kill the Angel and Roman. You, he wanted to keep. He thought if he forced Anastasia to come with him by threatening her parents, that Roman and the Angel would bring you with them and he could simply take all of you prisoner. No such thing happened, they left you on the dock. He had to force them to follow Anastasia, enter the castle of their own free will, so you would come looking for them. He already had Gavin in his back pocket as a contingency plan and he simply put that plan into effect and let you come to him. He needed you to come of your own free will."

"If he isn't following any other rules, or is going to break them all within the next little while, why was he so picky about us arriving at the castle of our own free will?" Lucy challenged, her mind working out all the details, trying to find holes, to prove that this must all be a lie.

"Because outside the castle," Abraxas replied as he pointed to the ceiling, "*they* can see you and would have intervened. As long as you went to the castle of your own free will, there is nothing the Angel Guild could do."

"They can't see us in the castle?"

In reply, Abraxas only shrugged, seemingly tired of this topic. "Malachi has put something over it. A shield, for lack of a better word. It is powers beyond even our comprehension."

"He's gone to a lot of trouble." Lucy murmured, almost to herself.

"He did it in the hopes that you were as remarkable as he suspected. After spending time with you, was elated to discover that you were far more special than he originally had anticipated." Turner waved at her like she was a fly. "Apparently, you are not only a genius, but philosophical, metaphysical, strategic and beautiful. You are simply perfect for his plan."

"Which is what exactly?" Lucy started, but then the pieces came together. "The tunnel," she whispered.

"The tunnel is not an entrance," Abraxas prompted.

"It's an exit." Lucy's voice shook.

"He will literally release the horrors of Hell upon the Earth and there is nothing we can do about it."

"There must be," Lucy pleaded. "There must be something that can be done."

"We have to make sure that the masses do not get through the tunnel when he opens it. All the Demons out and working together is bad enough, but we think we have enough men on the inside who can shut down the tunnel when the time is right."

"Okay, and?" Lucy prompted.

"You need to kill Malachi," Turner said shortly.

"You say that like I have to pick up milk at the store."

"It's that simple, if you can send him back to the depths for another century, that will solve everything. The uprising will stop in its tracks."

"No," Lucy shook her head, "I can't."

"You can and you will," Octavia pressed. "It's the only way!"

"If I murder then I go to Hell, right?"

"It would be worth it!" Abraxas shouted. "You are the only one he trusts completely. You are the only one who can do it. You might go to Hell but you will save humanity!"

"But then Malachi will only go to the depths for a century or so, right? Then he will come back and try to take over again!" Lucy countered.

Abraxas rolled his eyes. "I am tiring of your logical mind, woman. What do you care what happens in a hundred years? You won't be alive."

"But my children's children will be! I am not leaving a legacy like that behind! Plus, Roman will be alive too. Malachi will just go after him again."

"Roman killed your father!" Octavia exploded. "You can't possibly care if he lives or dies."

"Roman was doing what he had to. He didn't know that he was my father or that he would become my friend in the end," Lucy defended. "He doesn't deserve to be punished." They all stared at her like she was insane. "I used to want to kill Roman for what he did, I admit that, but I have come to realize that my anger doesn't hurt him. It only injures me." Octavia shook her head and Abraxas mumbled curse words under his breath. "I won't kill Malachi. I am no murderer."

Turner sighed as though she knew this would happen and was disgusted. "If you won't kill him, you have to find someone who will and not go to Hell for it. We will deal with him in a hundred years and stop him again if we have to." She shot Octavia a meaningful look. "We will help protect Roman when the time comes." Octavia rolled her eyes.

"An Angel could kill Malachi and not go to Hell. Nathaniel?" Lucy asked warily.

"No," Octavia sighed, "he is too weak. You have to get the other Angels on board."

"Where are they?" Lucy asked, "I can't believe that Heaven knows all this is going on and is doing nothing about it."

"Heaven knows you are all inside the castle, but because you all went in of your own free will, they have no recourse."

Turner replied, "They know nothing of the plan, of course, but certainly suspect foul play. They are bound by Guild laws and being Angels, certainly won't break them. You all entered the castle by choice, a forced choice, but a choice none the less. They will only know the truth if someone gets out."

"Where are they?"

"Swarming the castle."

"What?" Lucy was dumbfounded.

"They cannot see through the protective shields that Malachi has surrounded the castle with but they are there and waiting and watching and…" Octavia faded off.

"Praying," Turner finished.

"So how can I get to them?"

"There are some weak spots on the roof that have been developing, more every day as he diverts his power to the revolution. If Malachi is sufficiently distracted, then you might be able to jump off the roof."

"Jump off the roof?" Lucy looked back and forth between them.

"That's the only way you could break out of the shield," Octavia offered. "You have to use your free will and jump."

"But they would have to catch me."

Octavia nodded and shrugged at the same time. Agreeing and yet not really caring what happened to Lucy. Abraxas was right; Lucy's death might solve their problems too. At least that way, she would go to Heaven.

"How long do we have?" she asked.

"Tomorrow at noon," Turner replied, not sounding sure of anything. "It's the Spring Equinox."

"The Spring Equinox. Why?"

"The Earth is always on a bit of a shift at the Equinoxes and the Solstices, and the Guilds tend to use these days for change," Turner replied.

Lucy thought back. On Winter Solstice, Nathaniel and Roman had created the hurricanes that brought Fate, on the Fall Equinox, Roman had returned from his banishment in Hell, on the Summer Solstice, Nathaniel's ties had been cut with Heaven and on the last Spring Equinox, Lucy and Nathaniel had met. It had been almost one celestial year since she had run into him on the sidewalk outside the dorm. It felt like and instant and a lifetime since that day.

Lucy sucked in a deep breath. "Okay, so I need to figure out a way to distract Malachi tonight while you get everyone ready here to fake the invasion but actually close the portal. I have to distract the guards at the castle and get to the roof and attract the attention of the Angels so they can help kill Malachi and stop the Demonic uprising."

"Exactly," Octavia said sharply as she stood up.

"If we just stop the revolution, will he not just give up?" Lucy asked. "Rather than killing him?"

Abraxas threw his hands in the air, "Why don't we all just sit around and sing something. If no one is going to die, I'm out."

Turner raised a hand to him; he dropped his arms and stomped over to the fireplace. "Random seems to think that is possible. He can perceive things that no one else can. He is adamant that you are the key to it all and yet, offers no explanation beyond that. I can't see Malachi giving up on his plan, even if the tunnel is closed. As long as he has the support of the Demon's behind him, he will go ahead, unless he is dead."

"I will think of something." Lucy bit her lip.

"Well, you sound confident," Octavia shot back sarcastically. "Now, we need to get you back and ready for the night with him."

They all stood.

Abraxas moved back to the door and swept his massive hooded cloak back on. "I have to meet with the others to tell them the plan." He eyed Lucy. "When the sun is at its highest, make your move. If not, then I shall call you Queen for all eternity." He nodded to the other two and swept out the door.

Turner approached Lucy, and for a moment held the same sweet face of the lady who had lived on her street for twenty years. "I can tell you, dear," she said quietly, almost so that Octavia could not hear, "that Catherine the Great never showed as much courage as you have in the past few months and indeed the past few moments. I do think that if anyone can pull this off, it will be you."

"Well, thank you," Lucy replied awkwardly.

"But if you screw up," she added in her gravely hateful voice, "it's your own damn fault; you should have just cut his throat the day you met him."

"Again," Lucy replied dryly, "thank you."

Chapter Twenty-Three
Date Night

"I always play women I would date."
~ Angelina Jolie

"Come," Octavia cut in and motioned for Lucy to join her at the fireplace. Lucy moved to her side. "Step through quickly, don't hesitate. I will meet you there."

Lucy did as she was told with a half glance up at the portrait of herself. She prayed she would never be forced to see it again. She emerged in the den of the castle as before to see that the sun was beginning to set. To Lucy it felt like she had been gone maybe an hour, but in fact, it had been twelve. Malachi would be calling Lucy to dinner as soon as it got completely dark. They had very little time to hide the fact that Lucy had been away. Octavia appeared behind her and together they moved quickly to Lucy's rooms. Octavia ordered the girls to work resetting Lucy's hair and finding a new outfit for her.

"He is obsessed with her and will find the smallest detail out of place!" Octavia ordered, "She has to look her very best!"

"Wait!" Lucy grabbed the closest girl's hand as she was about the reapply the makeup that she just took off. Octavia shot her a hateful glare. "Listen," Lucy pleaded to her. "We don't have time. Let me try something." She picked up the blush brush and applied only a light touch to her cheeks and eyelids. She grabbed the mascara and quickly put only one layer on her lashes before applying a soft pink almost nude lip gloss to her lips. She ran some oil briefly through her auburn locks, causing the curls to tighten and splay wildly. Lucy dashed to the closet, selected an outfit and pulled it on before emerging back into the dressing room. "We will eat in my sitting room tonight. Burgers, fries and a movie." She thought for a moment. "The Manchurian Candidate," she said finally. "He will like that one."

She stood before Octavia in a tight white t-shirt, skin tight jeans and bare feet. Her makeup was subdued and clean, her hair wild and untamed.

"I hope you know what you are doing, Lucy," Octavia said with a smirk, "because in my opinion, you look like a dog's breakfast."

Lucy rolled her eyes. "This is how I look every day."

"Then I have no idea how you bagged an Angel."

"Thanks for your support."

"Whatever works! Just keep him busy while we prepare the last of the plans. He is very sensitive to everything that is going on in Hell and here. We will be preparing all of our defenses and we need him fully distracted so he doesn't sense anything." Octavia walked closer to her and looked her in the eye. Octavia's beauty was striking and Lucy doubted her plan for a minute. "Do whatever it takes," Octavia said with meaning. "He is very astute and will be able to sense deception. You must not let him question you for one moment. If he does, all of humanity will fail. You must be willing to go against your moral code if you have to." Lucy nodded but started to falter. What was she thinking?

There was no way she was going to be able to fool Malachi. "Octavia, I don't know if I can do this. He knows me very well. I have never shown any romantic interest in him, he will become suspicious if I suddenly change my tone. He's never going to fall for it."

The Demon threw her hands in the air, "So now I have to be your girlfriend?" she stalked over and gripped Lucy's shoulders tightly, her fingers digging into Lucy's flesh. "I can tell you that Malachi has had many women." She leaned in for emphasis. "Many. But no woman has ever had *him*. You, the bright eyed gal from Kansas with the photographic memory, *have* him. He is insane and has convinced himself that you are in love with him. He will believe almost anything you say he is so besotted with you and this plan he has concocted."

"Really?" Lucy blinked. "You sure?"

"I don't like you enough to lie to you." The Demon whispered. Lucy nodded and smiled, finding comfort in Octavia's bristly demeanor.

With a sharp nod, Octavia started to walk out the door but turned back again. "You know when we were talking about God's function? Of course you remember. I wanted to tell you a story that night." She looked sideways, her full lips pulled into a smirk. "I once saw a boy, maybe ten years old and completely paralyzed. He could feel nothing from his collarbone down. He was on the street in New York, singing at the top of his lungs and his voice was unlike anything I had ever heard, his voice struck me to the core. It was elating and yet startlingly sad. I found myself beginning to weep with emotion." Octavia looked out at the rising moon. "I understood that day. I got it. I looked up at the sky and said, 'Oh, *that's* what you do.'" She looked back at Lucy. "Please remember that if this all goes well. If it doesn't go well, remember that I was the one who helped you."

Leave it to the Demons to hedge their bets on all sides. There was a knock at the door. Lucy and Octavia locked eyes in a panicked second before Octavia darted for the window, opened it and slid out onto the small window sill. Lucy was convinced that she would fall to her death before a huge set of black wings grew out of the Demon's shoulder blades above her corset. She quickly climbed sideways along the windows with the agility of a cat. Just as she disappeared from view, the door opened.

Lucy turned quickly to see Malachi standing in the doorway. He wore a three piece suit of deep blue as he looked her very casual appearance up and down. Lucy sucked in a deep breath and tossed her head confidently.

"I thought we could have a casual night in," she said slowly in an effort to even her breath. She hoped it was coming off sultry rather than riddled with terror. "I like to dress up as much as the next girl, but this is how I look every day." She turned a quarter turn to show off the back of her jeans, and Lucy's best feature. "What do you think?"

Malachi looked her up and down. For a minute, Lucy was convinced that he was going to kill her right there. "I think I am completely overdressed," he said with a grin and the air exploded out of Lucy.

"Give me a moment please," he said and stalked out toward their adjoining room doors. Lucy collapsed on the sofa and forced her breathing to slow. She had to remain calm here or Malachi would suspect something was up. *This is going to suck*, she told herself. *But you have to do it*. Things felt so different now knowing Malachi's intentions and his actual identity. *The Antichrist.* Lucy thought over and over in her head. Panic rose within her. How far would she have to go?

"Is this better?"

Lucy looked up to see Malachi leaning casually against the doorjamb with his arms crossed. He wore a pair of jeans and a tight blue t-shirt. His hair wasn't slicked back like it usually was. Instead, it was loose and messy, giving him more of a boyish look. For the first time, Malachi could have passed for a regular twenty-something guy, a stunningly handsome one, but still a regular guy. Lucy couldn't help but smile.

"Love it," she said approvingly. "Thank you for indulging me."

"You will soon learn, Lucy," Malachi said as he crossed the room and sat next to her on the couch, "that there is very little I would not do for you."

Lucy just smiled coyly as their burgers and fries were delivered. Malachi seemed a little awkward at first, but as Lucy picked hers up and dug in, he smiled and followed suit. He started laughing after the first bite.

"What's so funny?" Lucy asked.

"I have never had a hamburger," he grinned, "and now it is my favorite food."

"Not too shabby, hey?"

They ate in silence for a while. They both finished at the same time and pushed their plates back to have them collected by the girls. Lucy turned and smiled at Malachi. *The Antichrist*, she thought again and shut it from her mind. She had to keep him distracted like Octavia had told her to.

"I have always thought, Lucy, that a woman could only look beautiful while in a striking dress," Malachi said, smiling. "I was wrong. You look stunning this evening."

"Why, thank you." She looked down and pretended to blush.

"Don't get used to it though." His bright blue eyes twinkled.

"Why not?" Lucy replied innocently, "No one sees me."

"Ah, but they will," he grinned at her, like he had a secret. "They will."

"What do you mean?" Lucy asked quietly. Was this the best way to distract him?

Malachi seemed to think for a minute. "Lucy, do you trust me?"

"Yes," she said quietly.

"I know things have not been perfect around here, but I need you to trust me. Please understand that everything is going to change and you and I are going to be at the beginning of something very wonderful. Lilith, it's going to be so splendid, you won't even think of your old life again."

"Lilith?" Lucy said, trying to sound light. Even though she knew this was coming, she had to still her heart from beating out of her chest.

"Yes," he said carefully, "I think we should change your name. I find that it suits you better."

"Really?" Lucy asked. She cocked her head for more of an effect. "I don't think so."

"Yes, don't you see? It's the perfect name for you," he urged while leaning forward and taking her hand. "One more day, Lilith, and you will be the happiest, most powerful human in the world."

"The most powerful human?" Lucy pretended to be thinking. It was like balancing on a sword. She had to sound doubtful and yet trusting. He would become suspicious if she didn't inquire further. "How? I mean, that does sound, well, interesting. But I don't know…." She needed to keep her responses short.

Anything longer and he would sense the deception.

"Don't worry," he patted her hand, "I have taken care of anything."

"But, I'm worried," she twisted her hands together, hoping to seem vulnerable."

He leaned close to her, his blue eyes wide with fervor, "Please trust me. I promised that I would never hurt you again, didn't I?"

"Yes," Lucy replied truthfully, "you did."

"Everything is going to be fine, wonderful in fact." He nodded encouragingly and Lucy smiled.

"Oh good," she breathed and decided to change the subject. "Shall we watch the movie? It's called The Manchurian Candidate, I think you will like it very much."

"Sounds lovely." He smiled at her.

Lucy motioned for the girls to start the movie as she lifted Malachi's arm and snuggled underneath it. To anyone, they looked like a regular college couple settling in to watch a movie on a Saturday night. *Antichrist*, Lucy's mind whispered as the opening credits rolled and she suppressed a shudder. They didn't speak during the film but Lucy glanced up at him several times to see that he was completely engaged. She relaxed and spent the time plotting out her next moves. Like their many chess matches, she had to both predict and counter his moves.

The movie ended and Lucy looked to Malachi for a response.

"Thoughts?" she prompted.

"Fascinating film!" he exclaimed and Lucy smiled. She had thought the brainwashing topic would get the wheels turning in his mind; anything to keep him talking. They discussed the show for quite a while, debating on mind control and its effectiveness in humans. Lucy still had several hours to fill before sunrise and, since she seemed to be driving the train tonight, she called one of the dead girls over and whispered a request in her ear. The girl nodded and left the room.

"What are you up to?" Malachi eyed her with a smirk.

"We are going to play a game that I suspect you have never played, but I think you will love it." Lucy smiled. "We are going to play Risk."

Lucy had played Risk several times with her father, but it was not her favorite game. A game of Risk can be anywhere from three to nine hours and Lucy had little patience for such an investment. It was a mental, time consuming game though, just what Lucy needed. The dead girls returned with the game and started setting it up on the large table. Lucy stood and pulled Malachi with her.

"I must express to you how impressed I am with you, Lilith," Malachi praised. "You have planned an entire night of pastimes to entertain me, and I assure you it is very much appreciated."

Lucy shrugged. "It's fun, don't you think?"

They passed by the huge windowed terrace and the moon shone in brightly. Malachi pulled on Lucy's hand, tugged her towards him and wrapped his arms around her waist. He pulled her closer and Lucy pressed completely against his chest.

"You are my everything, Lilith," he whispered heavily, "I want to be your everything. Could you try to forget everything before today? Could you try to leave him," he motioned with his chin toward the door and Lucy knew he meant Nathaniel, "behind? To move forward with me? I promise you won't regret it." He leaned forward and rested his forehead to hers.

Every single nerve in Lucy's body was screaming in protest

as she whispered, "I can try." She hoped the shaking could be mistaken for excitement. "But…"

"I will be your savior, your beginning, middle and end." Malachi almost growled at her, "I will be your anchor to this world and the next." Her photographic memory kicked into high gear and fired every image of her exchanges with Malachi. It too was protesting this behavior. It showed her the cat on the ledge, Anastasia rolling her eyes as she spoke of "Alexander," all the different ways he had tried to kill them, the theatre at Mulbridge exploding, Gavin's pained face at betraying her against his will, Nathaniel being beaten, his wings misshapen shards on his back and finally, it showed her his expression of glee as he slammed his fist into her face over and over again. Her memory was sending her a clear signal; this man is dangerous, run.

Then, Octavia's words came back to Lucy: "You must be willing to go against your moral code." For once, Lucy had to ignore her most precious gift and it was killing her. This wasn't just against her moral code. This was against everything she had ever wanted. It violated every bit of her internal compass. This was the most hateful, horrible, vicious moment in Lucy's life. Yet, to save them all, to have the possibility of a life to come, for Nathaniel, for Stasia, for Roman and for Gavin, for all of humanity, she lidded her eyes, tilted her chin up and whispered, "You can be my Angel."

He kissed her.

Lucy forced her hands to reach up around his neck, grateful that he could not see them trembling. She stilled the muscles in her neck and in her shoulders that wanted to pull away and run. She closed her eyes and tried desperately to convince her mind that this passionate kiss was coming from the love of her life and not the demented Antichrist. The restraint on her physical body was so much that tears began to tip out the sides of her eyes. Malachi pulled back and wiped her tears with his thumbs. Relief washed through Lucy when he smiled at her.

"Shall we play the game, darling?"

Lucy forced herself to smile and follow him to the table. She was behind him when something cold touched her hand and Lucy flinched. Turning, she was staring into the black eyes of one of the dead girls. She was squeezing Lucy's hand in comfort and reassurance. Lucy was so appreciative of this act of kindness from a creature she didn't even know could see, let alone feel anything. She nodded her thanks and headed to the table to get back to work.

The night could not have passed slower for Lucy. She dragged the game out as long as she could. She used every strategy she could, referencing hundreds of history books. She focused on the first and second World Wars, for she knew that Malachi would have been in the depths during that time and possibly not familiar with the strategies of Patton and Haig. This proved to be a good plan for the most part. Lucy had to work extra hard to keep Malachi winning and yet not let him win and end the game. It was an exhausting level of constant action. Several times, Lucy thought that maybe Malachi suspected something as he would pause and eye her carefully, but with each instance, he seemed to dismiss his own thoughts and move on.

Finally, and just as the sun was beginning to turn the sky a brilliant pink hue, Lucy allowed Malachi to overtake her armies and made several fatal errors that proved the demise of her game. Malachi took the moves offered, and beat Lucy soundly.

"Ha ha!" he clapped his hands with happiness.

"Good game," Lucy replied politely and offered her hand in sportsmanship.

Malachi, in full spirits, would not be content with a simple handshake. He leapt around the table and whipped Lucy up in his arms, spun her around laughing and planted a kiss solidly on her lips. Lucy again forced her body to respond. He finally put her back down on her feet and Lucy stifled a yawn.

"I'm so tired," she said softly. "I think I should sleep."

"Don't worry Lilith," Malachi smiled into her face, "After tomorrow, we won't have to worry about things like that."

"What do you mean?"

"Don't worry darling," he gazed at her longingly. "I will explain everything tomorrow night, at sunset. Have a good sleep."

Lucy nodded and pulled gently away.

"Goodnight," she said softly. To add to the authenticity, she even reached up and touched his face lightly, trailing her fingers over his cheek. "I will see you soon."

Malachi covered her hand with his. "I will come for you at sundown and we can begin our new life again."

Lucy grinned and stepped away to her room. The dead girls followed quickly behind. As soon as they closed the door, Lucy collapsed sobbing onto the soft carpet, the tension, fear and exhaustion of the last hours finally finding release. One of the girls guarded the door and another knelt down beside Lucy and offered a cold but somewhat comforting hand on Lucy's back as she sobbed silently into her arms.

"Is he gone?" she whispered to the closest girl. The girl looked at another, who darted out of the room to return moments later with a nod. Lucy sat back on her heels and calmed her breathing. "I swear to God," she hissed at the sky, "that creature will never touch me with permission again."

She stood and walked to the window at the mountains and valleys surrounding her. It was time to move on in the plan but again, she had doubts. Angels swarming? Really? Was that possible? Could she just jump off the roof of this castle and hope that someone caught her? It was the most insane thought she had ever had and yet it was her only option. She reviewed the conversation with the Demons against everything that Malachi had said last night. Everything they said to her had been true. It stood to reason that they had not lied about the Angels either. Lucy nodded as her plan cemented itself in her mind.

Chapter Twenty-Four
Hero

"Being a hero is about the shortest-lived profession on earth."
~ Will Rogers

She went back out to the sitting room. "I need to speak to Gavin," she said to the dead girls, "and I need a pot of coffee. Please." Lucy paced the room while she waited and eventually ended up back at the Risk Game, which was still set up. "It may look like you won for now, pal," she muttered, "but you are going to lose everything."

"Who is going to lose everything?" came a voice from the door. "Please tell me it's who I hope it is." Lucy grinned at Gavin and ran to hug him. It felt so good to have familiar arms about her.

"I've got ya, Red," he whispered into her hair. "You okay?" He could tell from the paleness of her face that indeed, all was not well.

"I need to fill you in quickly," she said as she crossed to the coffee being set up, "and then, my friend, we are all getting the Hell out of this crappy castle."

"Music to my ears." Gavin smiled as he took the coffee. "I told you, you would make an excellent BatGirl."

Lucy laughed a genuine laugh for the first time in weeks; it felt like she had breathed for the first time too. Gavin had a calming effect on Lucy that she cherished.

"Okay, so here's the deal," Lucy began and she filled him in on the last twenty-four hours of her life.

Gavin sat back stunned. "This adds a whole new level to this, Lucy," he said quietly.

"I know," she muttered.

"Like seriously," he leaned forward, "I thought we would just have to find a cell phone or a goat farmer or something to call the cops to raid the castle and Malachi would vanish in a pile of smoke cackling the whole time."

"That's what you thought would happen?" Lucy was shocked.

"Well yeah, Lucy!" Gavin half smiled. "I read a lot of comic books."

Lucy laughed. "You are weird. You and Ben need to figure out a way to spring Nathaniel and Roman. I assume that will cause enough of a stir to allow me to get to the roof."

"And jump off," Gavin finished for her.

"Yup."

"Nope."

"What do you mean? Nope?" Lucy rounded on him.

"I mean," he said calmly, "that you are not jumping off the roof of a castle in Bulgaria in the hopes that an Angel on the other side of the Demonic shield is going to catch you."

"When you put it that way..."

"I will jump off the roof," he replied with conviction.

"Oh I don't think so," Lucy shook her head, "no way."

"Why?" Gavin challenged, "Do you think the Angels won't catch me? Because I am pretty sure, Lucy, that they have to catch anyone who jumps off this roof, whether you are marked to be the fiancé of the Antichrist or not."

"Don't be glib about this, Gavin!"

"I'm not!" he yelled. "You are! Are you out of your mind? How do we even know that there are Angels out there?"

"I don't know for sure," Lucy faltered, "but we have no other choice." Gavin threw his hands in the air and Lucy leaned toward him. She grabbed his hands and held them under her chin. "Please, please don't fight me on this," she whispered, "I need you to make sure that Nathaniel gets out; there is no one else I trust with this. Please help me."

Gavin sighed, "I swear though, if you end up a bloody pancake on the ground, I am going to point and laugh."

"Duly noted." Lucy nodded and added a small smile. "Thank you."

"I guess we need to talk to our old pal Ben about this, hey?" Lucy nodded to the closest dead girl, who went out into the hall and came back with Ben.

"What are you two planning?" he asked wearily. "Because I gotta be honest, I don't really have the patience for any crap today."

"How would you like to make a great deal of money?" Gavin started and Ben rolled his eyes.

"I thought I already was making a great deal of money by keeping the redhead alive. That was the deal, remember?" His tone was one of warning.

"And you are, but that was just my parents," Gavin said smoothly. "I don't think you completely understand how wealthy Anastasia's parents are. Have you ever heard of the Rooke Hedge Fund?" He continued without waiting for a response. "It's one of the biggies, look it up if you want to. If you return their precious, only child to them, unharmed, then I can guarantee you my friend, you will be set for life."

"How will I know you will keep your word?" Ben shot back.

"You realize that if you help us escape, then you escape too," Lucy offered; to her, this was a no brainer.

"Maybe I can stop you all from escaping and get all the payments that the boss has offered me; a lifetime of money and freedom," Ben taunted.

"You really are a capitalist, aren't you pal?" Gavin said with admiration. "Here's the thing though, Lucy, Anastasia and I are lucid people, one hundred percent sane. The guys at the other end of that tunnel and the guy who is running the show? Not so much. I don't think you realize how bad a dude he is." He pointed to the closest dead girl with his chin. "Trust me on this, you want to stay on our side of the team."

"Hmmm," Ben seemed to be thinking, "Well, I would have to hear it from Anastasia herself."

"Sounds like a grand idea," Gavin said and he turned to the girl by the door. "Please go and get Anastasia."

"How many guards are in the castle right now?" Lucy asked.

"Four," Ben answered, "the other three are digging."

"What?" Lucy reviewed her memory. "There were at least twelve here when we arrived."

"They disappeared." Ben replied shortly.

"Ran away?" Lucy prompted.

"Or tried to run away," Ben shrugged. The girl returned moments later with Anastasia in tow who ran across the room to clutch at Lucy. Tears welled up in Lucy's eyes when she realized how much she had missed her best friend.

"Hey!" Stasia said, looking angrily at Lucy. "Where the HELL did you get jeans?"

"My closet," Lucy grinned, "help yourself."

Anastasia darted from the room followed by two dead girls who presumably didn't think Lucy and Stasia were even capable of dressing themselves anymore.

"I have to wait for her to change now?" Ben demanded.

"It's jeans!" Stasia yelled from the other room. "Put yourself in a corset for a day and you will totally understand, Jim."

"This one is Ben," Lucy called and Ben glared at her. "Then tell us your real name!" she pleaded but Ben shook his head.

"You will have to tell us eventually so we can write you a check, hero boy," Gavin replied.

"Hero boy?" Ben's eyebrows shot up in interest.

"Don't you see how this is going to go down?" Gavin replied, placing his hands up in the air like a movie director. "Picture it, five American university students, being held hostage by a crazed billionaire lunatic in a medieval castle in the Balkan Mountains, saved by one of the guards hired to watch them as his moral compass shows his heart the way. Are you kidding me, pal? This stuff is writing itself! We are talking book deals, interviews, purple heart medals, high schools named after you and the cover of a Wheaties box!"

"Buckets of money too," Anastasia added as she was coming out of the bedroom zipping up a pair of jeans and adjusting her new found t-shirt. "Holy crap that feels good."

"Exactly," Gavin leaned back in his seat and motioned grandly towards Stasia. "What did I tell you?"

"My dad will pay you anything you want if you bring me home safe." Stasia plopped down on the seat next to Lucy and poured a coffee. "For real, if he doesn't, I have a huge trust fund set up for me, and it's all yours, Jim."

"Ben," Lucy corrected and Anastasia shrugged. She could tell by the way Gavin and Stasia were acting that this had been a pre-organized plan. To Lucy, it felt like they were reading lines. To Ben, she hoped it looked authentic.

They all waited while Ben sat silently. All Lucy could hear was the ticking of the clock on the mantle.

Lucy ran out of patience. "Look, whatever your name is," she spouted and Gavin winced, "if you don't help us, all of humanity is going to suffer for it. Your boss is no regular guy. He's the flipping Antichrist and if you think he is going to set you up with a beach house in Maui and a harem of women after this, you are out of your mind. He is going to kill you or enslave you just like he is going to do to the rest of the humans on the planet and we are the only ones who can stop him. So are you in or are you out?"

"Not the approach I was going for, Red," Gavin replied tersely.

"Well seriously," Lucy exclaimed, "I don't have time for negotiations."

"I had it totally under control!" Gavin snapped at her. "And now he's all freaked out and thinking we are nuts and he's not going to help us at all and I don't think we can do it without him!"

"Well Gavin," Lucy exploded, "did you ever think to tell him the actual truth? Maybe you could try that!"

"Have you ever tried trusting another human? Maybe you could try controlling your temper every once in a while," Gavin shot back. "Sometimes it might work!"

"I trusted you and look where it got me!"

Gavin tightened his lips, "Well played, Red." He whispered as he tipped an invisible hat. "Well played, indeed."

Lucy opened her mouth to recant her words.

"I'll do it," Ben said quietly and they all stared at him. He looked up. "If you promise me that no matter what, I will get a Wheaties box cover."

"Done." Anastasia slapped the table. "If my father has to buy the company, then you will have your cover, my friend. Good choice." Gavin stood and walked away.

Chapter Twenty-Five
Explosives

*"Although personally I am quite content with existing explosives,
I feel we must not stand in the path of improvement."*
~ Sir Winston Churchill

"What is this place?" Gavin asked with raised eyebrows. They were in an area of the castle that they had never been to. The walls were narrow and moist; moss grew between the cracks. Ben stopped in front of a wooden door.

"Armory," he said shortly and after looking side to side, slid a key from his belt into the keyhole. He pulled open the door and led them all inside. Anastasia whistled.

"That is a lot of sharp objects." She gave Lucy a sideways glance. They were in a room roughly the size of school gymnasium and they were surrounded by racks and racks of swords, spears and clubs, all metal, all huge.

"There must be thousands of them," Lucy murmured. "What is he…" but she cut herself off. Of course she knew what Malachi was planning on doing with them. He was planning on taking over the world.

"What are we doing here?" Gavin asked.

"You wanted a distraction?" Ben prompted and pointed his chin towards the far corner. "This is where you will find it."

They all craned their necks to see, but Lucy and Anastasia just saw piles of wooden boxes.

"Explosives," Gavin whispered. He turned to Ben with a grin on his face. "Respect." And Ben nodded at the compliment.

"Does anyone know how to use that stuff?" Anastasia demanded. "Do we know what to do to *not* get ourselves blown to bits?"

Gavin shrugged, "I know that this isn't a part of general knowledge, but I am quite bright really and Chemistry is my strong suit. If all else fails, I'm sure there are instructions." He started walking towards the corner but Lucy grabbed his arm.

"Gavin, listen." She didn't want to leave things the way they were. But Gavin raised a hand to stop her.

"We are all on edge, we will talk everything over later."

She bit her lip. "Okay fine but I still don't think this is a good idea," she urged, "the other day, I saw a stress fracture in the glass in my room. Malachi has dug so deeply that the foundation of the castle is sinking. Any explosives in here are likely to send this place crumbling to the ground, with us in it!"

"Don't worry Red," he gave her hand a squeeze, "we will stick to the small stuff. Fireworks basically, just to cause a stir. Nothing major. You and Stasia guard the door while Ben and I figure this out."

"Guard it?" Stasia demanded. "With what?"

Gavin waved his hand out. "Pick your weapon." He winked at them and headed off to the corner with Ben.

Stasia nodded and reached over for a spear that was sitting close by. She picked it up in both hands and held it with appreciation. "If the dance girls could see me now." She smirked.

Lucy reached over and grabbed a knife from the rack to her left. It was about ten inches long with a solid metal handle. The weight of it felt wrong in her hands and she began to sweat. Still, she slipped it into her back pocket and crossed her arms as she glanced nervously out the door.

"Fill me in on the details," Anastasia whispered, "all I knew to do was to promise anyone money if Gavin prompted me to. What's going on?" Lucy filled Anastasia in on the new information. By the end, Stasia was leaning, wide eyed against the wall.

"I don't know what to say. I wish I could go back to the first time I met him and run him over with my car." She muttered and Lucy had to agree. They sat silently for a while.

"I've got a bad feeling about this," Lucy finally uttered.

"Me too," Stasia agreed. "I don't trust that Ben guy," she whispered.

"Mmm," Lucy eyed Ben as he and Gavin bent over a box of explosives. "Don't think we have a choice."

"Nope." They were quiet for a moment. "Hey Loser," Stasia whispered and Lucy looked at her, "I know that hanging out with Alexander or Malachi or whatever wasn't fun and I know that it was pretty rotten for you and I know that you got us a bunch of privileges and you got us to this point because of it." She reached over and took Lucy's hand. "Thank you."

Lucy felt tears brimming up in her eyes. "Thank you for thanking me," she whispered and gave Anastasia's hand a squeeze.

"And I don't think you should jump off the roof," Stasia added quickly. "I think it's a bad idea and I don't think it's going to break any shield or anything."

"I..." Lucy faltered, "it's our only hope. Roman and Nathaniel have tried getting out before and there is some invisible wall around this place. I have to use my free will to break through it."

Lucy watched as Anastasia physically bit her tongue.

"Get comfortable, ladies," Gavin called from the other edge of the room. "Turns out Brad Pitt had help when he made stuff blow up. This is complicated."

Time seemed to stretch on forever and although they were well ahead of their noon cut off, Lucy's apprehension grew with each passing second. What was she thinking? How did she know that this plan, if you could call it that, would actually work? How did she know that there were Angels on the other side of the wall? Why should she trust a bunch of Demons that had shown nothing but hateful disregard for her and the people she loved?

"I think we have something!" Gavin called as he and Ben walked towards them flushed and bright-eyed. Gavin held a bag slung over his shoulder. He opened the flap to show several small metal canisters.

"Will they work?" Lucy asked, trying not to let the doubt seep fully into her tone but not being able to stop herself.

"No way to test them," Gavin said. "We can only pray."

"Okay." Anastasia put her spear back on the rack. Lucy decided to keep her knife, because, although it made her uncomfortable, it did offer a weak sense of security. It wouldn't help though if she was plummeting to her death over the castle walls. "Lucy, you head back up to your room and pretend like nothing is going on. We will free the boys and wait for whatever signal the Demons are planning from the tunnels at noon. We will hopefully escape in the chaos of Gavin's little bag of tricks there and see you on the outside."

Lucy sucked in air; every time someone said the plan, it sounded worse.

"Yup," she tried to look brave, "sounds good."

Everyone was silent for a moment.

Gavin stepped forward and pulled Lucy to the side. Pressing his forehead to hers, he whispered fiercely at her, "You don't have to do this, Red. You really don't. I want to jump off for you. Please let me. You go with Stasia and whatshisface and I will just run up and jump off the roof. Please let me do this for you. Please let me show you." He paused and swallowed and left it there.

Lucy pressed her eyes closed against the swelling tears. "No," she whispered back, "I need you with Stasia to make sure that Ben stays in line. We wouldn't be strong enough to stop him if he decided to change sides again. You are the only one who can make those bombs work and you are the only one I trust enough to get Roman and Nathaniel out. I have a better chance of getting up to the roof. Malachi will kill you if he catches you. He won't kill me. Plus," she swallowed as her voice cracked, "I want to do this for you. I'm not just saving Nathaniel; I need to save you too."

"But why?"

"Because I do!" she yelled and hugged him quickly before stepping around him to Stasia and hugging her too. She angrily swiped her tears away. "If this works, I will see you all soon. If it kills me, I will still see you all soon." And with that she stormed away.

Don't cry don't cry don't cry. She repeated this to herself all the way back to her room. She would see everyone again, this would work. She quickly climbed the stairs, her bare toes sinking into the plush carpet. *This will work, just a little longer.* She pounded down the hallway towards her room. *You still have a half an hour at least before the sun is at its highest. Calm down, breathe.* She opened the door to her room to see Malachi standing in the middle.

You are going to die.

Chapter Twenty-Six
Faith

"Faith is taking the first step even when you don't see the whole staircase."
~ Martin Luther King Jr.

"Darling!" he called out, "Where have you been? Where are all the guards?"

Lucy blinked her eyes. What was he doing here? "I...I just couldn't sleep and went for a little walk." She nodded her head as if convincing both of them that this was true. "I didn't see anyone."

"It's almost time, Lilith!" His eyes were bright and wild. "Everyone is all set and ready to go, all we have to do is give the word and the world will be ours."

She had to stall him, "Are you sure about this? It sounds a little crazy."

"I know it does and I know it is hard for you to understand but I need you to believe in me and my powers. I know that you have your doubts but I will show you everything. Come with me, down to the tunnels and you will see."

"Of course," Lucy nodded and turned to walk back out the

door as panic surged through her. They would be too close to the dungeons, Malachi would sense that something was wrong and would know that Gavin and Stasia were trying to get Nathaniel and Roman out. The timing would be off. She wouldn't have time to get to the roof before he started the invasion. What was she going to do? Because her thoughts were so occupied, she stepped out into the hallway ahead of Malachi before she realized her mistake.

The knife.

"Lilith?" his voice sounded stern behind her, like a chiding father. Her heart stopped and her jaw clenched as she turned ever so slowly around to face him. Could she grab the knife in time? Probably not, and now that he had seen it, she had no chance at all. "Would you be offended if I asked you to change? I have a particular red gown that I have chosen especially for this occasion." Lucy saw the image of the portrait in Hell of her in the red dress. That must be it. He hadn't seen the knife after all.

She forced her breath to steady as she answered. "Of course, sounds gorgeous." She went to take a step back into the room but stopped in her tracks as a huge explosion rocked the castle. Lucy steadied herself to keep from falling. She heard a loud rumbling from all around as the castle sank in a little on itself. Lucy could almost feel the ground tip ever so slightly beneath her feet and she heard a loud crackling sound as all the windows in the room splintered in spidery cracks, some breaking all together.

"What--" Malachi started to rage, but Lucy didn't hear the rest. She was too busy running.

She sprinted as fast as she could to the stairwell. The castle groaned again as another explosion came from deep in the bowels. Before she reached the stairs, she glanced back over her shoulder to see that Malachi wasn't there. He would have had a challenging decision, go after Lucy or go down and stop whatever was trying to stop him. Lucy hoped it was the latter, but doubted it. She started to climb the stairs inside the turret. Cool, fresh air pushed at her cheeks and relief washed over her. This stairwell led to the roof.

Lucy scrambled up the stairs. The stone was slick and her bare feet slipped several times. Terror shivered down her spine as she kept climbing and climbing and racing to the roof. Finally, she could hear the wind she and increased her pace to get there faster. She didn't care where Malachi was; she would sprint off that roof. She emerged onto the top of the castle, felt the sun bathing down upon her and saw all of the mountains and sky beyond stretching as far as she could see. But that was all she could see. Lucy couldn't see any Angels or even hear the slightest evidence that anything was out there. All she could hear was the wind and the groaning castle. She hesitated in her doubt.

"Lilith," Malachi said from beside her. She was frightened that he would have turned himself into some monster to stop her. He could have morphed into anything he wanted to, anything at all, but he didn't. There the Antichrist stood, a twenty-one-year-old, handsome, blond-haired, blue-eyed man in jeans and a t-shirt regarding her with nothing short of sadness. "Why Lilith?" he asked softly. "Why are you here on the roof?"

Lucy swallowed as she looked out again at the vast emptiness beyond. "I need to escape," she explained and felt the lameness of this statement before the seemingly harmless man before her. "There are Angels beyond the shield," she finally blurted.

"Shield?" He was shocked. "What shield?"

"You have a shield up around this place," Lucy countered as she looked again at the sky beyond the ramparts of the castle. *Show me some sign*, she begged in her mind, *something to help me believe*. But there was nothing, not even a flicker of movement in the sky to tell her that anything at all was there. All she had to go on was the word of a couple Demons. The stones beneath her feet rumbled and shifted again, and Lucy struggled to keep her balance. Malachi stood still as a statue. The castle was collapsing. Lucy hoped everyone else was on their way out of the castle - that this was all worth it. All she had to do was jump and they would all be free.

"Lilith, have I ever lied to you?" he asked quietly. "Think back, use your memory, have I ever lied to you?"

Lucy did so, she rewound her mind to every encounter that she had ever had with Malachi and indeed, he had never lied to her. In fact, he had told the truth even when it was to his own detriment. She didn't respond and looked out again at the horizon.

"Lilith, my dear," Malachi said softly, "there is nothing there. No Angels have come for you and if you jump off this roof, you will die. Unless, of course, you hope that I would save you, which I could, Lilith, easily." He paused and Lucy's mind started to move at breakneck speed. It was as if her life was flashing before her eyes, but only the past year came to her. "I can save you, Lilith," Malachi continued. "I can even save Nathaniel if that is what you so desire. I can keep you all alive and happy, but I don't think you understand my vision." Lucy saw the day she met Nathaniel, her saying goodbye to Dr. Hannon in the auditorium, walking through the quad and slamming into Nathaniel. She saw his face as she had seen it that day, with that smile and his hand reaching for her. He had loved her at that second.

"The human race has gone off track, Lilith," Malachi explained. "The planet is at war, half of the humans are starving and the other half have so much to eat that they are dying from their own indulgence. There are children that have more fresh water in their toilets than some children drink in their entire lives." Lucy saw the first time Nathaniel kissed her, how he had grinned at her before lowering his lips to hers. She saw them talking all night long, laughing until their stomachs hurt.

"Entire species of animals are dying because of humanity's constant obsession with mastering the elements. No one believes in anything anymore. No one needs to, they just buy whatever they want and then throw it away when they are done with it. People throw everything away, even other people. What kind of world is worth saving when babies are found in garbage cans and murderers are set free?" Lucy saw Nathaniel leap off the cliff, terrifying her, and then appear again with his wings. She saw him at the summer solstice party, devastated that he was being returned to Heaven. She saw him walking towards her in the quad, the sun glinting off his hair as he walked with that easy gait of his.

"The world is out of balance, Lilith," Malachi continued. "Humans have spent the better part of the last century annihilating one of the most perfect living planets in the Universe. They have destroyed it to its very core and everyone on it, whether they understand it or not." Lucy saw Nathaniel with Roman, laughing at some joke. She saw him driving the jeep, grinning at her as he reached over and took her hand, the wind whipping at his black hair. She saw him racing through the quad, an unconscious Anastasia in his arms, concern pressed into his handsome face. She saw him on the dock with Roman, creating a massive hurricane, looking back at her with worry and determination.

"I just want to reset the clock, Lilith," Malachi pleaded over her thoughts. "I just want the world to get back in balance and give everyone a chance to thrive. The rich should not be the only ones with food and water and shelter. Humans need to start appreciating this sphere for what it is, the greatest gift ever given. You and I together can create a world that makes sense; that is free from chaos and the unknown." Lucy saw the butterfly Nathaniel sent her. She saw him in chains, being beaten and yet having a wink and a smile for her. She saw him during their one night together and warmth spread through her heart. She knew what she believed.

"Join me, Lilith," Malachi pleaded, "and you can have anything or anyone you want in this world. You will be the Mother of all humanity, revered and blessed above all others. You will be the greatest human that ever lived with the power to teach the world everything you know. I offer you the knowledge and learning of thousands of years of life and the ability to write the future as you decide. Lilith, please." Lucy looked up at him and gave a little laugh. Malachi smiled back, relived she saw things his way.

"My name," she spoke slowly as she began walking backwards towards the edge, Malachi following her, keeping his distance, "is Lucy Bower. I have the most amazing photographic memory ever recorded. I know many things, but what I know for sure is that I am in love with Nathaniel the fallen Angel and that he is waiting for me on the other side of this wall."

"How do you know that?" Malachi said with pity in his voice. They were getting very near to the edge. "How could you possibly know such a thing? There is no evidence to suggest that to be true. Use your mind, and realize that it isn't possible. It isn't logical." Lucy bumped into the rampart and reached behind to boost herself up on to the edge and stood, tall and straight. She glanced behind her at the ten story drop to the craggy rocks the castle stood upon. She looked back at Malachi and smiled. "Listen to me," he pleaded, "there really isn't anyone there! Do not jump off!" His eyes were full of worry and panic.

Lucy cocked her head in wonder at him. "You really *don't* believe, do you?" she said with awe. "You aren't lying when you say no one is there, because you really don't think anyone is there."

"Yes darling!" he exploded, "Because I can't see them and neither can you! It doesn't even make any sense and it's foolish and illogical to believe that something you can't see or hear or feel exists!"

"It may not be logical," Lucy said, "it may make no sense, but I still believe."

She turned and faced out into the nothingness beyond.

"But why?" he almost screamed in desperation behind her. "Why do you believe?"

Lucy looked back over her shoulder, a small smile playing on her lips and whispered, "Because I have faith." She dove with all her might off the top of the castle and into the sky.

Chapter Twenty-Seven
War

"All war is deception."
~ Sun Tzu

Lucy began to fall as she heard Malachi scream in rage and terror behind her. She heard him scrabble after her and a ripping sound as his own wings exploded through his shirt.

"Nathaniel," Lucy whispered into the crisp spring day, the wind almost stealing her voice, "I need you, can you come?"

She would only have to call him once and he would come. There was a rush of air and Lucy felt his arms around her and heard his wings beating into the wind. She slipped her hands around his neck and grinned into his shining gorgeous face. There was a flurry of activity and Lucy looked around to see hundreds of Angels teeming every inch of the castle. She looked back to the roof to see that now Malachi could see them too. It was amazing what one could believe in when finally forced to see the truth.

He no longer looked like the handsome young man he had moments ago. He had dropped the façade and become the monster he truly was. Malachi's face had molted, lengthened and deformed into something that looked half man, half goat. His eyes had turned black with dark red rims over a hooked nose and massively sharp fangs. His body shape had morphed into something only partly human. He must have grown to at least seven or eight feet tall, his muscles bulging about the shoulders but rapidly tapering towards his overly slim waist. His leg muscles were so powerful that they had ripped through the bottom half of his jeans, leaving them in shards at his calves. His veins were black as oil and crisscrossed his pale sweaty skin. His wings were an enormous bright red leathery appendage protruding from his back.

"Yeesh," came a droll voice beside them, "he looks like the Hulk married a farm animal." Lucy looked over and let out a squeal of glee to see Roman, healthy and floating beside them.

"Good to see you, Demon," Nathaniel grinned.

"Good to see you and your wings in one piece..." Roman's sentence was cut off as he suddenly pitched forward toward the castle as if being pulled by an invisible rope. He reached out but was moving too fast for anyone to grab him. Malachi was holding a hand out, his black claws beckoning his servant back. Roman looked at them just before he reached the castle and smiled. "Fly away, Angel," he called. Even from the increasing distance, they could see the sorrow in his eyes. "I have to join my own side. Watch over Stasia for me."

"No!" Lucy screamed as Roman flew right into Malachi's waiting claws and was struck down so hard his body lay prone on the stone castle roof. Nathaniel pulled Lucy tighter and he and the other Angels started to speed off. "You have to help him!" Lucy yelled, trying to get a better look over Nathaniel's shoulder.

"There is nothing to be done." Lucy saw Gabriel approach, flying on Nathaniel's right. "He is a Demon, Lucy, and cannot fight with the Angels."

"Fight?" Lucy asked. "Who is fighting? We stopped the flood of Demons, didn't we? Closed the tunnel? Gavin? Stasia?"

"We did," Nathaniel explained, "and Gavin and Stasia are safe and managed to close the tunnel." He and Gabriel shared a meaningful look. "So the citizens of Hell were prevented from invading the planet, but as you know, Demons do not require a tunnel to leave Hell and as you just saw with Roman, they are all at the mercy of the Antichrist. Most though, want a battle. We will have to fight." Lucy looked up at Nathaniel and smiled. He looked bemused. "What are you grinning about Lucy? Can I tell you that the Angels have had to stop time on Earth because the Demons are attempting to take over and all of humanity is at stake. What could you possibly be smiling about?"

"I jumped off the roof because I had faith that you would be there." She grinned at him. "I love you and we are together and to be honest, I think that is all that matters."

Nathaniel looked at her and winked as they flew. "Me too," he whispered, the wind whipping at his hair. He then reformatted his face into one of serious concern for the immediate attention of Gabriel. Lucy squeezed him tighter and inhaled him. For this moment, right now, she was safe and she was happy and her world was perfect. What happened before or after this moment was not a concern. She sighed contentedly and grinned at Gabriel, whose worry could not be masked. Lucy looked away, seeing that haunting fox in his deep grey eyes.

"Where are we going?" she asked as she gazed around at the thousands of Angels flying with them. Each Angel was more fiercely beautiful than the last.

"The Black Sea," Gabriel answered gently.

"Why the Black Sea?" Lucy asked. "How do you know that

is where the battle will happen?"

"There are some things we just know," Gabriel answered cryptically. He turned to regard Lucy more closely. "You have shown great strength and determination these past few months, Lucy," he said kindly. "We are all very proud of you." The Angels closest to them nodded in agreement. "I just need you to be strong for a little while longer and I promise everything will work out for the best. Everything will be as it should."

"I knew you were the fox!" Lucy smirked at him. "But everything *has* worked out for the best. Everything is going to be fine. You are going to win this battle and everything will be back to normal." Gabriel smiled at her but didn't answer. They approached the Black Sea and although it was landlocked, Lucy was amazed at the size and beauty of it. The Black Sea was more turquoise than anything, with long sweeping soft shores and gorgeous cliff faces. Surely, one would think, nothing bad could happen here. Yet Lucy saw a black mass emerging from a hole in the cliff face. Like oil from a spill, the Demons flooded out of the rock face like vermin. Lucy shuddered. "How many?" she asked. Nathaniel did not have to look to know what she was asking.

"I'm not sure," he replied, not making an effort to sugarcoat it. "But it doesn't matter, we are three times as strong," he added reassuringly.

Lucy's elated mood swiftly turned to one of worry. She had not considered that there would be a battle, let alone one that they may not win. She looked up at Nathaniel.

"You will win, won't you?" she whispered into his neck.

"For you, Lucy, I would do anything." He looked sideways at Gabriel again and received a reassuring nod in return. "Anything at all." They landed on the west end of the beach, near the cliff face and far behind the Demon battle line. Once they were near the ground, Lucy lost sight of the Dead Sea's other coasts. They might as well be on the ocean, it was so huge. Nathaniel placed Lucy gently on her feet. They were beside a large cave and Lucy heard a scream out of the darkness. Her heart froze in fear before she saw Anastasia emerge in a sprint towards them, accompanied by two Angels. Lucy ran to her friend and embraced her tightly.

"Oh you made it!" they said together and then laughed into each other's hair. Anastasia broke first, her face pulled into fear. "Did you see Roman? Did he make it out?"

Lucy looked to Nathaniel and Gabriel for help.

"Roman must fight with his own kind," Gabriel offered kindly and laid a hand on Stasia's arm in response to her gasp of terror. "Have no fear though, for none on our side will engage him in battle. We know him to be the friend that he is." Anastasia relaxed.

Lucy looked into the cave's darkness, hoping to see someone else emerge.

"Gavin is safe on the other side," Nathaniel explained in answer to her unasked question. "We thought it wise to separate you. We did not want the three of you together during the battle in case…" he trailed off.

"In case what?" Lucy pushed and Gabriel stepped in.

"We need to go now, Nathaniel will be back, soon," he explained. "Mathias and Sariel are here to watch over you and Anastasia." He eyed them carefully. "I expect you to stay in the cave until we drive the Demons back." His voice was strained and tired.

A roar sounded and Lucy peeked around the cliff face and paled at the sight beyond. Miles and miles of black leathery wings, as far as she could see stretched away from her to the east and along the shoreline. Terror gripped her as she glanced at the water to see the number of white soft feathered wings floating above it. It seemed like the Demon's outnumbered the Angels four to one. She looked up at him with tears edging out between her lashes.

"It will all be all right," Nathaniel said with a wink and a smile. "What will happen is what is best."

Lucy's mind flashed the dream she had experienced with the fox and rage bubbled up. "No!" she screamed. "What are you talking about? That is what Gabriel said in my dream. Everything is going to work out the way I want and everything is going to be fine and everyone is going to get out of this okay! Now promise me! I want you to say that you promise!"

Nathaniel chuckled at her. "Always the temper, my Lucy." He grinned as he picked her up in his arms. "Calm down. I love you and I will be back to get you and everything is going to be fine."

Lucy let out a gust of air and entwined her fingers in his thick black hair. "I love you, come back to me." She grinned at him.

"I will always come for you, Lucy," he smiled, "always." He ran his hand up the back of her spine and cradled her head in his hand before pulling her face to his and kissing her like he had never kissed her before. Every nerve in Lucy's body ignited as if on fire and her mind emptied of worries. Slowly, Nathaniel placed her upon the ground and broke the kiss. He ran his hand lightly down her cheek and Lucy remembered the first night she had met him and how he had done the exact same thing on the stairwell at the dorm. He had not done it again since. She opened her mouth to tell him this but he was already airborne, sailing to join the fight. She felt Anastasia tuck an arm in hers and sigh. Nathaniel hadn't promised.

Mathias and Sariel tried to steer Lucy and Stasia all the way into the cave, but both refused to go and the Angels, deciding against physical restraint, simply stood beside them.

"What happened back there?" Lucy asked Stasia.

Stasia all but growled in response. "Gavin should not be trusted with explosives, that's what. We figured we would use one of those tiny things to knock out the door to the dungeons to free Roman and Nathaniel. Useless Ben didn't actually have keys. Well, the damn thing nearly brings the whole castle down on our heads. I barely had time to hug Roman and Nathaniel because we figured our cover was blown. We all ran to the tunnel, met up with that Abraxas dude from down below who seemed quite pleased with everything and told us to toss the rest of the explosives down the path to Hell. We barely made it to the dumping tunnel and climbed out there. These two were waiting for us."

Lucy shook her head. "I'm so relieved that you guys are okay," she said as they leaned their heads together to watch the battle. Lucy watched as the last of the Demons spilled from the cavern onto the beach and the last of the Angels arrived on the sea. They all stood, the Demons growling and raging, eager to fight, the Angels calm, almost peaceful but fierce and determined. Lucy could not make Nathaniel or Roman out of either group. There was a war cry from high above and all looked to see Malachi the Antichrist sailing on his red wings to the middle of the Demon line, where he landed with such force upon the beach that the ground shook.

The Demons roared and cheered in response to his arrival, throwing their fists in the air and tossing fireballs in the sky. Malachi seemed unimpressed with the reaction of one Demon close to him and that Demon received a sharp claw across the face. The Demon stumbled but stayed upright and took his place back in line, it was Roman. He had been placed beside Malachi and was in the most danger. Even if the Angels did not want to hurt him, they would want to attack Malachi first and that put Roman at a greater risk. Anastasia saw the exchange too and derived the same result as Lucy had.

"He's going to be used as a shield!" she screamed. "Lucy! What are we going to do! He's going to die!"

Lucy dropped her head to think. There had to be a solution that no one had thought of yet. She saw Gabriel glide away from the Angel battle line over the water toward the shore, seemingly in a last ditch effort to negotiate. Malachi stepped into the air and sailed over the beach and toward the water to meet him halfway. Lucy reviewed everything she knew about the Demons. From Bael in the laundry to the attack on Dr. Hannon to her conversation with Roman in the wheat field, she thought about it all.

She remembered her talks with Roman in the concert hall and sitting on the porch of the cabin. She thought about every talk she had had with Malachi and the conversation in his Palace in Hell with Turner and Octavia. She thought about Purgatory and Roman serving that kid all those drinks so he could ultimately get into his car and drive into her father. Her mind raced and fired information and scenes at her so quickly she barely had time to process it. She reviewed her conversations with Malachi, and how enraged he was when Lucy tried to forgive Gavin in front of him.

Finally she saw Retep, the keeper of the Gates of Hell. "No Forgiveness, No Redemption, Pass and Suffer for it" was the mantra of Hell. Lucy had assumed that no forgiveness meant that the citizens of Hell were not forgiven for their crimes, but in her conversations with Nathaniel, he had made it very clear that God forgave everyone, no matter what. She thought back to Roman at the Gates of Hell, saying "Everyone here, chooses to be here. It is a difficult concept for us to understand as well." Well, of course it was, because it wasn't what they thought. What if Roman didn't need forgiveness at all? What if it was the other way around? What *was* the choice the citizens of Hell made?

The truth struck her as her hands began to shake. She knew

what she had to do. Lucy's toes bit into the sand as she bent her knees in preparation to sprint. She had to get to Roman and now. She had to explain, she had to make him understand. Slowly she looked back at the two Angels ordered to guard her, but they were watching the now heated exchange between Malachi and Gabriel. Lucy seized the opportunity and sprinted directly into the center of the battle.

For the first several minutes, the Demons did not seem to see her or did not care that she was there. But soon, they started to realize that a human had run into their line and not just any human; their Lilith, their savior. Interpreting her actions as support for their cause, they began to cheer and roar in victory as Lucy raced at breakneck speed towards the middle of the line. She saw Malachi out of the corner of her eye look back over his shoulder and spy her. A grin spread across his evil face and he raised one fist in triumph.

The Demons exploded in roars of joy as Malachi turned back to Gabriel with nothing but mockery in his stance. Lucy kept running. She looked back over her shoulder to see Mathias and Sariel standing there, watching her go, making no effort to stop her. Had this been the plan all along? Did Gabriel know Lucy would figure it all out? Had he known it was all in her hands from the start like Random had said? Finally, she reached where she thought Roman was, but all she saw was strangers about.

"Roman!" she screamed into the crowds of winged Demons. "Roman!"

An arm grabbed her from behind. Lucy jumped and twisted to defend herself.

"What are you doing, Lucy?" Roman yelled in her face.

Relief washed over her as she twisted and held onto his arms. "Listen to me!" she screamed over the roar of the Demons. "No forgiveness, no redemption is not from God! It's from yourself!"

He shook his head at her. "What are you talking about? You have to get out of here!" He started to pull her away.

"No!" she yelled, fighting him. "Listen to me! God has already forgiven you. It isn't about being forgiven, it is about forgiving those that made you this way and forgiving yourself for making the mistake in the first place! You have to forgive to be free from Hell. You choose to be in Hell, not only because you do not repent! You choose to be in Hell because you do not *forgive*! You have to forgive yourself and you have to forgive those that harmed you!" She stopped. Breathing heavily, she let this information soak in, but Roman did not understand. He shook his head uncomprehendingly at her.

"We create our own Hells, Roman! While alive and dead by not forgiving those who have hurt us the most! The power of Hell is in the citizens themselves and their inability to forgive. It is by forgiving that you are set free!" She swallowed the sob rising in her throat and grabbed his face so he would listen. "I know, Roman!" she screamed into the wind. "I know that you were the bartender who served the drinks to the man who killed my father. I know you are responsible and I forgive you, Roman. I love you and I forgive you for what you have done because you didn't know any different. You didn't know better! I forgive you!"

Those words rocked the Demon to his very core. Light dawned from deep in his eyes and when he blinked, tears spilled from the corners. He grinned at Lucy, grabbed her face and kissed her hard on the forehead before leaning back, turning up to the sky and laughing in joy at the clouds. He looked back at Lucy, teary-eyed with happiness. "I can take away his power over me!" he yelled as he turned and flew toward Malachi and Gabriel. "Then the Demons will see that this isn't worth fighting for!" Lucy jumped in joy as she watched him go. She should have run back along the beach to Anastasia. She should have run away, but she didn't. Until her dying day, Lucy would never understand why she didn't just run back. For if she had, everything would have gone differently.

Roman beat his wings as he reached the water's edge. For the first time in years, his wings felt heavy on his back, like the yoke they were designed to be. He understood now. Lucy was right. He had to forgive to be set free. He looked back over his shoulder at the Demons behind him, friends, foes and unknown masses alike. Could he ever make them all see what he now saw?

He looked forward to the rows and rows of Angels, knowing that his sister, Emma was somewhere in there and knew for the first time in his entire life that he was indeed blessed. He hadn't realized that before. He had always been blessed, even when he was a street urchin and Emma a maid for the aristocrats that paid her nothing. Even when Emma was hiding their bread scraps in her pockets to scurry them back to the tiny room under the bridge that they had claimed for their own. Even with the lice and the rats and the cold, even then, Roman, or Samuel as he had been known, had been blessed, but he had chosen not to see it.

The Antichrist saw Roman coming and his eyes narrowed in suspicion. Roman's insides tensed in fear. Malachi would rip him to shreds for this but at least he would be free, even if he went to Purgatory for a thousand years, he would be free from the weight of these wings and his soul might feel like his own again. Roman allowed hope to creep into the edges of his heart and for once, he did not push it back but allowed it to flower and open in his chest as he came level with the head of the Demons and the head of the Angels. Gabriel smiled at him, as if he knew what Roman was about to do; maybe he did. Malachi sneered.

"What do you want, traitor?" he snarled through his fangs.

More than two thousand years of hate and malice and fear had turned the Antichrist into a disgusting creature. He even smelled dead. Roman swallowed his fear down.

"I need you to know something," Roman announced, hoping that they did not hear the small quiver in his voice. Malachi shot one claw up and clutched at Roman's throat with it.

"No!" he screamed into his face. "You may not speak, Demon!"

Roman felt his throat collapsing under the pressure. He grasped at Malachi's claw with both his own hands and used all his strength to try to pull away. The result was less than an inch of airspace but enough for Roman to suck in a lungful of air and scream, "I forgive you for killing Emma!" Malachi tightened his grip, and Roman felt blood drip down his chest from the gouges the claws were making in his flesh. It was warm and smelled of salt. In a few seconds, Roman's throat would be ripped from his body. "I forgive you for hurting Anastasia, I forgive you for hurting Lucy, I forgive you for everything you have ever done to every soul on that beach!"

Malachi screamed as he tightened his grip and hit Roman's jugular vein. Blood poured over his hand in a wave. He grinned into the dying face of the Demon. Blood spattered out of Roman's mouth and his eyes rolled back in his head as he whispered, "I forgive myself for all I have done." His head fell backwards, lifeless and heavy as Malachi flicked Roman's body off his claw and let it crumple into the water. Blood ballooned like ink around Roman's vanishing face as he sunk under the water.

Anastasia's scream cut through the air, ripping everyone to their core. Lucy's hands flew to her mouth, what had she done? Malachi turned to Gabriel, his face a sneer as Roman's blood still dripped from his claws.

"You're next, Gabriel," he growled. "I have been wanting to

slaughter you for about two thousand years."

Gabriel smiled. "Oh, I think not," he said kindly and he gazed downward and grinned. The water began to bubble and boil, frothing and raging on the surface. Malachi followed his gaze and screamed in rage as he saw Roman's body emerging from the water surrounded by a bright yellow light. He rose out of the water completely transformed, his skin glowing and warm, his eyes bright and shining and his hair a more natural light brown. Roman stood, floating above the water with droplets of the Black Sea cascading off his perfect white Angel feathers.

"No!" Malachi raged as a bright white light appeared on Roman's chest, glowing from within. His soul, now at peace, shone almost brighter than the sun. He tilted his head back and laughed jubilantly into the sky. With forgiveness, for himself and for those who had hurt him the most, Roman had received redemption and was free from the powers of Hell.

Malachi stood stunned and even sank a few inches toward the water. His skin greyed further and his wings dropped down as he turned to see the line of Demons, no longer cheering, no longer following him, but showing him their black leathery wings as they turned from the battle, disenchanted with their leader. Roman had just shown them the truth. Hell was nothing more than a prison of their own creation and the Demons no longer wished to fight for it. The citizens of Hell always knew that they had, on some level, chosen to live there with their actions in life but now it was clear that they continued to choose this prison every day.

Roman and Lucy had just shown them that with forgiveness, it is never too late to make a different choice and with that forgiveness, comes redemption. The only power Malachi ever had over them was that which they chose to give him and he could no longer control them. Some flew off, others returned to the hole in the cliff from which they had emerged. Others still put their wings away and materialized regular human clothing on their bodies and simply walked away to continue their day.

Lucy looked over her shoulder to see Turner and Octavia walking toward her in regular clothes. Octavia wore jeans and an oversized sweater and riding boots, her hair pulled back in a tight pony. Turner was wearing a white lace apron over her sensible green pant suit.

"Well done dear," Turner whispered as they passed. "Well done indeed. We must go now, work to be done."

"But did you see?" Lucy stammered. "You don't have to…"

"Oh Roman?" Turner smirked. "Yes, I saw him. The balance though, still needs to be maintained. The Guilds still stand intact. You changed one Demon and gave a great many something to think about Lucy but you certainly did not change human nature. Hell will not be empty until the end of the human race." She looked wistfully over the water and for once looked old and tired. "Personally, I have far too many, shall we say, inner demons to be redeemed any time soon. Forgiveness is not an easy concept for souls like ours. Maybe with time, which really, is all if have."

She brightened and smiled kindly at Lucy, "And frankly my dear, I could not imagine any existence worse than that of an Angel." She and Octavia burst into cackles of laughter as arm in arm, they walked away looking like nothing more than a mother and daughter out for a walk on the beach.

Lucy grinned, her heart leaping in victory. They had done it. They had won! She squealed in delight as she turned to look out at the water, hoping to see Nathaniel coming toward her to sweep her up in his arms and kiss her deeply. Gabriel had been right; this had not gone the way that she had thought it would, but it had all worked out for the best.

Her grin was cut off, though, as she saw Malachi, in a fit of rage and bent on revenge, hurling towards her like a bullet. She didn't have time to run or even think about running before he slammed into her, grabbing her with one arm around the waist and pulling her with him towards the hole in the cliff. There was a roar from the Angels as they moved toward the beach in a battle line, enraged with this new violation. Lucy screamed and fought against his claws digging into her ribs, but she was no match. Nathaniel's face emerged from the crowd of Angels, flying faster than the rest, determination and fury pressed into his features, his dark hair whipping in the wind.

Malachi twisted so Lucy was shielding him as he darted toward the rock. As Nathaniel approached, a sword of ice appeared in his hand and with a roar he swung out and down, inches from Lucy's waist. Malachi screamed in pain as his arm and Lucy fell away from his body into the sand. He turned, a black triton appearing in his remaining hand that he then hurled at Nathaniel, who hit the triton away easily with his sword. Malachi produced fireball after fireball and hurled them at Nathaniel, who dodged them again and again. Lucy scrambled back from the arm still holding her and kicked it away. She looked out on the horizon and the Angels still coming.

"You are no match for me, young pup!" Malachi raged through a clenched jaw, his fangs flashing in the sun. "I am much older than you and far more powerful. I can best you with one arm and I will take my Lilith for my own!"

"Lucy is mine!" Nathaniel raged. He lunged, sword held aloft, ready to strike Malachi down. Malachi dodged sideways and was suddenly on top of Lucy again, struggling to grab her with his existing arm. Lucy wrenched away from him and onto her belly to try to squirm away. She could hear Nathaniel lunging again from the side, trying to attack but avoid hitting Lucy. She felt something on her jeans and screamed in rage as she reached back, but it was too late.

She had forgotten about the knife. She had never forgotten anything before and yet, she had forgotten that knife. Malachi sprung like a cobra as he twisted and jammed the blade into Nathaniel's side below his ribs. Nathaniel's body pitched backwards over the knife and Malachi laughed as he fell sideways onto the sand.

Lucy screeched as she scrambled toward Nathaniel. Blood poured out of his side, sinking into the sand turning it a deep black. The Angels descended finally upon Malachi, who hurled a few fireballs before realizing that he was outmatched. He screamed in rage and darted for the cliff, vanishing in its depths as the rock sealed itself behind him. Lucy held her hands around the knife in Nathaniel's side, trying to staunch the flow of blood, but it still surged undaunted over her hands. She leaned over Nathaniel, screaming for someone to help. Her entire mind splintered, leaving what felt like nothing but madness and shards of knowledge behind. Gabriel appeared beside her and she grasped at his arm, stamping slick bloody marks all over his skin.

"Help him!" she yelled. "Heal him quickly."

Tears poured from the Angel's eyes. "I cannot, Lucy," he whispered. "It is not meant to be."

"No!" Lucy raged and let go of his arm to return to her useless task of trying to stop the tidal wave of blood coming from Nathaniel. "You have to save him!" she sobbed. "Roman! Roman!" His face appeared beside her. "You have to save him! He saved you! I saved you! Please please please!"

Roman shook his head, his blue eyes wet with tears.

"No!" Lucy screamed. "He saved everyone! You have to

help him!" She slammed her fist into the sand and screamed.

"Oh, my Lucy," Nathaniel whispered and she looked down at his gorgeous face. Despite the pain he must have been feeling, he looked completely at peace. "This was the way it had to be," he whispered, and Lucy sobbed as she laid her head on his chest. He rested his hand in her red curls. "We were not meant to be together in this world, but we will be together one day. Let's be grateful that we got this one year together. One year of Heaven during our lives until we are together forever in Heaven itself."

Realization dawned upon her as she thought of Nathaniel's words and actions over the past few months. "How long have you known?"

"Since before the Winter Solstice," he whispered with a smile. "You are so clever, my Lucy, I could not risk you changing your path to try to keep me here."

"I would have gone with Malachi," she replied. "If I had known you would be alive."

"I know." He coughed and blood trickled out of the corner of his mouth. Lucy wiped it away with her thumb. "And I could not have that. Ours is a love that is not meant for this world; it is too big and too wide and too powerful to be contained on one planet. You just wait, Lucy, until you get to Heaven. But until then," he looked her in the eye, "you must promise to live the best life you can. You must swear to live every day with love and bravery, and when you are an old woman, warm in your bed surrounded by happiness and peace, you will close your eyes and I will be waiting for you." Lucy shook her head, silently refusing. Her tears poured out and splashed hotly upon his chest.

"I need to speak to Gavin," he said to the ring of Angels about them and Gavin appeared at their side and knelt beside Lucy. Nathaniel reached up and grasped Gavin's hand in a fist. "You love her, I know you love her. You would do anything for her." Nathaniel whispered to Gavin who nodded vehemently. "And so Gavin, I ask that you take care of Lucy for me, you must not let her die inside. You must spend your life making her happy and allowing her to make you happy." He took Gavin's hand and wrapped it around Lucy's. "You two were meant to be." Lucy knew now why Gavin had been kept separate from them all. He was being protected above all others today. Nathaniel had known how this all would turn out and didn't want Lucy to be alone.

"It would be an honor, dear friend," Gavin whispered through tears as he grasped Lucy's hand like a lifeline. She brought their hands to her head and sobbed against them, pain ripping through her soul. Anastasia appeared beside her and wrapped her arm around Lucy's waist, laid her head on her shoulder and wept.

"Roman," Nathaniel whispered and Roman knelt on the other side of him.

"I am here." Roman blinked back tears.

Nathaniel grabbed his hands. "You look good in white, Brother Roman or should I call you?" he paused thinking. "Samuel is it?" He grinned as Roman laughed out loud through his tears. "I think I like Roman better."

"I do too. It shall stay." Roman whispered.

"I hate to say it, dear friend, but I told you so."

Roman laughed ruefully. "That you did, brother, that you did, and I will ever be grateful to you."

"I need you to stay here on Earth and look after Lucy and the others. Are you willing to do that?" Roman hesitated and Nathaniel nodded. "I know the pull of Heaven is a powerful one. Trust me, I know." Roman looked at Anastasia, and the decision was then made. He looked to Gabriel who sighed but gave a weary smile.

"Very well," Gabriel agreed and raised his hands to Roman whose frame seemed to sink slightly. Lucy knew the movement well, his tie to Heaven had been severed. "You are now mortal Roman and although you will have some of your powers, you will receive no assistance from us and you are not bound by celestial law. Live well Brother."

"And don't get yourself killed like me," Nathaniel drawled. "Because as you can see, there are no second chances. Back to Heaven I go." Roman nodded and snuck a small smile to Anastasia who grinned back. Lucy cast them both an angry glare.

"This isn't fair!" She raged at Gabriel. "Why does Roman get to stay but Nathaniel has to leave?"

"We warned you both that Nathaniel was mortal." Gabriel replied softly. She opened her mouth to reply but her memory reminded her of the Angels words on the day Nathaniel's ties were severed with Heaven. He was right. They had been warned.

"Thank you," Nathaniel whispered to Gabriel who nodded sadly. He turned his attention to Roman again. "I will see you, dear friend, again when the time is right. Until then, I have a task for you." He pulled Roman close to whisper in his ear. Roman listened intently, his newly white wings fluttering in response. Finally, he sat back on his heels and nodded assent.

Nathaniel smiled at them all in turn.

"I love you all," he whispered with shuddering breath, "thank you for the best year I have ever known. I will see you soon." He looked to Lucy, his crystal eyes dulling rapidly. "Goodbye my Lucy, my love, my heart and soul. Know that you are so special and so wonderful and deserve every happiness in this life and the next. Live well, my Lucy, goodbye." And with that, he let out one trembling breath, closed his eyes and died.

Lucy screeched and Gavin and Anastasia held her tightly as

she tried to throw herself onto Nathaniel's body. "No!" she sobbed at the sky. "No."

"I've got you, Red," Gavin whispered in her ear as he rocked her back and forth, "I've got you." She hated herself for the comfort she felt in those words.

The Angels were silent as they moved forward to lift Nathaniel's body reverently. They raised him up to their shoulders and took flight. Lucy watched as an entire legion of Angels carried her love to the Heavens where he belonged. Light poured from his skin as they approached the clouds and the Angels vanished into the world beyond.

Lucy collapsed forward with her head in the sand and cried and raged and screamed into the bloody ground while her friends sat beside her, stunned and sad beyond words. When she could not cry anymore, Lucy just lay in the sand, spent. Finally, when she could think clearly, a small smile touched her lips, for she knew something no one else knew.

Chapter Twenty-Eight
Fallen

*"The drops of rain make a hole in the stone,
not by violence, but by oft falling."*
~ Lucretius

The students returned to the home with a well-rehearsed story about the mad billionaire that held them all captive and murdered Nathaniel when he tried to escape. The guard, who strangely enough was actually named Ben, was touted as a world-renowned hero and lived comfortably for the rest of his days on the funds provided by the Rooke and MacFarlane families. He also reaped the benefits of the tell-all book he wrote and (after much editing and rewriting by Lucy) published as a New York Times best seller that was sold in the same stores as his Wheaties box.

A beautiful service was held for Nathaniel and after some recovery time in Kansas, and rebuilding at Mulbridge, Lucy and her friends returned to school. Lucy's mother and Dr. Hannon asked few questions because they saw the pain in Lucy's eyes when they brought it up. The fact that she was back and healthy was enough for them.

    Lucy waited and waited and waited for the right day to come. She lived in a state of constant fog. Images of Nathaniel haunted her everywhere she went. She would see his back in a crowd, or the side of his face on a bus driving by. When she wasn't delving into her school work, she was forcing herself to act normally around her friends, who proved to be stalwart and unwavering in the face of her indifference. Gavin, loyal and determined, barely left her side and endured the rages and the wracking sobs as they came in waves over and over again. He outwaited her catatonic states with patience and perseverance. Lucy would flail at him, punching and kicking and screaming her pain as he absorbed it all over and over again. He proved his love endlessly without a care for himself and Lucy hated him for it.

    Finally, three long years and three months passed. Lucy had completed her studies and was graduating with every honor imaginable the next day. She had decided against any more schooling; she didn't want to pay for something she would not be around to use. Despite the fact that she was waiting for this moment beyond all moments, it still somehow, caught her off guard. She was in the mall, buying a dress for the ceremony the next day. The elevator was full and she had darted into the cement encased stairwell to get to the main floor of the mall. As she reached the landing, her phone rang, and she answered to Anastasia's incessant checking up on her. Smiling, she turned the corner for the second flight of stairs.

    She fell. Tripped really. Her foot slipped and although she might have been able to save herself, if she had the inclination, she didn't. So technically, it was an accident and that was how it had to be. By her estimation, there were twenty-five solid concrete steps on this staircase. As her body charged forward, her left shoe fell off and twisted lightly in the air behind her. As her mind registered this, a flash image came to her of the day she bought that shoe; it was during a better time -- a much better time. But now the shoe was off and she had tripped and because the stairs were made of concrete and numbered twenty-five, the fall would kill her. For that simple fact she discharged the better time - the shoe shopping time and she rejoiced. She felt joy in her own death; deep, full, unabashed joy. She was finally being let out of her own personal Hell and her soul grasped at salvation with everything it had left.

Seconds before her head hit the twelfth step, she twisted her body, looked up at the sky, smiled and whispered, "Thank you, thank you, thank God it's over."

Today was the Summer Solstice; she thought that was a nice touch.

She stopped falling. Smiling, she looked about her for Nathaniel, but what she saw instead made her scream in rage.

"Please forgive me," Roman whispered roughly as he cradled Lucy in his arms. "I promised him before he died. He told me I had to catch you. I'm sorry."

"No! No! No! I can't be here, Roman! I can't live. I can't. Damn you!" Lucy screeched into his face as she beat him with all her might. Roman just stood there and took it as tears ran down his face.

Epilogue

It took years of patience and a great deal of love for Lucy to finally begin to live again. She didn't know why or how it happened, but one day she woke up and took a deep breath and was ready to take on the day. She fell wildly in love with Gavin, for he was so easy to love. They married in a jubilant and crazy wedding a year before Stasia and Roman married on the beach in Hawaii.

They lived their lives to the fullest every single day and after the children came, time passed even faster. The days were long but the years were short, and they made each other laugh every single day. They stayed close to Roman and Anastasia and were a family of odd misfits and joy. Sometimes Gavin would see Lucy, her hair still wild and red and her eyes as green as emeralds, looking out a window or staring at a particular leaf or flower petal and he would know she was thinking of Nathaniel.

He kept his word though, and made Lucy very happy. Over the years she had done so in return. He never regretted one decision he had ever made and loved his life beyond measure. Gavin knew he was a blessed man.

Lucy had her memories; at the end of the day, that's all any of us have. When our last day comes, we are all only made of the stories we tell. She was eighty-five years old, secure in her bed, covered by quilts and soft warm sheets when she died. Gavin, their children and their grandchildren stood close by to say farewell. Lucy, as promised, had lived a life of love and bravery and now was ready to go. She smiled at her loved ones, closed her eyes and remembered each and every moment of her life and knew she had done well.

She had known two great loves when most don't even get one. As her mortal life passed from her eyes, she saw that familiar bright white light. Suddenly, she was back in the quad at Mulbridge University, walking along the sidewalk toward her dorm. She caught sight of her reflection in a window and saw that her silver hair had been transformed back to a flaming red, her skin had softened and flushed youthful and bright; she was nineteen again.

The night air was crisp and the lampposts twinkled in the darkness as she followed the pathway, the one she was destined to walk. There he stood, beside the row of Pagoda Dogwood trees, where he had been waiting for sixty-five years. His dark hair and crystal grey eyes almost glowing as he smiled that smile that was hers and hers alone. Lucy went towards her Nathaniel, her heart rejoicing, for it had once again found its soul mate.

In the end, Lucy travelled from Heaven to Hell and everywhere in between to save her true love's soul and by doing so, had saved herself.

The End

About the Author

Laurie Lyons is the author of *The Feather Trilogy* with Ring of Fire Publishing, "The Heart Tree" and "The Gatherers" short stories with Little Bird Publishing House, and "Bloodlines" short story with Twisted Core Press.

Laurie wrote her first story at the age of 8 and hasn't really stopped since. She lives in Calgary Alberta, Canada with her husband Trevor and their two clever children. She loves writing, reading and sharing her love of both with students during author presentations.

You can find more information on Laurie and her future works at *www.laurielyons.ca* and *www.ringoffirebooks.com*.

RING OF FIRE PUBLISHING

www.ringoffirebooks.com

Made in the USA
Charleston, SC
20 March 2014